Thick as Water had me on the edge of my chair and kept me quickly turning pages excited to discover what the next mystery might be. This book was both exciting and enjoyable and I highly recommend it to anyone that has the curiosity of "what if's"! Great story with a great ending. Ava Page might just be my new favorite author!

...It pulls at your emotions with every turn. Have a box of tissues ready because you will need them with this book.

— Amazon Reviewers

5 Stars - ...It was so riveting I found that when I finally made myself put it down I looked for reasons to pick it back up...

— Goodreads Reviewer

An intriguing observation of the dangers of technology compromising privacy told through the lens of family, love and loss.

— Sam Bland, Reedsy Discovery

the watcher

a killer is among us...

ava page

LAJOLLA
PRESS, LLC

La Jolla Press, LLC

1902 Wright Pl, Suite 200

Carlsbad, CA 92008

www.lajollapress.com

Printed in the United States of America

First printing, 2022

Library of Congress Control Number: 2022909279

ISBN-13 (Hardcover): 978-1-7372736-4-6

ISBN-13 (Paperback): 978-1-7372736-3-9

ISBN-13 (eBook): 978-1-7372736-5-3

author's note

This book is a work of fiction. All the characters and events portrayed in this novel are products of the author's imagination or used fictitiously. Sometimes both.

dedication

The Watcher is dedicated to the readers of my debut novel, *Thick as Water*. Thank you for giving me a chance to tell you a story and the confidence to keep telling them.

let's get in touch

Website: www.avapage.com
Newsletter: www.avapage.com/lets-connect
Facebook: www.facebook.com/TheAuthorAvaPage
Instagram: www.instagram.com/avapageauthor
Email: ava@avapage.com

also by ava page: debut novel

Thick as Water

Thick as Water

Ava's debut novel, published in 2021 is a contemporary fiction novel that will grab hold of the reader from start to finish.

I would like you both to come in. For Agnes and Liam, life is never the same after these words. In one afternoon, every vow in their marriage is a challenge: For worse. For poorer. In sickness.

Visit here or www.avapage.com/thick-as-water/ for more information.

also by ava page: one last call

One Last Call

One Last Call - **FREE**

Have you wondered if it's better to be born now with social media and phones, or before it was available? Read the novella *One Last Call* for free and see if it changes your mind. Free to download here **(if reading ebook)** or by scanning the QR code below.

Scan to download your copy today

coming soon

The Kat Eland Series...

Kat's husband is a detective of cold cases. He brings his briefcase home, and Kat is curious. What did curiosity do to the Kat?

fire and ice

Some say the world will end in fire,
Some say in ice.
From what I've tasted of desire
I hold with those who favor fire.
But if it had to perish twice,
I think I know enough of hate
To say that for destruction ice
Is also great
And would suffice.
- Robert Frost

prologue

. . .

MAGGIE SET the table for three and waited. The garlic and marinara scent of dinner wafted through the house. Trader Joe's meatloaf, mashed potatoes, and a salad would have to do. She plated the food and discarded the packaging. Her husband and his brother knew she couldn't cook, but she insisted on putting the food on her own serving platters, regardless. Tonight was special. She didn't care for meatloaf, but it was one of the few things she successfully kept down. For the last three months, chicken had sent her hurling over the toilet. Her husband would follow her, patting her back and holding her hair, as she vomited. It annoyed her yet she never said a thing. She did not want to diminish the already minuscule role of a husband as her pregnant body morphed into something neither of them recognized.

She bumped her tight, round abdomen against the counter. "I'm sorry, sweetie," she said to her tiny inhabitant as she rubbed her stomach.

Her phone rang.

"Hello?"

"Hi," the familiar tenor of her brother-in-law's voice, "I'm five minutes out. Can I bring anything?"

"Yourself," she said.

Her husband was late again.

A moment later, Chris stepped through the door bearing a bouquet of red roses, his apology flowers. His eyes, the color of the Caribbean Sea, were shocking against his jet-black hair. After nine years, those eyes still brought her to her knees. He went to her, his suit jacket open, and his yellow tie with tiny forget-me-nots dangling around his collar. She liked forget-me-nots better than roses. She hated everything about roses; the glaring reds, their musky scent, the cliche of them, but she didn't tell him that either. She greeted him halfway, and he tousled her chestnut waves. Her hair grew unruly since the pregnancy hormones coursed through her veins and she spent thirty minutes curling it just right. She caught an image of herself in the window. Thirty minutes of preening, and now she looked like a toddler waking from a nap.

She glanced at the pops of red apologies strewn with the silvery baby's breath between. The deluxe bouquet meant a big apology. "Oh no." She gazed up at him. The floral, earthy stench of the roses curled her stomach.

He frowned down at her, his square jaw set. "I'm sorry," he said, tucking her tangled hair behind her ear. She wanted to pull away but rooted herself in place.

"C'mon Chris, can you at least stay for dinner? Tonight is important. Paul is coming. We were going to ask him to be her godfather," she said as she rubbed her belly. "We can make it a shorter dinner. Give me half an hour. We can eat fast." The desperation in her voice irritated her.

Chris glanced at the table and eyed the three place

settings. He hit his head with his free hand. "Damn, I forgot. I'm sorry, love, I can't stay. You can ask him without me." His hand reached out to touch her belly but she brushed him away.

"Chris, this was supposed to be special." Her shoulders slumped.

"I'm already late. Look, this is the last project. No more after this. I promise. This, it, just has to get done."

Her voice hardened with a steely anger fueled by her pregnant hormones. "Don't say something you don't mean. You've been promising for over a year."

Paul opened the door behind Chris, his face stretched in an open grin. He wore khakis and a button-down blue checkered shirt with his sleeves half rolled up. He looked nearly a carbon copy of Chris, except his jaw was more rounded and his eyes were the color of moss. "Am I late? It smells delicious." Maggie glanced at him, and his face fell. "What's wrong, Mags?"

"It's nothing. Let me get these flowers in water. Just go, Chris."

She snatched the flowers from him. A single crimson petal came loose and drifted to the floor, and she defiantly crushed it beneath her ballet flat like a child. Chris leaned in for a goodbye kiss and she pretended she didn't see as she pivoted away from him. He straightened and turned to Paul. Maggie spun on her heel toward the kitchen, picked up the third setting from Chris's spot, and kept walking. She could claim the tightness in her chest was hormones rather than what it was, a blistering rage.

She set Chris's dishes on the counter, but she wanted to slam them into the floor and admire the porcelain scattering across the linoleum. Instead, she recalled the mantra her mother taught her when her anger bubbled to the surface. "Smell the flowers, blow out the candles," she whispered to herself as she breathed in and out. The blistering rage cooled to a fiery anger. She laid the withering roses flat on the Formica counter, trimmed the ends, and threw away the granular plant food so they wouldn't survive longer than they needed to. Heated hushed tones traveled from the living room, and Maggie stopped the snipping and listened.

Paul said, "Is this a bad time?"

"No, it's a perfect time. I've got a work project, and dinner is ready. Mags can use the company."

"What are you doing, Chris?" Paul asked.

"I've got to go. I'm already late," Chris said.

"You've got to stop this. Your wife is in there, seven and a half months pregnant, and you're always working late." Paul's tone was stern.

"Don't you think I know? I've got an issue at work, but I've come close to resolving it. No more after this."

"What work issue keeps you from your family all the time, Chris?"

"You wouldn't understand, but I have to finish this last thing," Chris said.

"I think I understand. Don't be like Dad. She deserves better," Paul said.

After, the voices grew too hushed for Maggie to hear. A tightness climbed into her chest and her daughter kicked her in protest. Their father left when his mother was pregnant with Paul. He became a shadow of a father, doing little more than taking his boys to the range every few months to shoot. Chris wouldn't leave her. Paul was wrong. He had to be.

She walked closer to the kitchen door and pressed her

ear to it. Maggie made out Paul's last words to Chris. "She's too good for you, you know."

"I do," Chris said. She heard the door close, and Chris vanished into the night.

Neither of them saw him alive again.

one

. . .

EIGHTEEN YEARS LATER...

He peered back at her from another photograph. This photo had been taken sixteen years ago, and over 800 miles away from home. But there he was, observing them from behind the balloon vendor. His baseball hat concealed his bristled brown hair, and his sunglasses obscured his muddy brown eyes, but it was him. The way he favored one leg, even when he stood still. His scarred hand was a collage of pinks and purples. He kept it tucked close to his side like a feral, wounded animal.

The burns on his hand were angrier in this photo than in the others she found of him. She studied him, the way he stood, his intensity, with his eyes on her family.

His unburned hand clasped the slight hand of an auburn-haired toddler. A child wedged between the man with the scarred hand and the balloon stand. The girl gazed up at the vendor's Mickey Mouse balloons, lost in a sea of her own desires. The only evidence they were a pair was their tethered hands. If not for that, the little girl might have floated away and Maggie thought he'd barely notice.

Almost two years since the accident, it had been her first real vacation alone with Emily. Maggie hoped it would distract her from the grief of Chris's death, but grief was a flexible thing. It traveled easily and folded itself inside her carry-on. For Emily, the wondrous world of the theme park was an exciting, albeit over-stimulating distraction from their home in Northern Virginia.

They both were eager for a diversion from their normal lives. Emily spent most of her weekdays at the Children's PlayTime Academy where Maggie dropped her daughter off at eight and retrieved her at five. Her position as a computer scientist with the Customs and Border Protection office kept her locked in a secured facility most days, but the daycare workers were kind enough to inform her in daily reports of the first steps and first words she missed. When she received reports like these, her resentment boiled over at Chris for having the nerve to die.

As she had done with the other photographs, Maggie cropped the man out and focused on her daughter. Emily wore a red polka dot dress with mouse ears to match. As she spun, her eyes were closed and faced toward the sun. The hem of her red polka dot dress flared up in the spin, showing off her chunky toddler legs, and the tiniest sliver of her white ruffled bloomers. Her blonde hair had darkened into Maggie's familiar chestnut and curled on the edges as her baby hair grew out. Maggie filed the photo in the stack of pictures she was planning to include in Emily's memory book.

For the last few years, Emily retreated from her mother, leaving Maggie to spend the empty periods strolling through memory lane. She tried to convince herself she did a good enough job with her daughter before she sent her off for her first year of college. Maggie hoped the memory book would be ready for her high school graduation, but there were thousands of pictures to comb through.

Maggie's stomach clenched when she dwelled on the coming fall and the long stretch of empty days ahead. She survived the weeklong summer trips Emily took to visit Maggie's sister in Idaho only by the skin of her teeth. How would she survive the quietness of the house when September arrived? She didn't know. Her daughter, the same little girl who used to hide behind her mother's legs when company came over, was about to journey into a world scarier than Maggie remembered. She lost herself reminiscing about the past as Emily drew back to launch like a rocket into her adulthood.

As she scrolled through the photos, her mind recalled when Emily was an extension of her. She yearned for the exhausting days that, when she was enduring them, she couldn't wait to be over. The days when she hid in the bathroom. Then, several pudgy fingers slid under the bathroom door, wiggling for attention, eager for closeness. In the years that followed, the roles had reversed. Maggie clung to any sign of attention from her ever distancing daughter.

There weren't many pictures of Maggie and Emily. Her brother-in-law, Paul, urged her to put down the camera, but she liked the weight of it around her neck. It felt like armor. Ready to take the next heartwarming moment and memorialize it. Now, she regretted the lack of pictures with her and Emily. Maggie snapped photos from her camera almost everywhere they went, imagining she was providing snapshots of life to Chris from behind the lens, straight to wherever dead people go. Maggie wished she had recorded Chris more and was determined not to make the same mistake with her daughter.

Maggie found the earliest picture of the wounded stranger among those taken at Chris's funeral.

Paul had handled all the arrangements. Maggie's exhaustion from giving birth, losing her husband, and learning to live a life alone was too much. He had set the funeral for a week after she and Emily came home after her premature birth. The photograph captured the man mid-stride from behind a tree. He wore the same sunglasses that he did in the Florida photo. His face turned toward the casket, and a bandage tightly wrapped around his hand. Emily nestled against Maggie's chest, snug in a blanket, and slept, oblivious to the seismic shift of their world. Studying the photo, Maggie still smelled the musky, pleasant scent of the earth. Paul's hand steadied Maggie at the small of her back. Her hair, the color of sand, grazed the silver casket splayed with white Calla Lilies, the universal death flower. The photo captured her bending to kiss the top of her husband's casket before the earth enveloped him forever. Her necklace dangled out of her shirt, the cross laid on the casket. She looked at the photo and gave a bitter chuckle at Christ's face planting on her husband's casket. After the funeral, she threw the cross, a gift from her first communion, away with her funeral attire, and her faith. She replaced the cross with Chris's wedding ring. One year after his death, her wedding ring joined it, yoked around her neck.

She focused again on the man in the photo. An unease prickled the hairs at the nape of her neck.

"Who are you?" she asked to the photo.

two

. . .

MAGGIE STEPPED AWAY from her computer and idly opened Instagram on her phone. She loathed the platform but checked in to bear witness to Emily's world as it orbited farther from her own. Maggie couldn't resist the opportunity to glimpse the mask Emily presented to the world. She scanned her daughter's feed and found the same stranger in the background of one of her pictures. It was an action shot in soccer. Her long dyed-blonde ponytail shot out like a comet to the right. The mud and grass stain on her shirt from a previous play obscured her number 88, while her leg flexed forward after kicking the ball. Her face stripped clean of makeup, contorted into deep concentration to score the winning goal. The reason Emily allowed the unfiltered shot on her feed was the glory of the winning goal. It had pushed their team to a championship victory.

Maggie refocused on the man in the corner of the shot. His gaze fell to the left of the play. His hand was not visible from the angle and distance, but Maggie couldn't unsee him anymore. "Enough," she muttered to herself. She shut her computer and walked downstairs to the kitchen to pour her third and last cup of black coffee.

Emily sat at the kitchen island with her face lit by her phone, sucked inside a world that didn't include her. Whenever her daughter's face lit up from her phone, Maggie remembered the ill-fated little girl in Poltergeist. *They're here,* Maggie thought and recalled her haunting, lilted voice. Emily absently poured a quarter of her creamer bottle into a cup of coffee without looking up. Maggie looked on as the black water turned a shade of milky brown.

Maggie walked to the pot to pour a cup. It was empty. Emily's new habit threw off the amount of coffee Maggie made for herself. She waffled about buying a bigger pot, like the kind they had when Chris was alive. But Emily would leave for college soon anyway, and Maggie would be all alone, throwing the ratios off yet again. Her daughter perched on her chair at the kitchen island, blowing her cream-cooled coffee.

Maggie decided against making another entire pot for a single cup. It was Saturday, with nothing important on her calendar. A brisk walk would help clear her mental fog. She regarded her daughter a beat longer. Emily did not acknowledge her mother entering the room. When the phone beckoned her into the highlight reel of classmates, acquaintances, and influencers, she wasn't aware of anything going on around her.

"Hey," Maggie finally said.

Emily jumped and bristled at her mother. "God, Mom, don't sneak up on me like that." Her eyes slid back to her phone.

"Like what? I've been standing in the kitchen for a while," Maggie said.

Emily blew out a sigh. "Fine, hey," she said. The familiar ding of a text summoned Emily back to her device. She crawled back inside the white light.

Maggie walked to Emily and leaned over her daughter's shoulder to glance at what captivated her attention. Josh again. The rapid-fire texts lit up her phone.

"What's going on?" Maggie asked.

"He's still trying to get the deposit paid for JMU."

"The due date is today, hun. I thought his parents said he was going to the community college."

Emily huffed, and said, "I mean, his parents let him apply to all these universities. He got in. Now they're saying he has to go to community college. He's been begging them to change their minds." Her lip turned up with disgust when her mouth formed around the words "community college."

Maggie sighed. "His mom's business failed. So, it isn't like they changed their minds on him. Things changed. They're doing the best they can. Community college is the same education at a fraction of the price, Em. No one predicted the pandemic." The pandemic was brutal to Josh's mother's sandwich shop, and she closed it in the ninth month. Her business sat in the heart of Arlington; the workers in the area were her lifeblood. When the telework days began, the workers' appetites were no longer available to pay for Josh's college.

When Maggie told Josh's mother she was sorry about the shop, his mother said, "Yeah, it's a real 'shit sandwich.'" Maggie liked her a lot.

Emily and Josh's relationship had thrust his parents on Maggie when their children began dating during their freshman year. But the trio instantly bonded and their children miraculously stayed together with limited drama throughout high school. Though his parents were fifteen years older, their laid-back ways were a rare treat in the D.C. area and it drew Maggie to them. Josh was a good kid, but Maggie sensed their journey together was coming to a close.

Emily said, "It isn't fair."

When Maggie's mouth opened to reply, her own long-dead mother's words popped out, "Sometimes, life isn't fair." Maggie bristled at the amount of privilege the kids didn't recognize they had. It was mostly her fault for giving in to her daughter's whims over the years; phones, endless activities, crammed schedules, sports, and clothes. All because the Joneses did it, and they needed to keep up.

In Maggie's desperate race to protect Emily from harm, sadness, and disappointment, she lamented the disservice. In her opinion, this generation was hurricanes of entitlement. They lacked the earned grit that can only come from harm, sadness, and disappointment. Those very things Maggie and her contemporaries strived to protect them from. Maggie peered over Emily's shoulder at her phone again.

Josh: It's total BS Danny got to go

Maggie heard the whine in Josh's voice when she read the message. He was born ten years after his brother as a surprise menopause baby. The death rattles of fertility gave his mother one last viable egg that became Josh. In typical baby fashion, he wasn't used to wanting for anything or having much oversight.

He was right, though. His brother, Danny, did graduate from JMU. But Josh conveniently left out that Danny also was born in a different era of his parents' lives. More rules, better grades, and athletic prowess. His baseball scholarship covered much of the cost. Josh's grades got him in but were not high enough for any scholarship. He played high school freshman football and the violin briefly, but his interests were fleeting. Chief among his hobbies was surrounding himself with all things about Emily.

Maggie changed the subject. "Is there more information about who broke into the school?" The local news had run a story about a high school break-in. However, Maggie could find no updates in the latest headlines.

"Ugh, no. It was a stupid senior prank. Some girl wrote 'Jensen High Sucks' in green paint on the gym walls. They brought me in for questioning."

Maggie startled. "They did? You never told me."

"There was nothing to tell. They said someone said it was me, but they couldn't prove it." Emily shrugged.

"Did they bring anyone else in for questioning?" Maggie asked.

"I don't know. None of my friends. They said once they proved who it was, they wouldn't be able to walk for graduation. Unless the person admitted it. They asked if I had anything to say. They showed me the video of the girl. It could have been me if I hadn't known I was with Josh. She wore a hat like mine, leggings, and a Virginia Beach sweatshirt."

Maggie said nothing, but doubt crept into the recesses of her heart.

She watched as Emily shut the messages from Josh and opened her Instagram. She had 37 DMs waiting for her attention after her last bikini shot posted less than a day ago. Maggie read the caption posted with the words "Take me Back to Golden Hour." When Maggie first saw it, she cringed. Maggie was becoming who she always feared, a mother trying not to judge her daughter through the eyes of everyone else. She recognized the picture from the previous summer. It was heavily edited, filtered, and cropped. She drew in her waist to anorexic proportions, her skin hue tanner, and her hair lighter than Emily's had ever been in real life (golden hour or not). The picture was of her daughter, but wasn't; a ridiculously cartoonish replica of the real Emily. The real Emily was much more interesting than the barbie doll temptress staring back at her. Maggie still kept the original photo on her phone. In reality, they were at a hotel in the middle of southern Virginia. They were on their way back from burying Maggie's grandfather; a man Emily only remembered through the lens of Alzheimer's. By the time Emily could remember anyone, her great-grandfather no longer could.

Maggie examined her daughter's picture as she scrolled through the comments. The familiar and awful twinge of envy pricked at her. As a widow and single mother, she had kept no companion in eighteen years.

As Emily scrolled through her social media feed, she got to the soccer photo. Maggie tapped Emily's shoulder and Emily shrugged her mom's tap off and turned toward her. "Are you looking over my shoulder, Mom?"

Maggie shrugged slightly, an apology. "Sorry, I glanced. I saw that photo and I don't recognize this guy. Is he one of the coaches or dads? I've seen him in a few pictures."

Emily turned her attention back to the photo and tilted her head. "Oh, no. He's Mr. Murphy. The janitor. Gosh, you don't know him? I feel like I've known him my whole life. In elementary school, a bunch of kids got in trouble for teasing him. He walks with a limp and has a bum hand. They followed him all around the school, walking like him and tucking their hands into their sides. I didn't tell you?" Emily chuckled under her breath.

"How awful. I think I would have remembered it. I guess it slipped my mind."

"Well, you were really busy working, and stuff," Emily said.

"I may have been busy, but I always made time for you. I went to every game and practice."

"Gosh, Mom, I get it. I'm just saying you weren't always the best listener."

"Fair," Maggie said. Emily already turned back to her phone and stopped listening to her mother.

Maggie recognized that Emily was right. She went to every event, teacher conference, back-to-school night, and game, but being present wasn't always guaranteed.

"I thought I was acquainted with nearly everyone at your school. Even the ones who are employees but not necessarily teachers. I mean, even the security officer, Kevin. He's a nice boy," Maggie said.

Emily snickered under her breath, "Real nice boy."

"What are you talking about?" Maggie asked.

"Mom, Kevin has been in trouble. I don't know how many times. He's always talking too much to the girls. He's creepy." Emily rolled her eyes.

Security officer Kevin was a derpy kid with an unfortunate smattering of acne across his face. Maggie had never considered him predatory. "Em, I heard nothing like that. How would you know it's true?"

Emily rolled her eyes. "Everyone knows. He has other security guards who check on him and do rounds and stuff. My friend Kelsey overheard two guards saying they couldn't fire him because of the union or something. They visit him often to make sure he stays out of trouble.

"You still talk to Kelsey?" Maggie asked.

"I mean no, I heard it from Sydney, who heard it from

Jessica, and she has Civics with Kelsey. It doesn't matter," Emily said, shrugging her shoulders.

Maggie ran into Kevin twice when she showed up to drop forgotten articles to Emily. With social media standards and makeup, the high school girls no longer looked like high school girls, but if Kevin was talking to them in school, then he didn't have an excuse.

Maggie looked at the photo of the janitor again. She breathed out a sigh. It explained a lot. The janitor was a member of the community. Of course, he would be in pictures. Besides, lots of families in the D.C. metro area escape to Florida for vacation. The janitor didn't attend the funeral. Maybe he had someone else there he visited. Gravesites were like train wrecks, people in the vicinity couldn't help but turn, watch, and be glad it wasn't them. When she visited Chris's gravesite to freshen his flowers, she was guilty of the same. A young mother, holding a baby and kissing the top of a casket, would have drawn her attention. It sent a shocking reminder that death and dying weren't always reserved for the old. But still, something didn't feel quite right looking at the man staring back at her through photographs.

three

. . .

EMILY DECLINED three FaceTime requests in succession and muttered, "He's so annoying." Josh again. Maggie gazed at her daughter and sighed. Emily grew out of his league. He fell in love with the mousy brown-haired girl with braces and pimples. Now, she was a blonde-haired beauty with a manufactured tan teetering on the edge of adulthood. Emily's future included sororities, parties, and handsome boys willing to give her all the attention she sought.

Josh changed, too. He grew taller (but not tall enough), wore his jet-black hair longer (but not styled quite right), and his complexion cleared (but small pocked scars peppered his cheeks). His limbs were still gangly, and he wore thick glasses.

"He's so dramatic, it drives me crazy," Emily said.

Maggie stayed silent as she navigated the emotional mines Emily planted throughout their conversation. As a mother, she teetered between listener and trauma dumping ground, all the while trying to avoid the rollercoaster of teen emotions. She kept telling herself, *Just because Em's invited me on the rollercoaster ride doesn't mean I have to get on.* But often she paid for the admission ticket and rode the waves of angst with her daughter. She wanted to worry less, and it was easier to worry less before Chris died. But now, bad things happened. In the middle of the night, police officers broke your world. These things happened and could happen again. She couldn't convince herself that worrying did nothing to help it.

"I just can't with him. He's so extra. Can't he be happy for me?" Emily said, a small discharge of an emotional mine left on the ground for her mother to sidestep.

"I'm sure he is, but he's having a hard time, sweetie."

Emily half-listened while she opened the comments on her bikini Instagram shot again.

She didn't look at her mother but talked to the air while watching her phone. "It's just that he wants to try the long-distance thing. Maybe we'll get back together later, but I don't want a boyfriend back home in community college."

"Em, stop putting down community college. It is a way to get an education. Not everyone has the same resources. Judging people by 'community college' is elitist. Everyone walks out with the same degree." Maggie regretted the counsel. It was a battle she didn't want to pick today. She longed for the now lukewarm last cup of coffee sitting untouched in front of Emily. But her daughter's judgment pricked at her nerves.

Emily rolled her eyes at her mother, and again Maggie pretended not to see. "I know you went to one. Things aren't the same. It's different. Like, no one goes to community college anymore. It's for losers now."

Heat crept into Maggie's cheeks. Who had she raised? This wasn't the person who used to help clean litter at the local park on weekends. A pit in her stomach formed as she watched her privileged daughter dive back into the pretend world of her phone. What had happened to her? She wondered. Her little girl used to be one of the most compassionate people. Maggie would lay down her life for Emily and her happiness. But, she hated to admit that she didn't like her daughter all that much lately. Maggie consulted and researched why her daughter's behaviors had changed so much in a small period, worried about her character. Emily was 'soiling the nest' to make leaving home easier for everyone. As much as Maggie wanted to keep Emily under her wing, she also looked forward to Emily flying away. Especially when she acted like this.

Maggie turned to go. She needed a vigorous walk through the neighborhood. She needed to jolt herself into the day after her daughter snatched her last cup of coffee. As her hand turned the knob on the front door, Emily let out a yelp, startling Maggie back into her daughter's universe. She ran back to the kitchen. "What is it?" Her voice threaded with panic.

"Oh, my God! I matched, I matched with a girl." She jumped out of her chair and stared at her phone.

Maggie's brows turned up. "What are you talking about? What do you mean, matched?" For a second, she thought she went to a dating site, but Maggie never suspected that Emily might like girls.

Emily read her mother's face and laughed. "No, not like that, Mom. I mean, I matched with a roommate."

"Wait, doesn't the college pick for you?" Maggie asked.

Her daughter glanced at her and laughed again. It stung Maggie. It didn't feel like a good-natured laugh, but one that suggested she was a relic of another time, a dinosaur.

"You're so funny, Mom." In a way that didn't mean she was funny at all. "We don't do it like that anymore. If you can find a roommate on social, you can go in with them. Now, we can pick who we're living with. Kids who are weird, don't have social media, or accept late are the ones who do it old school."

Maggie remembered her roommate in college during her freshman year, a girl whose breath smelled like eggs. She would have liked to choose a different roommate and ended up meeting and living with Jasmine her sophomore year.

"As much as I'm not an advocate for social media, I think this isn't a bad idea. Who did you 'match' with?"

Emily turned the phone toward her mother to show her a picture of a girl who looked a lot like Maggie. "Her name is Jenna, and she seems perfect. On top of everything, she's a Sagittarius and I'm a Capricorn, so we're pretty compatible. I mean, it would be tragic if she were an Aries."

"Hey, I'm an Aries," Maggie said.

"It's fine to be an Aries as my mom, but not a roommate. Family doesn't count on this stuff."

Maggie crossed her arms and raised an eyebrow at her daughter. "Those signs don't mean anything."

"You don't know what's real or what's not. I have never met a Sagittarius I don't like. So, that says something, doesn't it?"

"Correlation is not causation," Maggie said.

"Great Mom, coming at me with the big words. I'm not in college yet. Anyway, she's perfect."

"Oh? What do you know about her? How did you select each other?"

"We've been kind of chatting and feeling each other out. Some girls asked to match. They were kind of extra. Jenna wants the same sororities as me and we have a ton in common. Her socials look like she's my type. I'm so excited.

The only thing is she's majoring in information technology." She paused and said, "She doesn't look like a computer geek at all, so it's okay."

Maggie bristled. "What does a computer geek look like? Because it paid for this comfortable life, including your college." She bit her lip and tasted a warm, coppery drop on her tongue. God, could she let her daughter say something without correcting her? But nearly everything coming out of her mouth was offensive to Maggie lately. Her job in the lab wasn't just computers, but she did a fair amount of time on one. And her middle started to show that she didn't have a job with physical requirements.

Emily glanced at her mother and shrugged. "C'mon Mom, I didn't mean it like that. Stop taking stuff so personal. I'm saying some computer people have a certain look. I didn't mean you." She pushed the phone closer to Maggie's face for a better view, but the closer the photo was, the blurrier the girl became. She didn't want to tell her daughter she needed reading glasses. Through the blur, she could tell it was a filter-tanned girl with more golden locks than her daughter, posed while staring off-camera pensively in a bikini.

"Isn't she pretty? She has thousands of followers. I wonder how she got so popular..." Maggie noted the pinch of envy in Emily's voice as she scrolled the girl's profile for probably the 100th time.

"She is a pretty girl," Maggie agreed. They all were. With makeup, filters, and Photoshop, kids carbon copied each other in a Stepford child sort of way. Even young teens, children really, looked like they were in their twenties. Maggie noted her daughter seemed to be a little prettier than the other girl. Either from her mother-tinted rose-colored glasses or reality, she didn't know. This girl's platinum blonde highlights swum in an underlay of blonde hair. It contrasted against green eyes and her filtered or sprayed-on tan. Maggie looked at Emily. "You understand by now, popularity isn't a real thing, right?"

"I know Mom, you tell me all the time, it's a 'made-up social construct,'" she said imitating her mother's cadence, flinging her mother's words back to her in air quotes while flashing her well-manicured fingers. Emily rose from the kitchen island and left her barely touched creamer-filled coffee behind her. "I need to get ready for practice."

Practice wasn't for another forty-five minutes, and she needed fifteen minutes to get into her soccer uniform and make it to the field. But Maggie pricked a nerve and the two women did their well-rehearsed dance to avoid further conflict.

Maggie sighed and picked up Emily's coffee and poured it down the drain. She cleaned up the kitchen and the remains of last night's dinner. It was one of Emily's only chores. But homework, practice, or tiredness impeded the ten minutes it took to pick up after the dinner Maggie made. She was tired of fighting her daughter on it, so she reabsorbed the chore every morning. Emily never acknowledged the magical fairy who came in to do her chores each day.

She placed the last dish from the pasta dinner in the wash and sensed someone watching her. She peered out the window and saw Josh's truck drive by out of the corner of her eye.

Maggie called up the stairs, "Hey, Em, are you expecting Josh to come by?"

"No, why?"

"Pretty sure he just drove by the house," Maggie said.

"Doubt it, Mom. There are like 1,000 Toyota pickups

running around here. It's not like they're uncommon." She heard the impatience in her daughter's voice and knew she rolled her eyes again.

But Maggie was sure it was him. The house sat in a cul-de-sac and Maggie knew each car in the neighborhood loop. She watched him slow as he passed the house.

Stop it, she thought to herself. *Now, you're suspecting everyone of something.*

four

. . .

MONTHS LATER, Emily graduated from high school. Summer kept her busy with her job scooping ice cream, visiting with friends, and dates with Josh. She wove Maggie into the downtimes of her other higher priorities.

Maggie spent the long stretches of time that she wasn't working shut in her home office, scanning through more photos for Emily's photo gift. Move-in was only a week away now. Maggie took two weeks off work to help Emily pack, and to adjust to a quiet house. However, it didn't seem necessary, Emily's dance card remained full.

The long summer days were drawing to a close. Maggie clicked through the pictures from Emily's fourth-grade year and eyed a particularly charming one of a moment she had forgotten. Paul was hugging Emily after her class performance of the Gettysburg Address. She got the enviable lead-in line, "Four Score and Seven Years Ago." The picture showed Paul's back as he bent to hug the little Abraham Lincoln. Emily's face scrunched up in a wide smile, the beard pulled down like a furry scarf, the Lincoln hat sat askew on her head, and one converse sneaker was untied.

Maggie smiled and placed it in the memory book file. She heard a knock on her door and it creaked open. She locked her computer and turned to her daughter, peeking in. Emily stepped inside. "Hi," she said.

Maggie's eyes lit up and smiled. "Hi, stranger."

"I'm so behind in packing. I've only got a week until I leave." She wore her Jensen High soccer sweatpants and an old JMU sweatshirt she had stolen from her mother's closet. The past and the present wrapped up in her outfit. The messy bun perched on her head sat askew, and her face was clear of makeup. A blemish formed on Emily's chin. This was the Emily that Maggie liked best, flaws and all.

"Nonsense, a lot can happen in a week," Maggie said.

Emily circled her toe on the ground and stared at it, a nervous habit carried forward from her youth. "I know, but can you help?"

"Of course," Maggie said.

Emily walked back toward her room, and Maggie followed. Her daughter's typically neat room looked like her dresser exploded, flinging its contents on the floor. The top of the dresser held a collection of photographs of friends, but mostly Josh. The detritus of her youth spanned the carpet. There were several unlabeled empty boxes agape, waiting to be filled and carted off. Emily glanced at her mom and shrugged her shoulders. "I didn't know where to start."

Maggie rubbed her daughter's shoulder. "I see. Why don't we start with your clothes?"

"Okay," said Emily as she plopped herself up on the edge of the bed.

Maggie sat near the tallest pile of clothes and held up a Jensen High t-shirt. "This?"

"C'mon Mom, nothing with the high school on it," Emily said.

"That cuts out 50% of your wardrobe, so the rest should be easy," Maggie said, smiling.

"Fair." Emily smiled back, and Maggie placed the high school shirt in the 'no' pile.

After they finished sorting the clothes, they moved to accessories. A prickle of a tear trickled down Maggie's face. She swiped it away before Emily noticed. She packed up Emily's mammoth collection of sunglasses. There would be no one left to strew random items throughout the house. It had always annoyed her so much. Why? She stood to survey the rest of the mess.

Emily interrupted Maggie's thought. "Should I pack this? Do you think there will be room?"

Emily showed Maggie a framed picture of Maggie, Paul, and Emily from senior night. Maggie and Paul held up a banner of Emily's senior soccer photo. Paul's free hand rested on Emily's shoulder, and she beamed at the camera. "Uncle Papa gave this to me for graduation." Uncle Paul became Uncle Papa as Emily formed language. He was more papa than uncle and Paul adored it, so the name stuck.

"You'll be able to make room for it." Emily stood and handed it to Maggie. She wrapped it in one of the five sherpa sweaters Emily insisted on packing.

"Thanks, Mom." Emily pressed herself into her mother and squeezed. Maggie hugged her tight back, ignoring the sour smell of her daughter's greasy hair.

After a time, Emily wriggled to get free. "Mom, you're going to have to let go," Emily said.

"I'll never let go first."

"I have to get ready. Josh and I are going out tonight. We can finish packing all this stuff later."

"Fine," Maggie replied, but she didn't let go. Emily twisted out of her mother's embrace and headed to the shower.

Maggie returned to her office to continue her stroll through the past in photographs.

She thought back to the night she asked Paul to be Emily's godfather. He hadn't expected the monumental ask, but he never shied from it. It was the fateful night of Chris's last late-night meeting, Maggie and Paul ate, mostly in silence. Then, Maggie asked shyly, "Do you want to feel her move?"

His eyes lit up, and he moved his hands toward her taut, barrel round belly. She took his hands in hers. His hand trembled. "Are you nervous?" She chuckled.

"I mean, yeah, I've never touched a baby inside before," Paul said.

"Here, let me show you where she is. Press in a little. Don't worry, it doesn't hurt." She pressed over his hands and placed them firmly under her right ribs where Emily kicked.

His eyes widened when Emily rolled into him. "Oh my God." His mouth fell open, and his eyes glassed.

"Right? This is what I'll miss most about being pregnant. I'm never alone," Maggie said.

"Or she hates the meatloaf." He laughed.

"I have a serious question for you," Maggie said.

His moss-green eyes stared into hers. His hands still lingered on her belly. The intimacy of his stare and attention washed over her with warmth, then guilt. She reminded herself that he was her husband's brother.

Maggie cleared her throat. "Will you be our daughter's godfather?"

The glass in his eyes shed a tear. "Yes, of course." He bent over her belly and said, "Hi, sweetie. I already love you, you know." He tilted his head up and said, "May I?"

Maggie nodded. The warmth of his face thrilled her as he kissed her belly, and Emily's little foot kicked at him. It was one of the most intimate moments of her life. Before she could do something she would live to regret, Maggie rose and cleared the table.

She had not thought of this moment in a long time. The tragedy of Chris's death had nearly scrubbed it clean. Maggie shook her head, bringing herself back to the present. She returned to the picture file and found two newspaper articles. She opened them and read.

SUV Crashes Through Arlington Memorial Bridge Barrier: Lands in River

Crews construct a barrier after the first heavy snow of the season ends in tragedy. At 1:29 am an SUV heading southbound skidded off the icy bridge and plummeted into the Potomac River below. The victim, identified as Chris Becker, 24 of Annandale, VA, was recovered shortly after by the Park Police. He survived the initial accident but succumbed to hypothermia before authorities could arrive and rescue him. Park Police cite weather and speed as factors in the crash. No other vehicles or injuries were involved in the accident. Authorities expect lane closures and delays as repairs are underway.

"Why did I save this?" Maggie said out loud. Her universe tilted on its axis in one small paragraph. The bitterness in her gut twisted even now, reading it. But she couldn't bear to delete it, either. After all, it was a part of Emily's history, how her father died.

She read the article again. He wasn't going in the right direction. Chris shouldn't have been on the bridge at all. Through her despair, she never stopped to consider where he was. Her last words to him were, "Just go, Chris." And she denied him a last kiss before snatching his apology flowers from him and purposefully crushing a petal beneath her foot.

The next news story was how to survive a car careening off a bridge. "If it bleeds, it leads," Maggie said to herself and sighed. She wondered if perhaps Chris would have had this information, would he have survived? Did it save someone else from the same fate?

How to Escape from a Submerged Car

In winter, ice freezes on bridges first. While you never want to be in the position to know these tips, they can save your life if you find yourself in this situation. In the event your car is submerged, the best way to survive is to:

1. *Open the window as quick as you can before it is underwater.*
2. *Keep your seatbelts on until the water goes up to your chin. Breathe deeply and hold your breath.*
3. *Do not open the door until the flooding has stopped. It cannot be opened from the inside if the water is pressed up against the outside. If you have to break a window, aim for a side window.*
4. *Once the door or window is open, remove your seatbelt.*

5. *Exit the vehicle and float. Let your body do the work to take you to the surface. You do not need to know which way is up or down. Your body will float toward the surface. Don't fight it.*

Her mind returned to the happiest and saddest day of her life. After Paul helped her clean the kitchen that night, he left to go home. Maggie waited as long as she could for Chris to return to her. But pregnancy tired her, and she went to bed with the knowledge he'd be there by morning, and she let her mind indulge the guilty thoughts of Paul's comforting presence.

But instead of Chris walking into her room, she woke up to the sharp rap of a knock at her door. Maggie glanced over and his side of the bed remained empty. *He forgot his keys to get back in*, she thought. He carelessly woke her from sleeping. Chris knew how hard it was for her to sleep in this final trimester of her pregnancy. Maggie heaved and rolled out of bed and stomped down the stairs, ready to fight.

She opened the door and two uniformed officers stared back at her. The fight drained from her. "Are you Mrs. Becker?" The female officer asked.

Her sleepiness dissipated in an instant. "I am. Is everything okay?"

The female officer didn't answer her question. "Is there anyone here with you?"

"No." Maggie rubbed her belly and opened the door wide.

"I'm sorry, ma'am, but there's been an accident," The female officer said.

"What kind of accident?"

They still did not answer. "Is your husband Christopher David Becker?" The male officer asked and walked inside.

"Yes, oh my God." Maggie's throat closed.

"Ma'am, a car registered to him went over the Arlington Memorial Bridge. A body with his identification has been recovered," The female officer said.

The male officer asked, "Is there someone we can call?"

Maggie's knees buckled beneath her and she rattled off Paul's phone number from memory. A jolt like a rubber band snapped hard into her body. Maggie doubled over. Then a warm trickle between her legs. She gazed at the small puddle below her. "This isn't happening. It's too soon," she whimpered.

"I know, ma'am, sometimes these things happen. Can you come to the police station with us?" The male officer asked.

"Frank, I think she's talking about her baby." The female officer pointed to the puddle on the ground and crouched beside Maggie. "10-52. We need a medic here, premature delivery." She spoke into the radio on her shoulder.

The static radio replied, "10-4, medic en route."

Maggie held her stomach and a wave of cramps set in. Through blinding pain, she screamed, "She's too early!"

The walls closed in, and her mind faded to black. Maggie's next memory was lying in the hospital bed with Paul sitting at her side. His tear-stained face stared down at her as he ran his fingers through her hair. She opened her eyes and looked at him. He withdrew his hands and placed them in his lap. "Where's Chris? What happened?" she asked. Then the evening's memories snapped into place. Her hands settled over her deflated belly, and she tried to get up. "My baby," she croaked. Her head felt wobbly as a kite.

He gently pressed her shoulder, nudging her back into

the bed. "She's okay, Mags. You did great. She's in the NICU for a little more oxygen as her lungs develop. You did great. I'm going to get the nurse."

He tried to get up, but she grabbed his hand and yanked. "Paul, is it true? Was I dreaming?"

"I'm sorry, Mags. He's gone." His voice cracked.

She nodded. Her heart mirrored her deflated belly, still a part of her, but something alive was gone from it. The light in her dimmed.

"I'll get the nurse so you can see your daughter. She's perfect," Paul said. He disappeared out the door.

She stared at the ceiling and ached for the familiar rolling of her baby. She truly was alone now. Maggie's hand traced the familiar line of her abdomen and her finger caught on a bandage. A nurse walked in. "I see you're awake," she said brightly.

"Mm-hmm," Maggie replied.

The nurse looked at Maggie's finger tracing the bandaging on her lower abdomen. "You'll have some dressings there. Your daughter needed a C-section, but she is doing well. You'll get to see her soon."

Maggie's mind darted back to the present. Emily's unexpected arrival on the heels of her husband's death meant there were no pictures of Chris with Emily, and very few of Maggie. She stared at the earliest and only photo of Emily in the hospital. From the distance, she couldn't make out Emily's fine downy coating. Maggie remembered her shock. Emily's scrawny pink legs squirmed and her face squished red with rage at being thrust into the world too early. Maggie held her and smiled at the camera and thought, *What am I supposed to do with this?*

She studied the photo. Paul sat at her side. He appeared every bit a father, yet he was a grieving brother and godfather. He peered into the lens with red-rimmed eyes from grief and exhaustion, wearing a hospital band matching the one on his goddaughter's floundering ankle. Maggie didn't intend on having Paul present for the delivery, but when the police came and she went into labor early, her sister lived too far away, and her husband was dead. She saw her slack-jawed and puffy face in the picture with her Christ necklace poking out. She winced at the unflattering picture but put it in the 'book' file.

She decided not to include the newspaper article of Chris's death in her daughter's book. But she read it again and wondered out loud, "Why were you on the bridge that night?"

five

• • •

COMBING through photos was easier than facing Emily's boxes as she packed up her life. Despite the plausible explanations of the janitor, his presence still tugged at her. His image cropped up each time it settled in her mind that he was a coincidence. He became a staple, an absolute presence throughout Emily's childhood, and Maggie did not know he existed. She sensed someone watching her often, but what woman hadn't? Yet, something in her gut screamed.

Maggie couldn't unsee him anymore. She opened the school's website and searched for the janitor. There he was, Mr. Murphy, and his picture stared back at her. His mud-brown hair was messy and receding, unremarkable in nearly every way. The only fact she could glean from the school's website was he started work in 2017, when Emily began high school, and he planned to retire at the end of the school year. "Enough," she said aloud. Maggie would put this issue to rest for herself. She went to her Apple Photos People Album. She found the picture of him at the funeral and tagged him. The app ran a search and created a listing of 412 photos of this random man bearing witness to her life. In contrast, Paul returned 697, and Maggie only 212.

She considered that maybe he ran in a lot of the same social circles. But she knew better. No one in her community would include janitorial help. While she and her friends were left-leaning politically, no one wanted a Section 8 house in their neighborhood or had blue-collared friends.

In the next picture, Emily was in her daycare. Maggie snapped the photo from outside the fence before picking her up. Emily's legs dangled in the air as she swung high on a swing. Her half-opened mouth was caught in a laugh, and her two pigtails shot out behind her like a jet stream. Then she saw it.

"Damn it," she said out loud. He was raking at the right corner. Pre-school, even before school, there he was.

The pool of people who traversed pre-school to graduation shrunk substantially. Emily had five kids who started at the daycare center through senior year. Coincidentally, Josh was one of them. Maggie snapped this picture about a month before the Disney vacation, where the Watcher eyed her from beyond the balloon vendor.

Maggie went to her bookshelf and pulled all her daughter's yearbooks off the shelf, scattering them on the floor in front of her. The books grew increasingly thicker with each school. She opened each of the twelve books and went to the back faculty page. He was, in fact, the janitor at her pre-school, elementary school, middle school, and high school. Emily was right. Mr. Murphy had always been there right under her nose, invisible.

Maggie opened Google and typed 'background investigation.' No one would know, and what harm would it cause? Better to overreact than not react at all. She found a site where she needed to enter his name, location, and pay $19.99. Before she changed her mind, she entered her credit card information. A Black man with dark hair peppered with white stared back at her through kind eyes. His race, birth date of 1956, and death date of 2016 made him an impossible match to be even a family member of the common Murphy name. The sole thing the two shared was their town. She minimized the background investigation screen, $19.99 wasted on a picture.

The janitor's presence still pricked at her. Why follow her family? What was his fascination with Emily? She typed the words 'private investigator' in the search engine. "Stop it," she said, and shut the computer before she read the results.

six

. . .

MAGGIE GROANED as her body protested getting out of bed so early. But if she didn't run then, it wouldn't happen. She donned her running gear, reflective vest, and a small headlamp. And with her body still cloaked in darkness, she ran by moonlight to clear her head before the day's chores and Emily's worries took root to dominate her day.

The small splash of the puddles beneath her feet kept cadence with the music in her earbuds. She sidestepped a dark puddle winking back at her in the silvery moonlight. "Three miles," she breathed in deep, the thick air filled her aching lungs. Her feet slapped the pavement in rhythm with the bass beating fast in her ears.

"Mmmm, petrichor," she said out loud. She liked the melody of the word in her mouth; the smell of the earth after rain. While the thunderstorm staved off the heat of a Virginia summer morning, it did nothing for the claustrophobic humidity. She peered up at the trees; today they still held tight to the dark greens of summer. But fall fast approached, and soon she'd run with no one to return home to. One yellowed leaf tumbled down in front of her, a hint of the next season teasing.

The hairs on the back of her neck protested her route, so she turned right despite her normal route left. Turning right steered her by the police station, just in case. Her speed increased and her breath heaved with exertion, but she didn't dare glance over her shoulder. At the side of her eye, she felt a dark figure keeping pace. A stitch in her side pinched hard, and her chest tightened, but she did not break her stride. She arrived at the police station and doubled over to nurse her stitch. Crouching under the basin of moonlight, she glanced around, but found no one. She waited another twenty minutes and watched the dawn chase away the night's monsters. Then she tightened her shoelaces for the jog home.

"I'm so stupid," she said to herself. She taught Emily better than this. Even when walking Emily to the bus stop, Maggie taught her to cross if there was a van or car she did not recognize.

So why did she risk running in the early hours of the day, before the safety of the sun?

On her jog back to Emily she thought, *who would keep her company when Emily left for good? Could she date?* The idea of it made her want to throw up.

Her romantic life was as dead as Chris. Her loneliness loomed before her. *What's next for me?*

Once, a friend set her up on a date. The hassle of finding a sitter (she couldn't, so it was a lunch date); discussing why they were single (he divorced/her a widow); kids or no kids (her yes/him no). The thought of another wasted evening or afternoon filled with empty talk of getting to know somebody who was wrong for her was nauseating. The dating pool now was a dribble of nonstarters. However, with Emily going to college, Maggie was running out of excuses. The loneliness mounting before her seemed unbearable but it wasn't clear what was more daunting; dating or being alone.

Alone. Her sole identity of 'single mother.' But was she? Paul never missed an event or game for Emily. 'Uncle Papa' made himself available for every father/daughter dance and holiday. While Maggie and Emily visited Chris's grave each Father's Day, leaving behind a stone and flowers Uncle Papa would take them to dinner every Monday after. Emily handmade Uncle Papa's cards from when her pudgy fingers could draw, to now when her hands grew long and slender. They made the day after Father's Day, Uncle Papa's Day.

At three years younger than Chris, Paul never shook 'little brother' status. Those years were forever in high school. However, decades later, they seemed less important. Who was the big brother now? He was fifteen years older than Chris was when he died.

Maggie and Chris started dating freshman year in high school, much like Emily and Josh. They were everything to each other. Her sole heartbreak was when his car careened off the bridge. For Chris, she would forever be his first and last. Why did she expect herself to be lonely after Emily left? No one else did.

Emily never met her father, so Father's Day felt more like a passage or rite. Maggie needed something to do with Emily when all of her friends celebrated with their living fathers. Emily held her mother's hand as they stood at his grave and stared at his name etched in stone. Each year, Maggie cried, and Emily would cry too, but not for her father. Emily cried, watching her mother cry.

"Please don't cry, Mama. It's okay," Emily would say nearly every year.

"I know, baby girl, we're okay. It makes me a little sad he isn't here."

"But he is, Mama, he sees us from heaven."

"You're right, he sure does. Sometimes, I have to remember that better," Maggie said.

"I'll remind you."

Maggie allowed herself a day each year to let grief overwhelm her, and every year, she let Emily pull her to shore. A small selfish act.

Emily stopped going with her mother to visit Chris's grave when she got to high school. There was always an excuse not to hold her mother's hand and bear witness to her loss.

Maggie's mind returned to the present as she increased her pace to get home. It was getting late, and the sun brightened the cul-de-sac. Glinting with sweat and humidity, she glanced at the driveway, then at her watch. "Damn," she said. Emily had already left for practice. If she didn't take the police station route, she would have seen her.

Before jumping in the shower, Maggie sat with the photo book to cool down. She wouldn't let her paranoia stop her from the most meaningful gift she would give her daughter. Maggie opened her laptop screen, and the listing of private investigators shone back at her. She minimized the screen but did not close it.

Then, a photo cropped up of Maggie. The right moment, angle, and lighting. Maggie stood in a field, walking toward an outdoor concert. Her chestnut hair tousled over one shoulder in perfect beach waves. Her mouth open slightly as she glanced over her shoulder at a person out of the frame. The golden hour created a hue of tan she never had. No filter, but natural sunlight and a perfect angle in an ideal moment. Her jeans held tight to her middle, with flared bottoms and platform sandals. She wore a black sweater that slouched to one side, allowing her slim shoulder to peek through. Emily took the picture ten years ago when she still considered her mother cool. She said, "Mom, you look awesome." Maggie turned over her shoulder to thank her, and Emily snapped the photo.

She cropped the random people out of the picture and felt heat crawl up her neck as she admired the tone of her legs. Her mane of hair looked more like a Pantene commercial.

She sighed. "I don't look like that anymore," she said to the air. The twinge of wasting her most beautiful years alone as a widow, raising a little girl, haunted her. She felt the edge of resentment from her choices creep in. She loved this photo, and there weren't many of her to choose from. Somehow it struck her as wrong to smile and have fun while her husband was dead.

After Emily goes to college, maybe she'd put together a dating profile, she thought. She wouldn't use this picture. She was no catfish. Besides, the worst thing to happen would be for someone to show up and be disappointed in the non-filtered ten-year older version of her. She opened her phone and looked at herself in selfie mode. Her jawline grew softer, and her chestnut waves wilted a bit, but her hair was still full and only mildly streaked with gray that she colored regularly. The flared jeans were back in style but wouldn't fit now. Long ago, she donated them to Goodwill.

She vowed she'd take new photos with no filter, but there was nothing unethical about great lighting and generous angles. Maggie began a 'Maybe Later' folder for herself, hidden behind the 'Budget' file header. No one could access her computer, but if anyone came across a file with a bunch of pictures of herself in it, she'd curl up and hide.

She wasn't sure how Chris would feel about her dating. They were so young when he died that they never had the 'if I die' conversation.

The sweat had long dried off her, and she re-opened the golden hour picture to admire herself again. She heard the door creak open.

"Mom, I'm home."

Maggie quickly shut the computer and walked out of the office.

"Hi sweetie, how was practice?"

"It was fine. But..."

"What is it?"

"I don't know if I'm being paranoid..."

"Paranoid about what?"

"After you mentioned the whole Mr. Murphy thing, it was weird. I realized without ever noticing before he's at, like, every practice. So strange, huh? You kinda got me wigging out like you do."

"Yeah, strange. I'm sure it's nothing," Maggie replied.

"You're probably right. But I couldn't help but think he was there to watch me. I don't know why. He was cleaning the bleachers, but he looked up a lot. Every time I looked at him, he glanced away."

Maggie's stomach curled tight around itself. "Should we do some more packing today?" Maggie asked, changing the subject.

Emily shook her head. "Nah, I have to get ready. Josh and I are going out." She walked up the stairs.

Maggie had heard enough. It was time for action.

seven

· · ·

MAGGIE FOLLOWED Emily up the stairs to get ready. She peeled her running clothes off and jumped into the shower. The hot water pelted her scalp and chest, and the steam rose, clearing her head. She soaped up and washed quickly to save enough water for Emily's hot bath. Maggie put on a pair of leggings over her wet legs, and the sweatshirt they stole from each other constantly. It was a sage green Virginia Beach sweatshirt that used to be a darker color. A men's large, with holes where the cuffs met the sleeves. It belonged to Chris, but the two shared this one piece of clothing like sisters. It fit big with the stretch of time and the threads coming loose at the edges. She glimpsed at her profile in her bedroom full-length mirror. She appeared dumpy. But it was the one thing of his she let herself wear.

She wandered back to the office and opened the computer. The picture of herself with the favorable angles stared back at her. She felt heat rise to her cheeks and shut the photo before maximizing the private investigator search in Northern Virginia. She scrolled through pictures and profiles of the private investigators. The 'professionals' specialized in background investigations, insurance fraud, and a lot of work on catching cheating spouses. That was one service she didn't need. Cheating was a non-issue for the couple. Even when he was alive, the idea of cheating couldn't cross their collective mind. He'd been dead eighteen years, and while she'd nurtured thoughts and fantasies. Never once had she cheated, even on his memory.

"They all are sleaze-bally," she muttered. She scrolled through the headshots and found an attractive man. Dunn Investigative Services, LLC listed background investigations. Before she could hesitate or talk her way out of it, she dialed his number. On the third ring, the voice matching the romance-cover man answered, "Hello, you've reached Nate Dunn's services. How can I help you?"

She heard her heart beating in her ears and hung up. Maggie placed her phone on the desk and got up from her chair to pace. "Oh, God, what did I do?" She didn't get two steps from it and her phone rang, beckoning her back to the device. Maggie glanced at the screen. It was the number she'd just dialed.

She sat back down at her desk and picked up. "Hello?"

"Hi, you called me. I'm Nate. How can I help you?" Maggie noted he didn't say he was with a private investigation service.

"Oh, uh, I think I may have dialed the wrong number," she said.

He sighed back. "People say that a lot. How about we have a conversation?"

No harm in a conversation between two adults, she thought. She breathed in and started, "I don't think I'm calling the right place, or service or whatever..."

"Let's start with why you called, and we can take it

from there." His voice sounded like silk, and she wanted to tell him everything.

"Well, I'm putting together this photo album for my daughter, who's going to college. There is a man in these pictures. I don't know him, but when I asked my daughter about him she said he's the school janitor. It's crazy, and it's probably nothing, but he's been the janitor for every school she's been in, and he was in the background of photographs we took on vacation in Florida." She heard her voice climb a higher octave and speed up. Saying the words aloud, she knew in her gut something was wrong.

She didn't tell him about the pictures at her husband's funeral. Being a widow felt intimate.

"I wouldn't call a mother's intuition crazy. I'll tell you what. Why don't we meet in person at Buzz Off in an hour?"

His picture stared back at her from the website. His blondish wavy hair combed perfectly in place, no signs of a receding hairline or even gray. She wouldn't mind meeting him in person.

The coffee shop was neutral and public. Emily had just stolen and creamified her last cup of coffee again, so maybe it was a sign. "Sure, I can be there."

"Alright, see you in a few. Bring some pictures and what you know. It will give us a head start."

"Okay, I'll talk to you later, Mr. Dunn," Maggie said.

"Please, call me Nate."

"Thanks, Nate," she said and hung up the phone. That *voice* again, smooth talking. She looked forward to the cup of coffee now. She mouthed the words, "Thank you" to the sky, grateful that Emily snatched her last cup of coffee. Maggie programmed him in her phone as 'Nate PI'.

She checked the social media platforms to see if she

could find anything on Nate Dunn. The name was too common or and he seemed to have no online presence. Disappointed, she returned to her files and pored over the pictures to find which ones she'd like to give to Nate.

She didn't know which pictures to take. Each one appeared innocent enough. Was it the quantity, or that he gazed toward them in nearly every shot? She gathered a few where he looked the most menacing, but none were egregiously so.

Among the photos, she included the man watching her from behind the balloon vendor. Would the little girl holding his hand make her appear crazy for suspecting a father on vacation with his girl, stalking her family? Regardless, the information was important enough to include and she added it.

On the phone, she didn't share with Nate that the mysterious man appeared after Chris died. Why? Was it a crime to be a widow, or was it the constant stares of pity she received from everyone when they learned of it? She scoffed at herself for keeping Chris's death from a private investigator. Before they met, she was sure he'd have her social security number, salary, occupation, address, birth date, and whether she was allergic to bee stings, let alone a widow. She printed out her cursory $19.99 background check that returned a Black man twenty plus years older than the Mr. Murphy she knew and included it in the envelope. She also printed the photo of the man in the background as she leaned over her husband's coffin and slipped it in with the rest.

Maggie removed the towel from her head, and her hair peaked and twirled in all directions. She glanced at her watch, merely half an hour before she needed to leave. Maggie, a scientist, and widowed mother, did not follow the trends and appeared every day of her forty-three years. She embraced her age years ago, sort of, though she still hid her grays. She cursed herself for not going to the salon last week to touch up. There was a clear line of white/gray streaks about two inches above her root line.

To cover her age, she combed her hair back and plucked an abandoned headband out of the bathroom drawer, and placed it in her hair. Her complexion quickly evened with a small bit of foundation and bronzer. Then she applied a small swipe of gloss, mascara, and a hint of liner at the sides of her eyes to draw him in to her favorite feature.

She went to her room to find clothes. She dropped her towel to the floor and looked at her body. A bra would certainly help, but it wouldn't work the magic she hoped for. She found a plaid skirt that flared and landed above her knee, and a white button-down shirt. She slipped them on and put her feet into a pair of black pumps. Her feet already pinched in them.

She looked in the mirror. "What am I doing?" she said aloud. She went to her nightstand and slipped her pepper spray into her purse.

As she was leaving, Emily popped out of her room with a towel around her head. She looked her mother up and down and said, "Okay, Nancy Drew. That's kind of cringe, Mom. Where are you going looking like that?"

Immediately, Maggie felt ridiculous in the headband, and she knew it didn't fit her or look anything like her. It was too late to change it. She blushed and tucked her hair behind her ear. "I needed the hair out of my face," she replied. She didn't owe Emily an explanation. She walked down the stairs, less confident than before. She needed to see Mr. Dunn, Nate that is, for Emily's safety, she reminded herself.

Maggie caught her reflection in the car window, and she did, in fact, look like Nancy Drew. She turned back toward the house but received a text.

Nate PI: *I'm here - what are you wearing?*

Maggie: *I'll be there in five minutes. I'm in a plaid skirt and white shirt.*

She threw her purse on the passenger side, and all the contents clattered to the ground, spilling onto the floorboard. "Damn it," she muttered.

Nate PI: *Perfect, you'll be easy to find. I'll be waiting outside.*

She started her car and drove off.

eight

. . .

MAGGIE PULLED into Buzz Off and parked in front of the cafe. She eyed him from her car. He had propped himself against the brick building outside the shop. He wore a casual button-down, slightly wrinkled shirt, dark jeans, and loafers without socks. The top two buttons of his shirt were open, revealing a sliver of hairless skin beneath. Nate wasn't as young as the website photo, but it wasn't so out of date that she couldn't find him. Certainly not as old as the photo of herself she admired earlier.

Maggie restarted the engine and put the car in reverse. What was she doing here? Why did she reach out to an investigator over a few photos? Mr. Murphy was a janitor, a community member. Her car made a beeping noise as she put it into reverse to announce her changed mind. He caught her eye and mouthed, "Maggie?".

She smiled sheepishly back and nodded. "Too late now," she muttered and put the car back in park. Her hands gripped the wheel, and she breathed deep. Despite not appearing exactly like his picture, he was objectively handsome. Her attraction to his blond beach waves surprised her.

He approached the car while running his finger through his blond mop, appearing equal parts childish and handsome. Maggie stared and only realized as he approached her door that she had been slack-jawed. She clamped her mouth shut and smiled.

"Hi, I'm Nate," he said. His mouth opened in a wide smile, revealing a row of perfectly white and straight teeth. He opened Maggie's car door so Maggie could accompany him for coffee.

"I'm Maggie," she replied. Before getting out, she remembered her purse's contents were scattered across the floorboard. "Oh damn, give me a minute."

"No problem." He turned his face toward the coffee shop, but stood awkwardly, holding the door open.

Maggie unbuckled and leaned over to the passenger side to tuck away her tampons first. She was glad the pepper spray stayed tucked away inside the purse. All the other items could wait. She reached farthest for the envelope of pictures. Her lip gloss, mascara, grocery store lists, and gum remained strewn on the floor. She felt the blood rush to her cheeks, either from contorting into the awkward position to re-assemble her purse or mortification.

She stepped out of the car and looked at him. "Sorry. My purse spilled." Maggie bit her lip and smoothed her plaid skirt.

"It's okay," he responded. He shut the door behind her and walked toward the coffee shop, and she followed. He opened the door. "After you." She walked through, idly touching her headband. Maggie's stomach would not unwind from the dismal first impression she was making.

She approached the barista, a bored girl with blackish-blue hair, tattoos, and several face piercings. The barista's name tag read, "Sue."

"Good morning, Sue," Maggie said.

The barista looked confused, then down at her badge. "Oh, yeah, sorry, I forgot mine today, so I picked up one in the back. I'm Carly," she said, chuckling. Then she added, "I'm six hours into an eight-hour shift, and you're the first person to look at my name tag."

"Everyone is in a hurry these days," Maggie replied.

"What will you have?" Carly asked.

"A black coffee, please," Maggie said.

"Coming right up, and for your husband?"

Maggie was about to correct her, but hesitated. She heard Nate's silky voice from behind. "I'll have a vanilla latte, thanks."

Maggie glanced over her shoulder, and he shrugged and winked. He paid the barista, and they brought their coffees to an empty table for two in the back. She sat, pleased to be off her heels. Her toes pinched and she wanted to take the blasted shoes off.

As they sat, she noted how mismatched in formality of dress they were. She said, "I'm on my way to a conference after this."

Nate said nothing in return, and she knew he knew she was lying.

His shoe grazed the side of her heel as he leaned back in his chair. She didn't pull away, and neither did he. He leaned back and blew on his tanned brown latte.

"So," he said, lifting his mug to take a sip, "let's take a peek at those pictures you brought." He pointed to the envelope she had laid on the table.

"Oh, right," she said and handed over the envelope. Her hand trembled, as did the envelope as she handed it to him.

He smiled back at her. "There's nothing to worry about with me." He took the envelope into his well-manicured hands, "May I?"

"Of course," she replied.

He pulled them out one at a time and studied them. The first picture was of the man and the balloon vendor with the little girl. "So, he's a father?" he asked, studying the picture.

"I'm not sure. I mean, if you look at the picture, I know it's a moment, but they don't really seem together, you know?"

He nodded in agreement. "Maybe an uncle?"

"Maybe," she said, and it made her think of Paul. He wouldn't look detached from Emily. Why did she feel this meeting was more than business? And why did guilt crawl in when she considered Paul? She pushed the thought of Paul from her mind. "This was a long time ago, my daughter is now eighteen. She is about two in this shot. He looks different, but you can still recognize him."

Nate moved to the soccer picture, where he stood at the edge of the field. "Who took this picture?"

"I printed it from her Instagram. So, I don't know. Maybe the yearbook person?"

"Interesting," Nate said. Maggie's brow formed into a question. "Well, in the other ones, he looked toward your family. Here he isn't watching Emily at all. So, perhaps it's more coincidence. It's hard to tell in a snapshot." He flipped to the next picture.

As he flipped, her stomach flipped, too. The photo of her kissing the casket felt much too intimate now, and she wished deeply that she hadn't included it in her haste. It felt like a siren song of her widowhood. He scanned the scene for a moment and set the photo on the table between them.

"It was a long time ago," she said in her standard explanation.

"I'm sorry for your loss," his hand reached over to cover hers and gave a gentle squeeze.

She smiled shyly at him and felt a shame creep in. Was this what she wanted? To show off her dead husband to get attention from him? The pressure and heat of his hand let up, and he returned to the picture, focusing his attention on the man in the background. "Is this the first picture he's in?"

"It is," she said.

He nodded. "I see." Then, he pointed to his hand. "This injury he has is serious."

"Yes, I guess in elementary school, he walked with a limp. I'm guessing it's related," Maggie said.

"How do you know?"

"My daughter said the kids teased him."

"Kids can be cruel," Nate said.

"Yes, they can." She absently touched her headband and remembered her daughter called her 'cringe' before leaving the house.

Finally, he scanned the $19.99 background check. There wasn't much on it, but he scanned it and set it down next to his latte and took a sip. He leaned back, but let his foot stay connected. Nate said, "Okay, so it sounds like you have already completed a quasi-check and there's something about it that still bothers you. I'll do a little more in-depth research. Because I like you, I can give you an introductory rate of $500 for the first eight hours, but I'll charge $150 for the first three. I can get a lot done in three hours. You'll know if you want to pursue the other five. We can see if there is more to investigate. Is this something you'd be interested in?"

Maybe this was all business, she thought. The way he easily slipped into his sales pitch. She tucked her heel away from his and straightened in her chair. "I don't want to be rude, but I tried to find you on social media. I couldn't find anything. Can you tell me a bit more about yourself before we move forward?" Maggie saw enough MLM scams and money grabs to at least ask the question. She sipped her coffee and sat back in her chair, allowing him space to explain. Though $500 didn't seem necessarily egregious for eight dedicated hours. However, would he find more information he needed to investigate? The services he provided didn't lend themselves to reviews from customers. No one admitted to needing services like those he provided, which made it the perfect business to attract the scammers. No one would report that they hired a private investigator, and they were swindled. What made him qualified?

His smile grew wide, and she smiled back without a thought. "Of course," he replied. "You couldn't find me on any social media network because I worked in cybersecurity for the federal government under one of the three-lettered agencies. I know what kind of information they collect. You're right to be concerned and to ask questions. Many people in my field of work are moonlighting cops or convicts. Our business isn't widely regulated. I stay offline mostly because you can imagine there are several people who aren't exactly interested in being 'buddies' with me. Honestly, besides my website listing, I'm a ghost. I keep my notes longhand. Though, I'll type it up before you get it, of course, but aside from research that I use a VPN for, and my website, I don't exist. I have two phones. With my line of work, I don't want my clients or whoever I'm investigating for my clients to get a hold of my personal phone. The one I have is for family. Well, my sister. I'm not married," he clarified.

She smiled enthusiastically at his admission. "Well, that makes sense," she replied. Maggie shuddered, thinking of all the places across the internet where she'd left bits of herself, little pieces to be traced back, allowing someone to assemble every bit of her. A stalker could have unlimited access. And here Nate sat in front of her, the only person she knew without a profile page.

Maggie's text dinged, and she glanced down and muttered, "Oh shoot, I thought it was silenced." She put her finger up to Nate. "Sorry, one sec. It's my daughter."

nine

. . .

EMILY: *Mama I see UR at buzz off can I have a cinn dulce plz*
He shifted in his seat and sipped his latte.
Maggie: *Yes, I'll place an order and bring it back.*

Despite teen texting etiquette, Maggie obeyed the rules of grammar. But for Emily, periods and punctuation were signs of anger. Maggie tried to abandon her grammar, but her fifth-grade English teacher shouted back in her head and she just couldn't do it.

Emily: *No worries OMW I stop by and get*
"Ugh," she said aloud.
"What is it?" Nate asked.

"My daughter tracked me down. This is her favorite coffee spot, and she's on her way. So she can have a free drink. Teenagers." Maggie rolled her eyes.

"Teenagers," Nate agreed.

"I know this is going to sound awkward, but can I introduce you as a colleague?" Maggie sipped her coffee and tapped her foot.

His tongue absently ran across his perfectly lined teeth. He looked like a predator. Her paranoia crept into everything now. Nate said, "I beg your pardon? I'm not opposed to this, but why? I mean, I certainly won't say the services I provide. But why a work friend?"

Maggie felt him prying into her personal life, but she wanted to tell him. "It's my daughter and me. It's already going to concern her enough that I have a 'friend going to coffee with,' because you're, well, a man; she's going to be curious. Aside from my husband's brother, she has seen no one who might be a male, friend, date, or otherwise at our house or with me." She idly twisted their wedding bands yoked around her neck that clinked together in a familiar reminder of everything she'd lost.

His eyebrows turned up in the universal sign of sympathy again, and it fueled an ire within her. He repeated, "I'm sorry for your loss."

"Thank you. It was a long time ago," she replied.

He nodded and smiled. "Maybe we can have our next meeting over dinner?"

Electricity shot through her toes, and before she thought, she replied, "Yes, that would be nice." Had she agreed to a date or a business dinner? She didn't know.

"One more question. You said he had been the janitor at your daughter's school, but wouldn't that be the same for about 100 other kids?"

"Yes, I thought so. Then, I spotted him at the daycare. I researched, there are five kids who went to all the same schools and her daycare. Three boys and two girls."

"Well," he paused and scratched his chin, "that shrinks the pool down, doesn't it?"

"I know I sound paranoid. There's something in my gut. It's hitting me in a way I think it isn't right. I'll pay the cap of $150 to see what you can find in a few hours. If it's nothing, then we move on and I'll feel a lot better. Deal?" She held out her hand.

He extended his warm hand and clasped hers. "Deal." And he winked at her.

"Great, I'll bring the contract to dinner for signing. I don't like to deliver anything online on account of the kinds of things I deal with. I extract things online, but I never contribute to the matrix."

She breathed out a sigh of relief. There would be no evidence she signed a contract with a private investigator to research a janitor as her daughter prepared to leave for college. If it was a foolish mistake, she would forget about it and be $150 or maybe $500 poorer. Still, she couldn't figure out if the dinner was a date or a business meeting, or a little bit of both. Surely, she didn't need to go to dinner to sign a contract.

The door of the cafe jingled open and Emily breezed through. She wore a crop top, jean shorts, too much makeup, and hair straightened stick straight. She saw her mother first, then noticed Nate. Her eyes narrowed. She came to their table and stood, her arms crossed in front of her, leaning on one foot.

"Hi, Mom," she said, glaring at the man beside her.

"Hi, sweetie, this is N..."

"Nick," Nate finished. "I work with your mother. I've heard a lot about you."

Emily's eyes did not leave Nate, and said, "Oh, really? I've not heard a thing about you. Mom, is Uncle Papa coming over for dinner tonight?"

"Hmm, not that I know of," Maggie replied.

Emily tossed her hair away from them and headed toward the tattooed barista while glancing over her shoulder at her mother. Maggie knew Emily didn't have money in her account, so she was expecting her mother to follow. Maggie got up to accompany her daughter.

Nate followed and grazed Maggie's elbow, and a warm tingle ran through her body. He said, "I'll make those final arrangements with the client."

Maggie blushed and nodded. She mouthed, "I'm sorry."

Nate peered over at Emily and said, "It was a pleasure to meet you." His tone struck Maggie as offended.

Emily did not glance up from her phone as she stood in line waiting to order. Maggie elbowed her, and she briefly met eyes with him. "Yeah, good to meet you, um... what was your name again?"

"It doesn't matter," Nate said and walked out the door, and it jangled closed behind him.

"Emily Renee Becker, what got into you to be so rude?" Maggie asked. Her 'mom' voice boomed louder than she meant it.

Emily eyed her mother. "Mom, he's sleazy. You couldn't tell?"

"What do you mean, sleazy? I work with him, and we went to coffee," Maggie said. The lie caught thickly on her tongue.

"You haven't been out with a guy in a long time," she said. "Obviously, because he was gross."

"Emily, you do not get to dictate who I spend my time with, and you will not be rude to people because of their 'vibe.'"

The women were at the front of the line, and the barista looked between them and said, "Do you need more time?"

"No," Emily said. "I'll have the cinnamon dulce, in a large, thanks."

Maggie forked over the credit card to pay for her daughter's drink, and grumbled, "I shouldn't do this."

"Do what?" Emily asked.

"Pay for your drink after you behaved so badly," Maggie replied.

They walked to the other side of the counter to wait for her drink. "Mom, I just don't want you to get hurt. And he was no good. I'm an excellent judge of character."

Maggie rolled her eyes at her daughter. "You haven't lived long enough to be an excellent judge of anything, Em."

"Okay, Mom." Emily's replacement word for '*whatever*' after Maggie banned it. The barista called her name, and Emily picked up her drink, sipped it, and walked toward the door.

"You're welcome," Maggie said to Emily's back.

Her daughter raised her arm in reply and looked over her shoulder and mumbled, "Thanks."

Maggie got back into her car, settled in behind the steering wheel, and peered down at the remnants of her purse. Now, with no one watching her stuff her purse with her life, she could take time with it. After she fished out the lip gloss that rolled beneath the seat, she started the car. Before pulling out a text beeped in.

Nate PI: I shuffled a few things. Can you get together tonight? Since "Uncle Papa" won't be there? :)

Maggie: I'm sorry about that. I told you it would be weird for her to see me with any man.

Nate PI: No worries. Seven at Morgan's Steakhouse?

Maggie: Perfect.

Nate PI: Great, I'll have the paperwork and the first three hours completed.

Maggie 'liked' his text and headed home.

ten

. . .

AS SOON AS Maggie pulled into the drive, she removed the headband from her head and rubbed the pain behind her ears. She shook her hair and glanced in the rearview mirror, but the dent from the headband remained.

After straightening her hair, cleaning the house, reading, and strolling memory lane through photographs, she got ready for her second business appointment of the day. Or was it a date? Morgan's Steakhouse was nicer than Buzz Off and called for a classier outfit and lipstick. She opted for black slacks and a red silk shirt tucked in the front to flatter her fuller hips. She shoved her already aching feet back into a pair of black pointed pumps on teetering heels. As she slid her second pearl earring in, she caught her daughter's reflection peeking into her doorway. "Can I come in?" Emily asked.

"Of course. What's up?" Maggie asked.

"Nothing," she said as she plopped herself on the bed and gazed at her own reflection, then at her mother. "You look pretty."

"Thank you." Maggie slid a red shade on her lips and

they came shockingly to life. She licked the front of her teeth to catch any residual lipstick off her teeth. She once attended an entire wedding with lipstick on her teeth. No one told her, but it later explained why people kept turning awkwardly away. When she discovered the blood-like smear on her teeth, it relieved her. She thought they were turning from her because of her widowhood.

Emily looked at her mother's heels. "Where are you going?"

"Dinner with a friend."

"Is this friend Nick?" Emily said, glaring at her mother. "He's no good, Mom."

"If you have to know, no, it isn't Nick. I'm going with Carolyn." She instantly felt a pang of regret for her lie. She wasn't going with Nick, but she wasn't going with Carolyn either. His name was Nate, but Maggie knew who Emily meant.

"The one lady from work, who has the voice that drives you crazy, and talks too much? Why?" Emily recalled more of their conversations than Maggie expected. She pulled the first female name she fished out of her mind, and it was the one woman she would never have dinner with.

"Because, Emily, if you must know, you're leaving and I have to make a life for myself that doesn't revolve around you." Emily jerked her head back and looked at the floor, no longer staring at herself or her mother's reflection. Maggie paused and breathed. "I'm sorry, Em. I didn't mean to say it like that. I need to make more friends. Just like when you go to college. We're both starting new phases of our life." She slipped her heels off and sat on the bed next to her daughter and nudged her shoulder.

Emily nodded. "Oh, I get it." Then she paused, and added, "But what about Uncle Papa?"

Maggie felt the flurry of butterflies surrounding Paul's name. "What about him?"

"I just thought you guys spend so much time together that he was like your best friend."

"He is, but I need more than one friend, Em."

"I don't want you to be lonely. I feel bad sometimes for leaving. It's been like just the two of us. I want you to spend time with people you like. Not the Carolyns of the world."

Maggie laughed. She shouldn't have said Carolyn. The woman really was dreadful. But she said what she said. "I know, baby. I'll be okay. Don't you ever feel guilty for going to college and living your life. It's what I want for you." Maggie leaned into her daughter and squeezed her shoulders.

Emily said, "You smell nice."

"Do I normally stink?"

Emily laughed and pulled away. "No. It's just that I can't remember the last time you wore perfume."

Maggie glanced at her watch. "Shoot, it's late. I've got to go, sweetie." She grabbed her black purse, flung her phone and lipstick in it, and slipped the uncomfortable but flattering heels back on. "What about you? Where are you going tonight?"

"I'm going to see Josh," Emily replied.

"Okay, don't be home too late," Maggie said. She blew Emily a kiss and walked out the door.

Maggie arrived at the restaurant, glanced in her purse to make sure her pepper spray was still there, and briefly wondered what the hell she was doing there. The steakhouse sat in the middle of the strip mall but was widely considered to have the best filet mignon in town. She walked over to the hostess, a pimply faced girl with frizzy mouse-brown hair.

"Do you have a reservation?" she said without looking up.

"Yes, I think it should be under Nate Dunn," Maggie said.

"Hmm, do you mean Nick Dunn?" the hostess replied, smacking her gum.

A smile passed over her lips. Nate was playful and coy. "Oh, yes, I'm sorry, Nick," she responded.

The hostess glanced up, bored. "He already arrived. I'll take you to your table." The hostess snaked through tables covered in white tablecloths. She walked impossibly fast in her black sneakers as Maggie followed, teetering on heels.

They walked to a table in the corner. He smiled as they made their way to him. He stood, and said, "Hi, Maggie." And tilted his head.

"Nick, it's good to see you," Maggie said.

"Ah, I'm glad you noticed the name on the reservation." His smile brightened.

The hostess pulled out Maggie's chair and hustled away before Maggie sat. He'd ordered a bottle of pinot noir and a full glass was sitting in front of her. She didn't care for red wine; she liked chardonnay. *It was presumptuous to order any drink*, she thought. He didn't know if she drank at all. Unless of course, he used his detective skills to find out. Though, then, he would have known she liked white wines.

"I ordered wine for the table," Nate said.

"I see, thank you." Maggie swirled the deep violet drink and took a small sip. Here she was, accepting a drink from a stranger in an unattended glass. Exactly what she asked Emily never to do. The tannins nipped and dried her tongue. This varietal tasted earthy to her, but not pleasantly so. More like drinking a mushroom. She picked up the menu and quickly glanced at the wine price list. It was a

$50 bottle. She eyed longingly the $40 chardonnay beneath it.

The waiter approached the table and asked, "Would you like to hear our specials?"

Nate said, "No, we'll be having the Caesar salad, bread, and the marinara pasta."

She smiled weakly back at him. Is this how dating went now? She didn't look at the menu. He ordered Caesar dressing, which made her gag since she got sick on it in Cabo during her honeymoon. *Maybe she could eat around the dressing,* she thought.

The waiter bowed slightly and said, "Very nice choices, sir." He didn't look at Maggie and walked away. Her hopes of trying the filet mignon drifted away.

Nate cleared his throat. "Anyway, where were we?"

"Before we get started, I wanted to apologize for Emily's behavior. She's not typically so rude. Lately, she's been a little hard to deal with." She sipped the acrid red liquid and tried to swallow it down without a grimace.

"It's no problem. I have nieces and nephews. They get snarky when they're teens." He leaned forward and put his hand on hers.

Maggie chafed and pulled her hand back. "I don't know if snarky is the right word. She is protective."

"Understood." He leaned back and took a long sip of wine.

The Caesar salad arrived at the table and she took a few small pieces of lettuce and a couple of croutons and placed them on her plate. He studied the leaves on her plate. "You don't need to eat like a rabbit, you know."

"I know. I am saving my appetite," she replied. Maggie crunched the flavorless lettuce and popped in a crouton chaser. Her belly growled for more, but her stomach stiffened at the scent of the Caesar dressing.

Nate cleared his throat and pulled a few leaflets of paper from his briefcase. "So far, I don't have too much. I confirmed what you provided. He has floated from school to school for the entirety of your daughter's childhood. My initial research was on how many people started at the school and are graduating. I did research on how many children went from the preschool to graduation, and you were right. Only five."

Maggie sipped her wine. He got no farther than she did in the few minutes it took for her to research, and it cost her $150. Worried mothers seemed as effective as full-time private investigators. "Do you think it is a coincidence?" she asked.

"It really may be. There could be perfectly logical explanations for all of it. But I don't like that he suddenly appeared at your husband's funeral, and this doesn't explain Florida either. I would recommend signing on for the $500, and I'll do additional research. But I can keep digging up to the $500 and we can go to dinner again to review?"

"What more will you research?" Maggie asked.

"His family, why he has burns, and why he's in so many of your photos. I would like to see if he poses any sort of threat. If he does, I'll notify the authorities. Especially before your daughter goes away to college," Nate said.

Her stomach curled at the thought of leaving her child vulnerable in college if there was any doubt or concern about a stalker was a nonstarter. She cleared her throat. "I think that sounds good." Maggie poked around her plate for a dry piece of lettuce.

"Good, good." He slid the contract across the table. It

was a single page. There was a limit of $500 with the total due at signing. She signed the contract and pulled out a checkbook.

"I'm sorry, I should have mentioned. I really prefer cash. Taxes, you know." He shrugged.

"Oh, uh, okay. I never carry cash. So, we'll have to go to an ATM after this." She tucked the checkbook back into her purse.

"No problem, I know one that is close by," he said.

The marinara and pasta appeared, and she took a bite. It tasted like the Prego she could throw together at home. They ate for several beats of silence, and the waiter returned with the bill. "No rush," he said before skittering off.

Maggie reached for it, and Nate batted her hand away. He winked at her and said, "We'll charge this as a work dinner."

Maggie thought Emily's intuition was right. It was still unclear if this was a work dinner or one of a more personal nature. Each time it was going one way, he pulled it in another direction. The idea of doing a walk of shame to the ATM to pull out $500 to fork over didn't please her.

After dinner, she gathered her purse and asked him, "Do you know where the nearest ATM is?"

"Yeah, there's a CVS two blocks up."

She did not expect to walk two blocks up and back on her heels. Her toes crammed tightly, begging for relief. "Great." She smiled through gritted teeth.

Nate kept a steady and quick pace. She did her best to keep up with the pinching pain but slowed. He said, "Sorry, I'll slow down. I forgot you wore stilettos. They're nice." And he touched her elbow.

"Thanks, they aren't very practical, though," she admitted.

She walked up to the ATM, withdrew $500, grabbed the cash without counting, and gave it to him. Maggie felt like an accomplice, but if so, it was a $500 lesson learned. He took the money without counting it and slipped it into his pocket.

"What's the next step?" she asked as they left the CVS and headed back to the parking garage. Maggie wished she was alone on the eternal two block slog back to her car; she vowed not to wear the stilettos again. Her heels would need Band-Aids, and her toes screamed with pain.

"Let's meet again in a couple of days and I'll give you what I've found. Dinner again?"

Blush burned up into her cheeks. "Sounds great." Nate leaned in for either a hug or kiss, and Maggie introduced her hand instead to shake. He shook it but held her hand briefly to his lips and kissed the top. His warm breath on the back of her hand both excited and repelled her.

eleven

. . .

NATE'S FACE WAS LIKABLE, but something about him struck her as *off*. It was rude to order a grown woman's dinner; it made her feel powerless and resentful. Is this what the dating pool had come to? If she knew for sure the transaction was solely business, that was navigable terrain. The mixed signals knocked her off balance.

Maggie would not tell Emily it was Carolyn again; her daughter was nearly too smart for the first fib. But she wouldn't admit to it being Nick/Nate, either. She couldn't pinpoint if she liked him enough for a second meal. Next time, she'd show up first and pre-order the wine. Even if she paid for it herself, she would not muscle down another pinot noir.

As she got ready for bed, she replayed the night's signals. A date or not a date; he loves me; he loves me not. Nate paid for the dinner but called it a business expense. He pre-ordered everything, and they signed contracts and exchanged money. But he kissed her on the hand and asked her to dinner again. Not coffee, not lunch, but dinner. He also liked her stilettos, which she resolved were no longer worth the effort.

The next morning, she rolled out of bed with a splitting headache from the wine and wished she had pre-treated with Advil. She headed to the kitchen to make coffee and received a text from Nate. He, too, was an early riser.

Nate PI: *Hi Maggie, hope it isn't too early. Can we talk tonight? May have found something. Sparkettos?*

Maggie's heart skipped. What did he mean he may have found something? She knew he wouldn't discuss it unless they were in person. It was no use to ask him.

Maggie: *Tonight is perfect.*

Nate PI: *Great, 7?*

Maggie: *I'll be there.*

Tonight was not perfect. She would have to cancel the Sunday night dinner with Paul. Maggie liked that Nate was not afraid to choose which restaurant. When Chris lived, they could never decide where to eat. The conversations were much the same; "Where do you want to go? I don't care, where do you want to go? How about there? I don't want there. Then where? I don't care." And this would continue into an echo chamber until they had settled on a place that would neither offend nor please either of them.

She nursed her headache and rapped her fingers on the countertop, willing the coffee to brew faster. She would be there at 6:45 to pre-order the wine she wanted. Maggie texted Paul next.

Maggie: *Hi Paul, can we push tonight's dinner to tomorrow? I have a work issue.*

It was a Sunday. She never worked on Sundays.

Paul: *No problem at all. You okay?*

Maggie: *Yes, sorry about the last minute change up.*

Ol' reliable, she thought. He liked the text message but

didn't reply. He was annoyed. She didn't blame him. She'd be annoyed, too.

Mercifully, Emily was out for the day. Emily could not corner Maggie into making another fictional dinner partner up. As she slipped a blue silk blouse over her head, she looked in the mirror. The lines around her eyes were more pronounced. She wasn't tired, but she looked like it. She spread concealer and smoothed the fine lines out. A real-life filter. Maggie thought absently about making an appointment for Botox. She had the money for it, after all. Her gray slacks snugged around her waist, and she made a mental note to start her diet again tomorrow. Finally, she stepped into her black ballet flats, which were much kinder to her aching feet, and spritzed a bit of the perfume she never wore on her neck. In case it was a date, after all.

Maggie ran a brush through her thick chestnut waves and pulled her hair back in her trademark ponytail. However, it made the grays more apparent in the light. She glanced at her watch. There was time to do better. She plugged the straightener in to see if she could do something more presentable.

At 6:45 she arrived at Sparkettos and the hostess sat her at a table close to the kitchen. She ordered a mid-priced bottle of chardonnay for the table and sipped water and waited. At 6:50 she received a text.

Nate PI: *I am running a little late get some wine for the table and an appetizer. I have to make one last stop.*

Maggie: *Should I be concerned?*

Nate PI: *I think after this last stop, you won't have to worry anymore about anything after this contract.*

Relief poured into Maggie as the chardonnay arrived at the table. She gave herself a generous glass and took a long buttery sip. *Ahhh, much better*, she thought.

At 7:15, the waiter came by again and asked if she would like to order anything. Maggie ordered calamari. The waiter glanced at the untouched silverware and glass across from her. "He's running a bit late," Maggie said.

Nate said he'd be late, and she had been early. Though it wasn't fair to him; it made him feel more late. When the calamari arrived, her stomach grumbled toward it. She felt a little dizzy from the chardonnay on an empty stomach, so she noshed the salty crunch of the calamari. She ate more than she intended, which would surely give her heartburn. She washed it down with a second glass of the chardonnay. At 7:30 she texted.

Maggie: Should we reschedule for another night?

He did not text back. Mortification set in as she shuffled in her seat, staring at her phone. Did this guy take her for $500? The room spun from the chardonnay again. She poured another glass. The waiter came by twice more.

At 8:00, the waiter stopped by her table for the last time with the bill. "Should I leave this here?" he asked, as he looked everywhere except the empty chair opposite her.

Maggie handed the waiter her card. "There was an emergency." She lied.

"Of course. I'll get this right back to you." He vanished behind the door as quickly as his feet could carry him.

"I can't drive home like this," she mumbled. She knew she could Uber, but texted Paul. He lived six blocks away, and she wanted to see his face and apologize for flaking. She'd stood him up for the first time in eighteen years.

Maggie: I was at a work dinner but they had an emergency. I'm afraid I've had too much wine to drive.

Paul: Where are you?

Maggie: Sparkettos.

Paul: Stay put, I'm on my way.

Maggie sat back in her chair, waiting for the receipt and Paul. "Nate's a jerk," she said to the air.

The waiter came back to the table, and she signed the bill. "Would you like me to send this bottle home with you?"

She looked at the bottle. It was three-quarters gone. "No, I think I've had enough." She smiled back.

"Very well." The waiter smiled sympathetically.

Paul came in behind the waiter and looked down at Maggie. "Sorry, I'm late." Paul's Washington D.C. hoodie, running shorts, and shoes looked entirely out of place. The nape of his neck glistened with sweat.

The waiter's eyes narrowed at him. Maggie's mind felt wobbly. She sloppily smiled at the waiter. "Don't leer at him. He's not the one who stood me up." And held up her glass and took another sip.

Paul looked at the waiter. "I'm sorry, I've got it from here." And the waiter skulked off.

"Hey Mags, what's going on?" The softness in his voice reminded her she had canceled on him, and he should be mad.

"I was going to this business meeting, but I kind of also wasn't sure if it was a date or not. But he never came," Maggie replied.

Paul's face fell, and he held out his hand to her. "Let's get you home."

"Okay." She leaned on him hard while he walked her out the door, as upright as she could be. She said, "Yesterday I was wearing stilettos. That would be a shit-show right now."

He patted her hair. "Yes, Mags, yes it would. Where's your car?"

"You didn't drive?" she asked.

"I was on a run and just ran here instead of home. You didn't sound great, and I'm glad I'm here."

She leaned into him. His sweat smelled fresh and healthful. "Ah, you smell nice." She stumbled into him and breathed in.

He chuckled. "Let's get you home."

She led him to her car by pushing the key fob and waiting to see which white sedan blinked back at her. He opened the passenger-side door, and she climbed in and buckled up.

"I'm sorry I canceled on you," Maggie said.

"It's okay, Mags," Paul said.

"I shouldn't have done it."

Paul stared ahead for the thirteen minute drive home. By the time he pulled into her drive, her head bobbed back and forth as she alternatively dozed and woke. She woke herself up with a snort.

Emily's car was still not in the drive. He circled around to her side of the vehicle and gently nudged her shoulder. "Hey, Mags, we're here."

"Thanks, Chris," she said as she rubbed her eyes.

Paul looked at his feet but said nothing. In the recesses of her mind, she put herself on repeat. What did she say that caused his face to fall like that? *Chris*, she called him Chris.

She took his hand and got out of the car. They were close now, and she was uncomfortably close to his face. "I'm sorry, that was an accident."

"I know." And he walked her to her door.

"So," she said, half closing her eyes, "Do you want to come in?"

"I'd love to, Mags. But not tonight. I'm going to Uber home." He kissed her on her cheek and closed the door.

Maggie locked the door and walked up the stairs. Was she planning to destroy her whole life in one night? She'd apologize to Paul in the morning. Tonight, she wanted to crawl into bed and sleep. Forget about the mystery janitor, the hot private investigator, and her brother-in-law.

The next morning came too soon. The sun pierced through her blinds and reminded her there was a price to pay for two late nights filled with too much wine.

Maggie missed a text from her daughter fifteen minutes ago.

Emily: *On run before practice*

The county implemented new rules on how many hours the coaches could have the athletes on the field. Most of the coaches finagled their way around it by giving the girls a pre-workout with a running app required for submission.

She'd be gone another thirty minutes. Enough time to have her last cup of coffee poured.

As Maggie lifted her first cup of coffee to her lips, another text rolled in.

She screamed and dropped her mug, shattering it into several pieces, burning her toes.

twelve

. . .

"SHIT, SHIT, SHIT," she yelled at the hot liquid scalding her feet. She jumped back and sliced the bottom of her right foot on a shard. She knew immediately the fragment went deep. Maggie grabbed the dishtowel from the stove and hopped to the dining room chair with her phone in one hand. She stared down at her foot, breathed in quickly, and pulled the glass wedge out. It was like an iceberg, much more beneath the surface than she expected. It wiggled and cut her on the way out. She began hyperventilating. "Stay here, it's almost out," she said to herself. Deep blackish crimson poured from her foot and spilled to the floor. She took the gray towel and applied hard pressure and stared back at her phone.

Nate had sent a news article to her.

Nate PI: *Check out this article...* **Local Private Investigator Dead**

Confused, and with shaking fingers, she clicked the article.

44-year-old local private investigator, Nathaniel Dunn, was pronounced dead following a suspected botched robbery attempt last night, police said. Mr. Dunn was found in his car in the parking garage at Sparketto's just after 10 p.m. The victim leaves behind a wife and three children. The crime is under investigation. Police ask anyone with information to contact the Arlington Police Department. Do not approach the assailant. Due to the nature of the crime, the suspect is considered armed and dangerous.

"Oh, Nate," she gasped. Who sent her this text? Nate had a wife and three children? She doubled over and howled from the pain in her foot and the text. He wouldn't have been at the parking garage if they didn't have a meeting, or was it a date? Heck, he wouldn't have been a target at all if she never contacted him. Based on the text, she knew that now. He died because of her. His three children lost a father because of her, and his wife joined the unenviable club of widowhood. Why did she think he was asking her on a date? But he told her he wasn't married. Maybe he was protecting his family? No that wasn't it, because he tried to kiss her. Nate was a creep, but he didn't deserve to die.

Maggie's fingers trembled, and she texted Nate's number back.

Maggie: *Who is this?*

Nate PI: *Tsk, tsk, no it won't be that easy. Three kids without a father. Just like Emily.*

Maggie drew in a sharp breath and felt the blood leave her face. Emily. She was still out on a run. She tracked her daughter, and her phone dot was about where she should be.

Maggie: *What do you want?*

She loosened her hold briefly on the dishtowel, and blood dripped to the floor again. She re-tightened her grip.

Nate PI: *I sliced his throat. If you want to be in the next* *news story, keep asking questions. Go to the police, and I'll slice Emily's throat before the police can find me. I'm watching you.*

The article didn't mention how Nate died. Mr. Murphy walked with a limp and had a poorly functioning hand. The private investigator was fit and could easily outrun or maneuver him. The text beeped again. This time it was a picture. She let out a cry.

Emily, deep in concentration mid-run. Her earbuds tucked into her ears, oblivious to being watched. The black top she wore swooshed to the right, revealing her fit abdomen. Her leggings clung tight to her legs, and the killer had caught her thick golden ponytail in mid-swoosh.

Nate PI: If you tell the police or Emily, she'll be gone before they find me. Do you understand?

Maggie: I do.

She couldn't go to the police. Maggie didn't know exactly who it was anyway. Could the police track his phone? Could the killer ditch the phone and kill Emily before they found him? It wasn't worth the chance. If it was Nate's phone, why hadn't the police tracked him?

Maggie tightened the bandage around her foot and hoped it would stop bleeding soon. She recalled sitting in the restaurant getting drunker and madder at Nate. The entire time, he was dying in the garage, steps away from her and her calamari and chardonnay. She texted again.

Maggie: Please, what do you want from me?

Nate PI: I'll let you know soon enough. Be patient and keep your mouth shut for now.

Maggie: Yes, of course.

The phone slipped from her slick hand straight into the drops of blood forming a shallow pool on the ground. She leaned over and picked it up, using the side of the towel to wipe the blood off. It created a brown-red smear. She opened the Find My app and traced her daughter again, willing her to return.

thirteen

. . .

MAGGIE'S FOOT WOUND CLOTTED, and she used the dishtowel to wipe the rest of the blood from the floor. She hopped to the kitchen, coffee long forgotten, and cleaned up the mug remnants, blood, and coffee.

She then hobbled up the stairs, putting most of her weight on the handrail, hopping and leaning hard on her other foot. Careful not to drip a trail of blood that she would have to explain to her daughter as she tried to choke back tears, but they fell anyway. She couldn't tell if she was crying for Nate, for fear of Emily, or because of the throbbing pain in her foot.

She limped to the bathroom, closed the toilet lid, and sat down on the cool surface to investigate her foot. The angry, jagged cut hurt like hell. But the glass was completely out. She bandaged herself up and tried to come up with the right next step. She tossed the blood-soaked dishtowel in the bathroom trash.

Maggie hobbled back to her bed and crawled in, keeping her phone glued to her face. She refreshed Emily's dot over again, watching her progress. Emily was still heading for home. Either that, or she was dead, and the killer was making progress toward the house.

"No," she said out loud. If the killer wanted them dead, they would be. He wanted something else. She'd have to wait and see. Pushing him might drive him to hurt her family.

Maggie watched Emily's dot on the tracking app until it landed on top of her own. She heard the door open, and Emily's voice yell, "Mom, I'm home." Maggie nearly cried with relief. She hoped Emily didn't come into her room just yet. As selfish as her daughter had been behaving lately, she was still an Empath. Emily sensed her mother's mood like an arthritic old man sensed changes in the weather.

"Okay, sweetie," Maggie called back and heard her voice crack.

Emily's footsteps came toward her room. Maggie kicked off the covers and swung her legs back to the floor. Her face scrunched with pain when she lowered her throbbing foot.

Emily knocked and let herself in. "Mama... wait, what happened to you?"

"Oh, it's nothing. I cut my foot."

"It doesn't look like nothing." Emily's brows turned up with concern.

Maggie felt a rush of gratitude for her injury. Her foot would be explanation enough for Emily, and she wouldn't pry about her red-rimmed glassy eyes.

"It's okay, Em. You needed something?" Maggie asked.

"Maybe I just came in to say hi," Emily replied.

"No, you call me Mama when you want something."

Her daughter grinned and hopped onto Maggie's bed. The jostling made her wince. "Oh, sorry," Emily said.

"It's okay."

"I know you helped me most of the way, but I was going to ask you if you can help me finish the packing today, but with your foot, maybe later?"

Maggie got up and balanced on her good leg. She raised her arm for her daughter to support her. "We don't have later. You move tomorrow. Don't worry, I'm good, I'd love to help you finish. It sounds like a great distraction from... this."

She rested some of her weight on Emily's sweat-cooled shoulder, and they moved like a tripod into Emily's room. She smelled like she ran four miles. But Maggie didn't mind. The days where only a wall separated them were coming to an end.

They hobbled together to Emily's room. It looked more empty than before. Much of what made the room Emily's was tucked away in the boxes.

Emily had a pile of items in the middle of the floor. "I know. It's such a mess, but I got overwhelmed."

"This isn't so bad, Em. Moving is a messy business."

"It is," Emily agreed.

This time, Maggie sat on the bed while Emily sorted the last few items. Something else was on Emily's mind. Maggie needed to wait it out to find out what it was. She hoped it was nothing related to Nate or the killer.

Emily interrupted her stream of worry. "Mom, don't look so sad. I will only be a few hours away."

"I know, I'm just going to miss you," Maggie replied.

She could tell her daughter sensed something was wrong, but it intermingled with the adolescent idea that Maggie's world revolved around her. While Emily inferred correctly that she held the sun, moon, and stars, that wasn't what troubled her. She folded the last of her sweat-pants and gave her mother a sideways glance. "Mom, tell me more about the guy in the coffee shop. Nick, I think his name was?"

Maggie grimaced. "I introduced him to you when you were there."

"I know, but who is he really? You wore heels to meet him there. Are you... dating him?"

"No, honey." Then, she repeated what she now knew. "He has a wife and three children."

Emily blushed. "Sorry Mom, I was rude to him because I didn't like his vibe. Now I feel bad. I thought he was coming on to you. I misread him."

"Don't, Em, he has already forgotten about it," Maggie said.

Emily taped the boxes and glanced at her mother. "It would be okay, you know?"

"What would be okay?"

"You... dating," Emily said quietly and turned away from her mother.

"What are you talking about?" Sickness crawled in her stomach. The man she thought she might date was lying in a morgue waiting for his wife and three children to bury him.

Her daughter walked to the bed and took Maggie's hand and said, "You know, Mom, no one expects you to be lonely. Not Dad, me, Uncle Papa, or anyone. If you decide you want a, you know, a companion, no one can blame you. I mean, I didn't like the vibe of that work guy, but there are others. I think you should look around. Maybe someone you already know?" Emily shrugged and let her mother's hand go.

Maggie laughed and reached for her necklace to rub together the two wedding rings. "Don't worry about me. I'm going to be okay. Let's focus on you, and getting you moved in to college. This is supposed to be an exciting time for you."

Maggie thought, *how could she allow her daughter out of her sight when this person watched them? Could she take her daughter and run?*

Emily turned from her mother and taped another box. "Josh has been getting really pissy lately."

"Oh?" Maggie asked.

"Yeah, the closer it gets to move-in day, the more he is trying to take all my time. Like, the other day he asked me to skip practice to go hang out at his place. He knows I'd never do that. And he just went off about it."

Maggie's ears pricked up. "What do you mean, went off?"

Emily turned around and sat on the bed next to her mother. They both stared at the taped boxes, Emily's life all packed and ready to go. "Just saying stuff like, he doesn't want me to leave, and he's going to miss me. He cries a lot. It's honestly kind of annoying."

Josh wore his emotions out where all could see. Maggie witnessed him cry at least three times in four years, and Emily witnessed it far more often.

Maggie said, "I'm sure it's got to be hard for him to see you're moving on, and he's staying here. For now, anyway."

"I guess. I think we may try the long-distance thing. He's worn me down." She gave a weary laugh.

Maggie turned to her daughter and put her hand on her shoulder, turning Emily toward her. She leveled her eyes at Emily. It was not the time to play coy or be a cool mom.

"Being worn-down is not a start to a successful long-distance relationship. It isn't fair to you or him."

Emily shook her mom's hand off her shoulder and got up to label the clothes box. "God, Mom, I was kidding about the worn-down part. Sometimes you take everything so literal."

Maggie blew out a sigh, propped her foot up on the bed, folded her hands over her stomach, and stared at the ceiling. She realized she sounded like a nag but found it impossible to hold her tongue.

Emily rummaged through her dresser to find her practice uniform. "Anyway, long-distance worked for you and Dad," she said in almost a whisper.

Maggie closed her eyes. "It was a different time, Em." She knew her daughter was not like her. There was not a wild oat in Maggie's body that needed sowing. As soon as Maggie and Chris met, they were settled. That was not where Emily was at. Maggie overheard enough conversations between her and her friends to know parties, boys and more parties were on the horizon. A long-distance relationship had a less than zero chance of survival. Emily was avoiding doing the hard, adult thing of having mercy on Josh and ending it.

Maggie liked Josh, but Josh was not the boy for Emily. In the last three years, her daughter quickly outgrew the high school and the town. Even Paul sensed Emily was ready to spread her wings and start her own life. If her daughter kept a relationship with Josh out of guilt, it would be full of lies and ultimately her daughter would be the villain. But Maggie kept her mouth shut. Teen romance would not be the hill she planned to die on today. She hoped she could keep her family safe and not die on any hill soon.

"I've gotta get ready and get to practice. Josh and I are going to meet up for coffee beforehand," Emily said.

Maggie's eyes were still closed. "Okay, hon. Have fun." She knew she'd track her the whole way. Everything had to appear normal even though it no longer was.

"Are you going to stay in here?" Emily asked.

"Maybe for a little while, I propped my foot up. So, yes, until the Advil kicks in." The Advil she took for her hangover had not worked its magic yet on her foot.

Emily leaned over and kissed her mom on the head. "Okay, Mama. Feel better."

Maggie opened her eyes and smiled. "Thanks, sweetie."

Emily patted her mother's shoulder, went downstairs, and Maggie heard the door click behind her. Maggie opened her eyes again and stared at her phone. Did he know Emily was going to college? Regardless, she had to pretend all was normal so Emily had to go. In the event he didn't, she would leave early, and get Emily out of harm's way. Maggie tracked her daughter again. She was at Buzz Off. Maggie just needed to keep her safe until tomorrow, because the killer couldn't be in two places at once. She texted her daughter.

Maggie: *We are leaving early tomorrow. Avoiding traffic.*
Emily: *plans with josh how early*
Maggie: *Five.*
Emily: *KK thats not bad*
Maggie: *No. 5AM.*
Emily: *Mom WTF?*

No matter Maggie's response, Emily would be angry. So, she didn't respond at all. They would leave before daylight, and the roads would be open. She would recognize a car following her. Even killers slept. If the killer followed, she would take down the plate and drive right to the police station.

She called Paul. "Hi. I was wondering if I could borrow your brawn?"

He laughed. "Of course. When?"

"Well, we're leaving before five tomorrow morning, so maybe tonight? I cut my foot, and I'm not getting around very well."

"Oh my God, do you need to get to the doctor? I can pick you up now."

"No, no, it's not that serious. I can barely feel it." She lied.

"You sure? I can come by on the way home. I'd love to see Em and say goodbye. Will she be there?"

"Honestly, probably not. She's pretty upset about the early wake-up call. But, traffic. And she's trying to spend the last moments with the boyfriend."

"Still the weepy one?" Paul asked.

"If you refer to him as the weepy one with Emily, she'll get us both."

He laughed again. "Of course not, Mags, that's between us. I'll swing by in a few hours."

"Thanks again," Maggie said.

"Anytime."

She hung up the phone and felt spent. Paul was as much an Empath as Emily, but with the foot and her daughter going to college, he'd hardly expect a stalker/killer.

Maggie needed to start her day. She hadn't eaten or finished her cup of coffee. The cut was worse than she thought and bled again in the shower. The blood formed a small whirlpool around the drain. So much blood for a tiny cut. She wondered how much blood Nate spilled before the sweet relief of death set in. She was alone. It was okay to scream in the shower, and she did.

After she dried and re-bandaged her foot, her stomach demanded she make breakfast. She hadn't been shopping in a couple of weeks. Emily was out all the time on her 'goodbye to friends' tour. She found Emily's favorite, Kraft Mac & Cheese, and the salty carby noodles beckoned. Maggie made them often because it was secretly her favorite, too.

As expected, after practice, Emily didn't come home but texted that she'd be out with Josh. Maggie tracked her the entire day.

Paul knocked on the door and let himself in. Maggie rinsed away the evidence of her childlike dinner. He smiled at her, and the box of Kraft Mac & Cheese she had left out. "Whatcha got there?"

"Comfort food," she replied.

"I see that." He walked to her, and she put the weight of herself in his arms. "How you doin,' Mags?"

She let a tear slip out of her eye. She felt safe in his arms, safe for the first time today. Maggie wanted to tell him, but the killer had been clear, tell no one. "I've been better." He pulled her closer, and her tears soaked his shirt. He smelled like cedarwood and mahogany, and she breathed in deep. She pulled away and wiped her nose with her sleeve like a toddler. "I'm going to miss her so much." She cried. And that part was true. She would miss her.

"I know, I know. You sit down, and I'll get her things to the car and come back. I don't want you going up and down those stairs on that foot." She didn't argue. Her foot hurt, and the stairs were difficult to navigate.

Paul made three runs to get the bags and boxes in the car and sat on the couch next to her. Maggie leaned her head on his shoulder. He said, "You worried about tomorrow?"

She was, but because she wanted to get Emily as far away from danger as she could. "No," she replied.

"Liar," he squeezed her shoulder and said, "I'm going to head out and give you two your last night."

She smiled at him, and he got up from the couch just as Emily came through the door. Maggie sighed with relief. Emily's eyes were red from her own goodbye tears for Josh.

"Uncle Papa," she said, and ran to him with her arms outstretched. She toppled into his arms. "I'm going to miss you so much." Maggie could see her daughter's eyes pinched tight as she held him like she was drowning. Maggie couldn't recall the last time Emily hugged her that tight.

Maggie stayed up for the night. When her eyes drifted closed, she'd jolt awake and glance at her phone. By three, she gave up and took a shower. At 4:30 she tiptoed into Emily's room. Patting her feet, Emily kicked back and grumbled, "Too early."

"I know, baby. But it's time. We've got to go."

"Please Mama, I need more time." Her voice sounded like the little girl Maggie woke for daycare.

"I know. You can sleep in the car. Grab your blanket."

"Okay," Emily relented.

Maggie grabbed her daughter's toiletry kit and pillow. She put the pillow under her arm and hobbled down the stairs. The pain in her foot had turned to a dull ache. She was grateful it was her left foot and she could still drive. Maggie didn't want anyone else to have to drive them. She wanted these few moments for just her and Emily.

Emily nodded off in the front seat with her blanket and an eye cover. Maggie left the music off so her daughter could rest, and her light snoring punctuated the silence of the night. The car's lights created a pool of light in the inky darkness of the road ahead. Maggie's eyes constantly darted between the road and the rearview mirror. The roads were desolate with several stretches without another car in sight. The further Maggie drove from home, the more her anxiety eased and her heart lightened.

Maggie heaved a sigh of relief.

fourteen

. . .

MAGGIE STOPPED at a Starbucks for coffee and breakfast. After she parked the car, she nudged her daughter's shoulder as she snored beside her. "Hey, we're at Starbucks."

Emily snorted awake and pushed her eye cover into her hair. "Really? How close are we?"

"About ten minutes from the school," Maggie said.

"What? What time is it?" Emily asked.

"We made great time. It's just past seven."

"Oh my God, Mom, I told you we should leave later." She pushed her seat up and stared at her mother. "I could have seen Josh today." She crossed her arms over her chest and glared at her mother.

"There would be traffic later," Maggie said.

"Who cares? Are you trying to get rid of me? Keep me from saying goodbye to Josh?" Emily threw the accusations at her mother as she rubbed the sleep from her eyes. She pulled down the sun visor and flipped down the mirror, staring at herself, and ran her fingers through her messy hair. "I look like crap. I can't show up like this," Emily said.

Maggie expected Emily's attitude and was glad now that she slept most of the way. She ignored the accusations lobbed at her and opened the car door. "One cinnamon dulce coming up. Do you want to come in or wait here?" she asked with false cheer in her voice.

"I'm coming. I have to brush my hair and teeth in the bathroom. Geeze, Mom, I can't show up like this. I feel like an animal getting ready in a Starbucks bathroom." She rolled her eyes.

"Okay, I'll make the orders and you can head to the bathroom." She grabbed her toiletry kit, a pile of bundled-up clothes, slammed the car door, and stormed into the Starbucks.

Maggie sighed and shuffled toward the entrance after her daughter, strongly favoring her right foot. She felt lighter and giddy with relief, despite her daughter's attitude. Emily would understand one day when it was over.

A soft jazzy tune filled the air, and the smell of coffee greeted her at the door. No one was there except the barista, and she hardly peeked up from her phone at their entrance. Maggie cleared her throat lightly to demand attention. The girl wore a pixie cut with tufts of dark hair poking everywhere. She seemed not far out of high school herself. She glanced up at Maggie, uninterested, snapped her gum hard, and stepped toward the register. She placed her phone down beside the register, but still trained her eyes toward the glowing device. "You ready?" the barista asked.

"I am." Maggie ordered both their coffees and breakfast sandwiches. The barista turned her back and began to prepare the order.

After ten minutes the order wasn't ready and Maggie was still waiting for Emily to emerge.

"Meggie?" the barista called with her order. Sometimes Maggie thought the baristas purposefully got customers' names wrong for their own entertainment. She was the sole customer in the shop. Maggie limped toward the pickup area and the barista's demeanor softened. "Do you need a drink carrier?"

"That's me, and yes, that would be nice." Maggie collected her drinks and sandwiches, sat at a table at the back window, and waited.

Emily took another ten minutes, and Maggie gave up on waiting. She didn't like to drink it cold. She could tolerate a cold sandwich. Emily finally emerged from the bathroom with her hair pulled back in a tight pony, leggings, sneakers, and a new JMU sweatshirt. She appeared every bit like a college student. Maggie wished her daughter would wear less makeup but said nothing.

Emily plopped down in front of her mother, unwrapped her sandwich, and took a giant bite. With her mouth still full, she said, "Thanks, Mom. I didn't realize I was so hungry." Her tone softened.

Maggie took a small bite of her own. Finally, she let out a breath. The killer sat in Northern Virginia while her daughter would be safe in her dorm.

"Jenna texted last night. She's already there and moved in. She sent pictures of the room. It looks smaller than the YouTube videos I watched."

"I thought move-in was today?" Maggie asked.

"Yeah, but she got an exception because her parents aren't with her. They are like in Africa, saving the world or something."

"Oh, well, that'll make it easier. You won't have a bunch of people in the room trying to set up," Maggie replied.

"Yeah, I guess." Emily took the last bite of her sandwich and washed it down with her cinnamon dulce.

"What do you mean by that?" Maggie asked.

"It's just... what if she's already made friends? Like, first impressions are important. I don't wanna be like a third wheel." Emily tapped her feet and slid her eyes away from her mother.

"You will not be a third wheel. You two have been talking nonstop since you matched. Meeting a few people who got to come early won't change that," Maggie said.

Emily didn't reply and sipped her coffee again.

After they finished their breakfast, they drove the ten minutes down the road, and the campus was buzzing with life. Maggie watched children with parents in tow carrying IKEA and Target bags, boxes, and pillows. The kids budding into adulthood looked frightened, impossibly young, and euphoric. Many dads smiled, and a few mothers swiped tears from their faces as they orchestrated the logistics. Tectonic shifts coming to thousands of families, and Maggie was in a sea of the same. But for her, it meant she'd be alone. No Emily. No Chris. Just her, and maybe a killer.

After the 'street team' unloaded the car, they parked and trudged up to the dorm. The building looked more institution than apartment as it towered over her. She crossed her arms over her JMU MOM T-shirt and wished she had brought a sweatshirt. Emily's gait slowed to a crawl. Maggie with her injury could easily keep up. Emily dragged her roller bag behind her with slumped shoulders and stared at her feet.

Maggie put her arm around her daughter's shoulder and put a little weight on her as they walked up the hill. Emily said, "Mom, I don't know if I'm ready for this."

"Em, you are. There are thousands of kids here thinking

the same thing." She smiled but thought about how ill-prepared Emily was. Maggie hadn't put her daughter in enough uncomfortable situations to help her deal effectively with discomfort. "You're going to be okay."

"I know, this part is just, it's hard. I don't know anyone, and I miss Josh," Emily said.

"I know you do. But you'll be home before you know it. We have parents' weekend in about six weeks, then another few weeks and you're home for Thanksgiving. When you're home, you are going to be begging to come back here."

"I hope so." Emily sighed.

Maggie and Emily navigated the throng of frenzied mothers, fathers wielding tools, and the constant hum of teenage nervous chatter. Emily shrugged her mother's arm from around her, and Maggie withdrew and hobbled, unassisted. She understood about first impressions but wished she could sit. The long walk to the dormitory damaged her foot more. She felt a warmth and wetness in her shoe. The cut had re-opened, and she hoped she wouldn't track blood through the campus. Emily's dorm door was open and a girl with a high tight blonde ponytail wearing a JMU sweatshirt and jeans with more holes than denim sat at her desk with her laptop lighting up her face.

The blonde looked up, and she squealed, jumping up from her desk and running to hug Emily. Maggie smiled as she watched her daughter's shoulders relax as the anxiety melted from her. She noticed the roots of Jenna's hair showed. Emily insisted on getting hers done right before school. They dyed their hair similar shades of blonde with similar shades of brunette beneath, like over half of the girls in the dorm. Emily's straightened hair curled at the edges with the humidity. She inherited her waves from Maggie. Maggie embraced her waves but only after fighting with them for far too long. She knew Emily would do the same, but not while straight was the trend.

Jenna beamed at Emily. "I feel like we've known each other forever."

"Same." Emily smiled back.

Maggie examined the room. Jenna took the side without a window, leaving her daughter on the superior side, a smart way to make friends. Aside from the stack of books on Jenna's desk and the partially opened desk drawer, there was nothing out of place. She made her bed with golds and blues and an old, worn Snoopy dog. Emily brought blue bedding in almost the same hue.

Emily looked at Jenna's bed. "You've got to be kidding me."

Jenna straightened and said, "What? Do you want that side of the room? I can move."

Emily smiled. "No, no, not that. You have a Snoopy. None of my friends back home even know who Snoopy is. I have one, too. But I left it at home."

"That's crazy. My dad gave it to me. I've loved on him until you can barely tell it's Snoopy anymore," Jenna said, smiling. She pulled it from the bed and showed one ear to Emily. "This is where I got the ear re-attached. Snoopy went in the wash and came out with one of his ears missing. I cried and cried."

Emily giggled, and Maggie smiled. Her daughter would be safe here with her new roommate.

Jenna looked over at Maggie. "Oh, I'm sorry. I'm so rude. Hi Ms. Becker, I'm Jenna." She held out her hand to Maggie.

"Hi Jenna, you can call me Maggie. It's nice to meet you." She searched for something more to say and noticed

Jenna's necklace. It had the letter M on it with a tiny diamond winking back at her. "I like your necklace."

Jenna glanced down at it. "Oh, thanks. It's my mother's. But when she's traveling, they aren't allowed to wear showy stuff. So, I'm holding it for her until she comes home. I know it sounds lame, but it's the only way I can reach her. She's in a remote area with no contact."

"That is so nice of you, it's lovely," Maggie said, and brushed aside the pinch of envy.

The girl blushed and she glanced around the room, following Maggie's. "What do you think?" Jenna asked.

"I think you did a great job."

"Thanks," Jenna said.

Emily interrupted, "Sorry your parents couldn't be here." Maggie took a step back and let her daughter enter her own world. As she said, first impressions were important.

"Yeah, right before it was time to go to college, my parents deployed to Ethiopia with Doctors Without Borders."

Maggie's eyes widened. "Wow, it's so great that they help people. One day I might do that."

Jenna shrugged. "Yeah, I spent most of my summer with my grandmother. My parents met in the Peace Corps right out of college. After that, they kept traveling. Saving the world one medical emergency at a time. So, I was mainly homeschooled, but all over the world. I'm excited to have a real school experience for the first time. The school let me move in early because I didn't have anyone to help me."

"We could have helped," Emily said.

"Maybe next year, my parents are gone for like eighteen months," Jenna said.

Jenna walked to her bedside table and picked up a frame. It held a picture of an impossibly beautiful couple. The blonde smiled at her husband as she sat on a red rock. She held the hands of a man who was kissing the top of her head. "These are my parents. I took this picture. We were on a hike. They can never keep their hands off each other." Jenna rolled her eyes and smiled at the picture.

Maggie suddenly felt out of place against the picture of the power couple saving the world with their model good looks. Suddenly, she couldn't recall if she brushed her teeth this morning. Her leggings and college t-shirt on move-in day felt completely underdressed against the beautiful couple who sat on Jenna's side table, assessing her from behind the glass. She swallowed down her envy. "Your parents look lovely."

Jenna put the frame down and said, "They really are." She smiled at the photo and touched the smiling blonde mother's face.

Emily interrupted again, and Maggie felt her daughter trying to gain her footing. "You can spend the holidays with us." Looking at her mother. Maggie nodded and took another small step back.

Jenna demurred, "Thank you so much. We'll see. I never know about my parents' schedule. I'm going to grab some coffee and breakfast. Give you guys a chance to settle in." She hugged Maggie and then Emily and disappeared out the door.

"She seems great," Maggie said.

"She does, but you hogged so much of the time," Emily said.

"What do you mean? She showed us a picture of her parents. What do you want me to do? Just stare back at her?"

"It's fine, Mom. It's fine. She's probably already meeting friends for coffee. I'm behind."

"Emily, move-in day is today. She came in early. You're not late."

"Let's just unpack," Emily grumbled at her mother.

The soiling the nest thing was getting old. Maggie said nothing and opened the clothes box. As she stood, she lost her balance on her good foot and tried to put the weight on her bad one. She stumbled and her elbow bumped the open drawer in the desk. The contents of Jenna's drawer tumbled out.

"Ouch, son of a biscuit." The searing pain shot up into her shoulder as she held her funny bone. There was nothing funny about smacking the tiny piece of bone.

"Jesus, Mom, all her stuff here is out. She's going to think I went through her things."

Maggie crouched to gather the colored pens, pencils, scissors, and a blue clothbound book. "Ah, she keeps a diary. How nice. Maybe you should consider that too, Emily. Maybe something to look at later and reflect on."

Emily's face burned red. "Mom, stop, just get all this stuff back in her drawer. She's going to think we snooped and then I'm going to know no one. She'll tell everyone and ask for a different roommate."

"Calm down Em, this isn't that big of a deal. Stop," Maggie said.

Emily blew out a furious sigh and opened the next box. "Just sit, Mom, and visit. I don't want you knocking something else over."

Maggie did as she was told and watched her daughter put her things away, vacillating between excitement and anxiety. Emily placed the picture Paul gave her of senior soccer night on her nightstand, and Maggie smiled. Sure, they weren't the model family opposite Emily, but Maggie was proud of the life she created for her daughter just the same.

Emily smiled at her mother. "I'm sorry. I've been so awful lately. You know how I get when I'm freaking out. It's a lot."

"I know, baby." Her daughter stepped into her embrace as she opened her arms. "I'm so proud of you."

"Thanks, Mama. I feel like this is going to be an awesome year."

"Me too. Can I get Jenna's number? Give her mine too, in case she needs anything with her parents gone."

"Of course," Emily sent Jenna's contact information. Maggie wiped a tear from her eye. "Don't cry Mama, you're just a FaceTime away," she said to her mother.

"I know. These aren't sad tears, they are happy ones."

Emily pulled away, and Maggie grabbed her purse. They walked to the front of the dormitory, where Emily stopped. "Do you want me to walk you to the car?"

"No, it's okay. Maybe you can text Jenna or finish settling in. I'll manage," Maggie said.

Emily nodded. "Thanks, Mom. I love you." She hugged her mother again, and Maggie didn't want to let go. Emily pulled away.

"Love you too, sweetie." Maggie limped out the door, feeling lighter on her feet. By the time she walked downhill to the car, she thought she could also move in the middle of a different night. Maybe then she could escape having to face the situation entirely. Before starting her engine, she already knew it was an impossible solution. She would have to face this situation. Somehow.

Maggie scanned the parking garage, still busy with the mothers and fathers pulsing in and out. *Wait*, she thought, *a parking garage.* She glanced at the back seat, half expecting to see the killer there with a knife, but there was no one. If he wanted her dead, she would already be dead.

Maggie put the car into reverse and drove off. She felt her shoulders inching toward her ears with tension. She stared straight ahead at the road. "Okay, just breathe," she said to herself. "Smell the flowers and blow out the candles." It was an exercise she'd used with her daughter as a child. Before each soccer game, Emily would freeze in fear. Maggie would hold her shoulders and look in her eyes and together they'd breathe in and out while Maggie said, "Smell the flowers, blow out the candles." Even now, before a game, her daughter breathed in and out, mouthing the words, *smell the flowers, blow out the candles* from the sidelines before they called her in to play.

Maggie held back her tears and left her daughter at school, safe. As she headed home to face the man who was threatening her.

fifteen

. . .

THE FARTHER MAGGIE got from the school, the lighter her heart became. Her anxiety melted away, and she realized longing would replace it. But now, it was time to figure out how to deal with the stalker.

She hadn't told Emily yet, but she considered selling her childhood home. She put the plan in place several years ago when she spotted the home prices rising in value. They owned the smallest house on the block. They'd renovated it by adding the finished basement and a pool. All costly items that drained a large part of their savings but would pay off handsomely when she could sell. She would use the funds to start a new life, far from the eyes of whoever watched.

Maggie pulled into her driveway, and she heard the familiar text notification. She smiled. Maybe Emily already missed her or forgot something in the car. She looked at the phone and her heart sank.

Nate PI: *Congratulations to Emily! Looks like she's going to have a great first year.*

Maggie chilled at the message. How could she have thought it would be so easy to keep her daughter safe? And now she was hours away, vulnerable and alone. She punched the steering wheel and cried out.

Nate PI: *What's wrong, cat got your tongue? Did you really think that I wouldn't know exactly where you are... And exactly where she is?*

Flattery, Maggie thought. I have to flatter him, to keep my baby safe.

Maggie: *I know you're smarter than that. I wasn't trying to do anything. You told me not to tell her, and she knows nothing. So, life had to be normal.*

Maggie forgot the digital trail she and her daughter left behind, the ones the dead Nate warned her about. Pieces of their lives were scattered all over the internet like beach glass in the sand. If one looked hard enough, one could easily find the jewels glittering in the sun waiting to be discovered. "No," she said out loud. She would not blame herself or Emily. Everyone shared the mundane pieces of their lives, eager to connect. Nate's internet anonymity hadn't kept him safe either.

The three dots on the screen that appeared from the killer were replaced by a photo of Maggie and Emily from the morning. Her arms were wrapped around her daughter. Emily's eyes were squeezed shut, just like in her last hug to Paul. Her daughter's face scrunched tight deep in her mother's embrace, and safe. She appeared younger than her eighteen years, even with her makeup on in this photo. If not for the sinister message behind it, the picture was quite good. Had it come from any other place, it certainly would have been in her Christmas project for her daughter.

Maggie was always behind the lens, and people rarely

photographed her. For once, she saw what other people saw. Two women who fiercely loved each other despite the paths diverging in front of them. While Emily's personality and high cheekbones favored Chris, from this angle, she saw her nose in Emily's profile. All the times Maggie felt unneeded and unloved, this picture proved it false. This girl loved her, and she would keep her safe if it meant she'd die trying.

How could her spider-sense be so off? She hadn't felt anyone watching them or taking a photo. She kicked herself for being present in the moment, letting her attention slip away from her surroundings, only seeing Em. She let the organized chaos of goodbyes, hellos, and moving her baby to college distract her.

Maggie: *What do you want?*

She waited five minutes with no answer. Maggie wanted to FaceTime her daughter, to lay eyes on her one last time. But it would raise suspicions. Instead, she sent her one last text.

Maggie: *Made it home - call once you're settled in. I love you.*

Emily responded immediately.

Emily: Kk met up with J to check the dining hall luv u

Kk, with no punctuation. All signs pointing to it being her daughter. Kk was better than Okay, Ok. Or OK—all of which would have meant Emily was mad or annoyed. All texts she received from her far too often.

Maggie got out of her car and spotted a package of coffees and breakfast she nearly tripped over. It was a delivery, and judging by the time stamp on the ring doorbell, it had arrived about fifteen minutes after they left. She studied the ring recording and saw a hooded figure she didn't recognize leaving it on the porch.

Inside the bag sat a cold coffee and note that read;

Good luck today moving in. Miss you already.

It was not signed, but she assumed it was Josh, or the killer, sending a message to Emily. She opened the coffee and smelled it. Cinnamon dulce, her favorite. Emily hadn't mentioned him leaving anything. Did Josh know what time they were leaving?

"Enough," she said out loud. Paranoia set in. Everyone was a suspect, and Maggie could barely keep her eyes open. She threw the delivery in the trash, limped up the stairs, and collapsed on her bed. The dull ache in her foot had subsided, but it was the only improvement in her life at the moment.

While trying to solve the puzzle of who was trying to hurt her family, she dozed off.

Maggie woke with a start and looked at her watch. It was 8:00 AM. She'd slept for eighteen hours. Her stomach growled in protest at food she hadn't eaten for almost twenty-four hours. Except it wasn't her hunger that woke her. She spotted her phone glowing. A new text came in. Maggie's chest tightened before looking at it. It was too early to be her daughter, unless it was bad news. She already knew in her heart who it would be.

This time it was a picture of her daughter in what appeared to be a party outside in a park or off-campus somewhere. She wore leather pants Maggie knew her daughter didn't own and had not packed, and a tube top that she did. She was draping one of her thin arms around the neck of a boy Maggie had never seen, and his arm was slipped around her waist. Emily's eyes were half-closed and her mouth was open wide in a laugh.

Maggie studied the picture. Her daughter did not appear like the angsty teenager who stormed off to the Starbucks bathroom to get ready. She looked relaxed and happy. It was a side of her she rarely shared with her mother. But as Maggie studied the photo more closely, she could see that Emily's hair was disheveled, her eyeliner half-melted off her left eye, and her bright crimson lipstick smeared. While the boy and she smiled, his fingers curled around her, squeezing into her waist as if holding her up. A red solo cup lay on the ground at her feet.

Maggie sunk her head against the pillow. Was this an innocent teen boy, or someone more sinister? What did the killer want from them? Maggie wanted the killer to be here, far away from her daughter.

Nate PI: Don't worry about Emily. I'm keeping a very sharp eye on your little girl. Wouldn't want her to be a victim of a 'botched robbery'?

Botched robbery, exactly what the newspaper called Nate's death. She texted back.

Maggie: Please, what do you want?

Nate PI: What does everyone want?

Finally, a quasi-answer. Perhaps he was ready to tell her, if she could guess right. She ignored the growl of her stomach and texted.

Maggie: Love, money, power...

Maggie hunched over the three dots.

Nate PI: Two of the three are right. One I already have. I have power. Which one do you think I want between love and money?

Maggie: How much?

Maggie wasn't rich. But in death, Chris cared for her. He left her a $500,000 life insurance policy. In the blur of Maggie's pregnancy, her mind and body were caught up in the seismic shift of bringing a human into the world. So, when Chris insisted on life insurance, she never questioned him. Her husband bet against his own life and won. The life insurance payout allowed her to maintain their home in a town perched on the outskirts of Washington, D.C. just outside the Beltway. But she worked to maintain their lifestyle.

Nate PI: $250,000.

Maggie broke out in a cool sweat, her stomach's protests forgotten. Half of the inheritance was not left. That money had gone to Maggie's leave of absence when Chris died, soccer lessons, tutors, babysitters, vacations, and Emily's college.

Maggie: I don't have that kind of money right now.

Nate PI: You don't need it yet. For now, I'll watch Emily to make sure you don't get out of line.

Maggie: When?

Nate PI: I'm not a terribly patient person, and I can do a lot to Emily without actually killing her. One week.

Maggie's stomach twisted into a hard knot. What plans did he have for her?

Maggie: Please leave my daughter out of this.

Nate PI: Get my money.

Maggie grabbed her pillow, buried her head in it, and screamed until the energy drained out of her. If she found the money and delivered it to him, what would make any of this stop?

Maggie opened up her investment accounts. She tied most of her money up in the house. The home renovation three years ago cost more than she expected, but their home was the smallest on the street, so she justified it as an investment. But installing the pool was a bad idea. They never used the pool, and the water was passable as refreshing for about three months a year. Maggie thought it would drive her daughter closer to her, and have the kids hang out at her house. With a neighborhood pool down the street, no one gathered in hers. What she hadn't expected were the costs of opening and closing it, chlorine, and the sky-high electric bills to keep the algae at bay. The pool's expenses nearly ran her in the red each month. Pool installers were liars. They said it would increase the value of her house, and she didn't bother to get a realtor's opinion.

$250,000 was more than she had lying around. She checked her retirement account. She could get almost $125,000 there, and she had another $75,000 stashed in her daughter's college account. That money she scrimped and saved over eighteen years. But if Emily died, she wouldn't need it, anyway. Maggie could liquidate the account and when she sold the house, pay for Emily's college. She'd need to sell the house sooner than she wanted to, which was the least of her problems at the moment. Still, she was $50,000 short. Was the price of their lives negotiable?

Maggie wished instead of the constant improvements to the house, she had sold it like she meant to do for years. The idea of erasing Chris was too much, but now what did that delay cost her?

Could she refinance the house? With the market, it would take thirty to forty-five days. Time she didn't have—didn't want to take negotiating—with a killer watching her daughter.

Maybe it was time to involve the police, she thought. If the person watched her as closely as she thought, then Emily would be dead or at least seriously hurt before the police would issue a useless piece of paper as a restraining order.

The private investigator gave his life to be nothing more than a warning to her.

No solution came to her. She was $50,000 short, which could cost her daughter her life. Maggie picked up the phone and called the one person who was there for her through it all.

sixteen

· · ·

THE PHONE RANG ONCE and Paul's gravelly voice answered, "Hi Mags."

"Hey. What are you doing?" Maggie asked.

"Mowing. Wait, what's wrong?" She regretted the call in the tiny instant it took him to know. *Smell the flowers, blow out the candles,* she thought to herself.

"Nothing. What do you mean?" She lied.

"Mags, I can hear it in your voice." His voice pitched upward with concern.

"I'm sorry, I shouldn't have called." She hung up the phone and swung her legs to the floor and stood, forgetting about the cut on her foot. She cried out; too much weight too soon. She went to the bathroom to brush her hair and teeth. Paul lived twelve minutes from her suburban house, so he'd be at her door within fifteen. In the recesses of her mind, she knew he would come to her, and it was exactly what she needed.

She glanced in the mirror and stopped. The woman who stared back was a haggard ghostly shell of the person she was. Paul would recognize this Maggie as the one he lived with for eight weeks during the throes of her grief, with a newborn baby. Red-rimmed and baggy eyes, unbrushed dull brown hair, now with streaks of gray instead of the honey highlights, and colorless lips. She was dehydrated from tears and grief and now dehydrated with the fear of losing everything.

She pulled her hair into a ponytail and applied some makeup. She looked every bit her age, and tired, but much more presentable. With ten minutes left, she navigated the stairs with her foot a bit quicker today, put the coffee pot on, and waited for Paul to arrive.

The knock she expected came, and he opened the door. He stood there wearing his gray sweatpants stained green at the bottoms, a hoodie, and his dark tousled wavy hair. He was unshaven, and Maggie noticed the gray specks in his whiskers that had not been there before. His outfit screamed teenage boy, but his face and concern were anything but. He looked like a pleasant mix of her husband if he'd survived, and Paul, the man who was her constant longer than she had been married.

"Mags, what is it?" he asked, his forehead wrinkling with the worried question.

She didn't look at him and walked toward the coffeemaker. "I brewed the coffee for us," she replied.

He walked toward her and patted her elbow. A pulse of electricity rushed through her. Electricity buzzed every time he touched her. Could it be his close resemblance to his brother? She tamped down the thought. There was no room in her heart for anything beyond saving Emily and herself.

She did her best to ignore his touch and reached for two coffee mugs. Her hands trembled with them. Just two days ago, she received her first text from the killer using Nate's phone. When her world fell off its axis, she was about to have coffee.

Paul took the mugs from her hand and filled them to the brim. "Go sit down. We can figure out whatever this is."

She nodded and limped lightly to the couch, where he followed with the coffee. He sat close to her, their knees touching. He set the mugs on the coffee table in front of them. It was still too hot to drink.

He faced her. "Do you want to talk about it?"

Maggie's face crumpled and tears flowed. She knew she cried ugly, but had no effort for pride. Paul scooted closer and opened his arms, and she curled inside. He patted her hair and said, "Hey, hey, it's going to be okay. Is this about Emily? She'll be okay."

How would he know Emily would be okay? Maggie certainly didn't. She couldn't get the words out. Sometimes people die and things happen. If anything happened to Emily, she'd throw herself off the bridge to be with her. Sometimes everything is not okay. She sniffled and wailed and nuzzled deeper into the crook of his arm.

He held her for a long time before she caught her breath enough to speak. Paul whispered under his breath to her, "Smell the flowers, blow out the candles." Soon, her breath followed his rhythmic inhales and exhales with the mantra. She breathed in his scent of sweat mingled with the earthy smell of grass. She pressed her nose tight against his collarbone, and she didn't pull away. He smelled safe.

How did he know the calming breath mantra? She tried to recall, but he had always been there. It could have been any time. Maggie claimed she was a single mother and did everything herself, but it wasn't true. Paul stood next to her and walked the journey of child-rearing in her shadow, a stand-in for his big brother. He didn't take credit for being a father. Like a shadow, he retreated when the sun shone high, but as it lowered, he'd come in and be her sturdy support. Paul gave her space as she required, but more often than not, he was there for both her and Emily.

She exhaled and took a sip of her coffee. Finally, she pulled out her phone and told him about the pictures, the janitor, the private investigator, and, finally, the text messages. His eyes widened with each layer of the story, and she handed him her phone.

He scrolled through the messages. His eyes darted and quickly scrolled past the picture of Emily taken without her knowledge. He sat quietly and turned to Maggie. "Have you talked to anyone else about this?" he asked.

"No. I don't know what to do. I mean, you read the article about Nate, and the killer has Nate's phone to communicate with me... So I know he can find me. You read the message. He'd hurt Emily before I could do anything," Maggie said.

Paul scratched the stubble on his chin as he considered this. "Why aren't the police tracking Nate's phone? Isn't it evidence of a crime?"

"I considered that too. He mentioned he had two phones, one for his work and one for his family. I'm guessing his wife and three kids didn't know he had two phones. I'll be honest, when we went to dinner, I couldn't really tell if it was a date or not. He gave me a strange feeling. And he distinctly told me he was not married. I don't know if it was to protect his family, or if he wanted to have an affair."

Paul's eyes lowered when she mentioned a date, and she immediately felt regret for saying it. It wasn't time to hold anything back. It was a date. Maggie's lie detector for men was out of practice, but she wasn't naïve. Outside of

Paul, who she only dared to think of that way in the dark recesses of the night, there had been no one else since Chris died. While Nate was a cur for what he did to his wife, and probably did with a lot of clients, he didn't deserve to get his throat sliced for it.

Maggie broke the silence. "This was the dinner where I was stood up and you ran to pick me up. He was there, dying in the parking garage. I feel awful. Nate had a wife and three children." She remembered how Paul smelled of sweat because he ran six blocks to get to her.

"How awful," Paul said.

"I know. When you came for me that night, my car was in the parking garage. The newspaper article didn't say where his car was parked, and I never knew what he drove. We could have walked right past the killer. He could have been with us."

Paul put his arm around her and said nothing. "It's okay, I'm here now."

She leaned her head against the weight of his arm, and he rubbed her shoulder as she closed her eyes. "What am I going to do?" Maggie asked to the air.

"Well, we can't go to the police," Paul agreed. "You don't know how close this person is to your life. And he wants money. How much do you have?"

"I checked, and I'm about $50,000 short if I drain my retirement and Emily's college. I don't have time to sell the house and get the money in time. He wants half of the inheritance, but I spent almost all of it living. I guess I could have been more careful with my money. That damned pool, I should never have put it in." Maggie rambled.

He squeezed her shoulder and stopped her. "I can get $50,000," Paul whispered.

How could she say no? Maggie didn't realize she asked

him for $50,000 before it came out. She gulped down her pride. "I can pay you back as soon as the house sells."

"Don't worry about it now. Let's focus on getting the money together to get out of this. How long will it take you to have your money together?" he asked.

"I think maybe a few days. How about you?"

"I can have it to you anytime," Paul said.

"After he's paid, how do I know that this guy will leave me alone?" Maggie asked, throwing her arms up in frustration.

"One step at a time. We'll get through this." Paul hugged her. Maggie noticed a set of scratches on his forearm.

"What happened to you?" Maggie asked.

"Oh, it's nothing. It will sound cliché, but the neighbor's cat was stuck in the tree. So, I got my ladder and took her out. She didn't take kindly to it." He chuckled.

Could Paul be more perfect? His handsome face commanded the attention of every single woman around, and a few married ones, too. She noticed the way the women watched him during Emily's games. One of the few men watching the girls kick a ball around the field. More than a few women remarked on Maggie's luck of marrying such an engaged father. She never corrected them. Maggie didn't want the women to know he was, in fact, single. She felt a twinge of guilt when she did so because she denied him the happiness of finding his own partner instead of being a stand-in for herself and Emily. But could she see him as someone separate, someone not standing in the shadows of Chris's memory? Her fingers traced the scratches on his arm. She hoped the cat didn't leave a scar. He pulled his arm back and reached for the cooling coffee.

"I can't think of any enemies I have. Or anyone who

would want to hurt me. It has to be Mr. Murphy, right? If it's him, this will be easy. Why would he want to hurt me? I don't know who he is? But I can call the police when I know where he is."

Paul took a long sip. "You could. But what if it's not?"

"Right, what if it's not?" A chance she couldn't bear to think of taking.

"I think I should probably spend more time here," Paul said. "Just until we have this sorted out, and you and Emily are safe."

"I'm frightened he'll hurt you, just like the private investigator." But she admitted to herself she wanted him there more than she was concerned for his safety. Paul was stronger than Nate. She wanted him with her like in days past. The ones marked with the nothingness of grief, motherhood, and an endless supply of tears, diapers, and formula.

"Don't be. I can take care of myself," Paul said.

He was as constant as the moon, waning and waxing whenever she needed him, and she needed him now.

Maggie gazed up at him. "So, what's next?"

"Well, I think I need to get to the bank and get the money together. Sounds like you do, too." Paul said.

She nodded her head in agreement. "How will we get the money to him?" she asked. "Isn't everything traceable?"

"I'm sure he has a plan. He'll send instructions."

Maggie shrugged. "You're probably right."

Paul finished his coffee and stood. Maggie rose, and they walked to his car. He opened the car door, and she caught her reflection in his window. She looked twenty years older than she had a few days previously. Maggie squeezed Paul's shoulder as he turned toward the car and whispered, "Thank you."

He turned back to her and embraced her, kissing her head. Paul never kissed her anywhere, but he kissed Emily's head often when she hugged him. A comfort, that's all it was, Maggie thought.

Paul gently released her from his embrace and asked, "You going to be okay?"

"Yeah, thanks for coming by," Maggie said.

"Of course." He lowered himself into the car, rolled down the window, and waved to her as he pulled away.

Telling Paul was the right thing to do. They shared the burden now, and it felt lighter. Besides, she needed more money, and he offered it without her asking. As soon as the house sold, she'd pay him back, she promised herself.

Maggie turned to head toward the house, and she heard a familiar engine rumble toward her. She turned, and Josh's truck drove past. They lived in a sleepy cul-de-sac with no other friends or classmates. She would find out why he had been driving past for months, and it would happen now. "Hey, come back here, Joshua Greene," Maggie called out. With an emphatic clap of her hand, she pointed at the driveway at the empty spot Paul vacated. She didn't know his middle name, else she would have used it.

His truck looped in the cul-de-sac and slowly drove toward her.

seventeen

. . .

HE PARKED his red truck in the driveway and rolled down his window. "Hi, Ms. Becker." His voice strained with nerves.

"Get out of the car, Josh. I'd like to talk to you."

He turned the key, and the engine shut off. He fumbled with the door latch. Josh got out of the truck and stood before her like a toddler caught drawing on the walls.

She cleared her throat and peered up at him. He seemed taller, more filled out than she recalled. She'd always seen him through the lens of her daughter's childhood sweetheart, never a threat. Now, she wasn't so sure. "Why are you driving past the house? Where are you going?"

"I'm sorry, Mrs. Becker. I was in the neighborhood. Did Emily get my delivery from DoorDash? I had coffee sent before she left, but she didn't text or anything. I haven't heard from her. It won't happen again." Josh scratched at the black hair stubble on his chin and stared at his shoes. The stubble on his face seemed strange to Maggie. Emily hated facial hair. He kicked an invisible stone in the driveway and a blush blossomed up his neck as his eyes remained on his feet. This kid was equal parts fascinated and maddened by Emily, as Maggie was. The last people on her daughter's mind were her mother and hometown boyfriend. She had a picture sent from a killer as proof. Josh and Emily were coming to an end; unrequited love was desperately painful for the one left behind. She reminded herself, Josh was not capable of harming Emily.

Maggie stared at him and waited. She learned silence encouraged confessions. He stammered on, "It's just she hasn't really been returning my calls or texts. I wanted to drive by. See her place, her car." His eyes were watery.

Please Josh, don't cry, she thought. She didn't have the emotional energy or patience to deal with it. "Josh, I've seen your pickup before she left, driving by. A few times. This isn't just because she's gone to college. She has only been gone for a day."

It was his turn for silence, an admission.

Maggie sighed. She hated to deliver hard truths to her kid, and especially to other children. At eighteen, he appeared as much a child as an adult. "Josh, you can't guilt her into staying with you."

His eyes widened. "Did she say that? I never guilted her. I just... I just miss her is all."

"I know, me too. But she's been gone less than twenty-four hours." Maggie patted him on his shoulder. It was the first time she touched him, aside from shaking his hand. It felt inappropriate and too familiar. She dropped her hand.

He shrugged. "I know. But as soon as I couldn't go to the same college, stuff was different. She always talked about moving, and her new roommate, and sororities, and things I won't be a part of."

"I get it. She's excited about this time in her life. She's settling in, and you need to focus on your own community college experience. Soon, you'll be away at a university too, but everyone is on their own timeline. It's going to be okay."

Josh nodded, his chin scrunched like he was about to cry. His voice turned into a whine. The back of her neck inched up with irritation.

"I know, I know. I just, I just thought we'd get to go do this together, you know?"

The whine in his voice felt like claws raking across the chalkboard. She breathed in. "I know, but you have to relax a little. I know it's hard but focus on what you've got to do here in your college."

"It's just community college. It isn't real college."

"Community college is the same education as the university at a fraction of the cost," Maggie said.

"You sound like my mom," Josh replied.

"Because your mom is smart, and it's true," Maggie said.

"Why didn't Emily pick that?" Maggie sighed. "Everybody has their own opportunities and life paths, Josh." When she said his name, his eyes dropped to the ground again. She breathed in. Losing her patience wouldn't help anything.

"Yeah, I know. It's just... I wanted to go with her. We were supposed to go together."

Maggie refrained from rolling her eyes. Josh and Emily weren't scholars or athletes who got scholarships, and the pandemic was harder on many of their peers. Unfortunately for Josh, the pandemic struck his family's business and community college was what they could afford. There were far worse plights. His whining would only get worse when Emily finally found the courage to set this kid free.

Maggie didn't answer. Sometimes she learned it was

best to let the words lie. Josh said, "I guess I better go." And he climbed back into his truck and started it.

She perched her hands on the passenger-side open window. "I know you miss her, but sometimes life doesn't work out exactly the way you plan it. You need to stop driving past the house, Josh. It's not okay, and it can scare people."

She really didn't know if she would react the same if the texts never came. But they did, and she did not know who may lurk around. Her anxiety didn't need Josh's truck slowing rolling past the house. Why would he want to hurt Nate, anyway? It made little sense. *He's a heartbroken kid figuring out how to move on without his childhood sweetheart,* she told herself. It wasn't fair for her to suspect a kid she'd known for years and treat him any differently. *Stop with the paranoia,* she thought.

His face flushed. "I didn't mean to scare you, Ms. Becker. I don't want to be a creep."

She had been harsher than she meant to. "I didn't mean it like that. You need to focus on yourself. I know you and Emily were inseparable, but long-distance relationships are hard. If it's meant to work, it will. Chris and I had a long-distance relationship for a time."

"Thanks, Ms. Becker, I appreciate it." Josh glanced over his shoulder to pull out, and Paul's car pulled around and back into her drive. He parked next to the pickup truck and got out. Paul's mouth was a straight line as he approached Maggie. She sensed a rush of security in his presence. She considered Josh harmless, but she also trusted Nate, who had a secret wife and three kids who were burying him. She removed her hand from the passenger window of Josh's truck.

"Hey Mags, I forgot my phone." Paul eyed the truck and met eyes with Josh.

"Oh, no problem. You remember Josh, Emily's boyfriend?"

Paul's voice dropped an octave as he approached the truck, eyeing the boy. "Hello, Josh. I remember."

Josh's hands fidgeted on the steering wheel. "Hey, uh, yeah, hi, I gotta go. Gonna be late to work."

Paul took a step closer to the truck before Josh pulled out. "Okay, nice to see you, kid. Maybe next time call before stopping by."

"Yes, sir." Josh didn't check behind him, shot the truck in reverse, and left quickly.

His truck barely stopped at the sign at the end of the drive and his tires squealed as he pulled away fast. Maggie looked at Paul, both annoyed and appreciative. "He's a kid. You didn't need to say that."

"Yeah, I think I did. Did you hear those tires skid out of here? That kid got spooked. He needs to stop coming by unannounced. He knew Emily wasn't around. It may be innocent puppy love stuff, but it may be something more. You can't be too careful, Mags."

"You don't think..." She couldn't finish her sentence. It was too foreign to consider Josh a threat.

"No, I don't, but I don't know for sure. And honestly, having an eighteen-year-old man— yes man—swinging by your house, that just isn't normal."

Maggie considered this. But she also remembered when Chris joined the Army Reserve, he went to Bootcamp for eight painful weeks. Occasionally, she would go to his house and hang out with Paul and their mother to feel closer. "He misses her. Josh is harmless. He loves Emily, and not in the boil the rabbit, fatal attraction kind of way. More the, I want you so close to me we breathe the same air, and I don't know who I am without you, way. Probably both unhealthy, but not equally so."

"Is he though?" He started toward the house to get the phone and she followed.

"Frankly, I don't think he has the heart or the brains to do half of what is happening. It's too intricate, and he loves Emily too much."

"Maybe." He grabbed his phone from the couch, then changed the subject. "Dinner on Sunday?"

"Yep, just like every week." She smiled back at him and he walked out the door. It wasn't often the two dined without Emily, and something stirred in her with excitement. She'd make something nicer for him, and maybe see if their future might look different.

The quiet of the house felt suddenly deafening to her. She, too, knew she would struggle to adjust to a life without Emily wafting in and out. The lack of laundry and empty glasses scattered throughout the house was nice, but also a stark reminder of how empty it would be.

Ding, a text. Her toes curled at the noise. She used to love the beep of someone thinking of her. Emily or Paul, her sister, anyone reaching out to say hi or share something funny. No more. Her hands trembled as she picked up the phone.

Nate PI: *One week from today, Wednesday.*

She realized exactly what it meant. Maggie had one week to get the money and figure out who her stalker was. It would be the longest week of her life. Too long. She responded.

Maggie: *I can get it sooner.*

Did she appear too eager? Like there was more money

to be had? *Damn it*, she thought. She should have waited and talked to Paul.

Nate PI*: I have some things to arrange. We're working on my timeline, not yours.*

The terse response kicked her in the gut. Next time he texted, she promised herself she'd wait. Until she knew who he was, there was no trying to figure out a motive or what might set him off. Nate was a message delivered. The killer was serious, and she needed no more messages.

Maggie*: Of course. One week, I'll be ready.*

eighteen

. . .

DINNER WITH PAUL, alone. Maggie chose the Beef Wellington recipe from his mother's cookbook. She'd been meaning to try the ambitious recipe, and with the long afternoon opened out before her, there was time and she could use the distraction. The cookbook was one of the few things left from when Chris and Paul's mother passed away. She died not long after Chris did. The doctor called it a sudden heart attack, but Maggie knew it was from a broken heart.

The grocery store was mercifully light of customers. On her way to the checkout, she picked up a rich Cabernet Sauvignon. A heavy beef/steak night called for stepping away from her typical lighter wine fare. Besides, it was Paul's favorite, and she owed him. They were on sale, so she put a second one in the cart. Maggie lined up for the checkout and an elderly gentleman with kind eyes and shockingly white hair ambled up behind her with flowers and cider.

"Please, go on in front of me," she said to the old man. He grinned at her and nodded, shuffling his feet forward.

"Thank you, kindly. It's our fiftieth anniversary." The corners of his eyes tugged up in a smile.

"Happy anniversary," she said.

"Thanks, she's in a nursing home and doesn't remember me most days, but the flowers sometimes spark a memory. They're her favorites." His eyes were shiny.

"Fifty years is a long time. I hope you have a great evening."

He smiled and glanced at her cart. "You too."

She felt the heat rise to her cheeks. "Thanks."

Maggie examined the two cuts of filet mignon, the wine, butter, and salad. The man's blue hyacinth bouquet winked back at her and she half-considered buying a bouquet of her own, but pushed her cart forward.

A text chimed in, and her stomach curled before reading it.

Emily: going to concert tonight close to home J and I coming for dinner ok?

Maggie: What concert? You don't have any tickets or money for tickets?

Maggie's gut twisted at the thought of Emily's college fund. She kept a close eye on Emily's account. They barely had enough for the tuition and mandatory costs. Definitely not a concert unless she got a job. But in a week, Maggie's money problems would be substantially worse.

Emily: Jenna's parents bought them as surprise we'll be there at 5 is uncle Papa coming

Maggie: Yes, he should be here. Are you staying the night?

Emily: no we're going to the concert and meeting Andrea and staying there and taking the train back tmrw

Maggie: Okay, sounds good. Please be careful.

Maggie looked down again at her cart and spun it out of the line to put back the fresh cuts of meat. The fancy dinner would have to wait. Instead she gathered the pork and beef to make the meatballs her daughter loved. She went to the Italian aisle and bought noodles and her daughter's favorite marinara sauce, Prego. She kept the salad, but added an extra bag for Jenna and Emily, and grabbed an onion. She kept the wine bottles in her cart.

Emily: *awesome see you soon can you pick up from train station*

Maggie: *Of course, text when you're here. Love you.*

Emily: *ilysm*

A few hours and many times tracking her daughter later, Maggie donned the apron her daughter made her with her Uncle Papa on Mother's Day thirteen years ago. The onions and mushrooms were on the cutting board to dress up the Prego sauce. It was Emily's favorite, and no matter how Maggie tried, she couldn't replicate the sweet tang of it, so she gave up on it years ago and added vegetables and spices to make it her own. She skinned the onion and heard Paul's familiar knock and her stomach flipped. Right on time, like always. She opened the door, and he blushed, holding pink-hued Asiatic lilies.

Aside from Chris's funeral, Paul never brought flowers to her. He wore a dark green button-down shirt with pale orange flowers, dark jeans, and dress shoes. At forty, he could have passed for his early thirties except for the gray patches of hair formed at his temples. He combed his dark hair back, and his face was freshly shaven.

She took the flowers from him. "These are lovely. Let's get these in water. Asiatic lilies are my favorites. How did you know? They last a long time." Paul leaned in for a hug. He smelled of Irish Spring and his mahogany cologne.

"I've been around long enough to know, and you're consistent. You mentioned it when you were talking about what to put in your wedding bouquet." She nodded and turned on her heel to the kitchen, and he followed.

"Paul, that was over twenty years ago," she said over her shoulder at him.

"You're right, it was a really long time ago."

He let the answer dangle between them. He reached for the white vase in the top cupboard, filled it with water and the packet to keep the flowers fresh, and handed it to her. His steely eyes looked at her, searching. Her nerves prickled, and she felt her heart pounding against her chest wall. She grabbed the scissors to cut the stems of the pink lilies for distraction. Why was she nervous? He turned away from her and went to the onion and chopped it. He made it almost possible to forget what they were dealing with.

"I don't remember that conversation," she said.

"Well, I do," he paused and added, "I remember every conversation with you."

"Pink means long-lasting love, you know? I'm sure I've told that to you before," Maggie said.

Paul continued chopping but said nothing. They worked in silence with only the sounds of the onion chopping and the snipping of the stems. Maggie arranged them, tucking the baby's breath between the pops of pinks.

"What do you think?" she asked Paul.

He put down the knife and walked over to her, closer than normal, and leaned in to smell the flowers.

Maggie felt the heat of him but resisted the urge to kiss him at the moment. "They don't have a fragrance," Maggie said, clearing her throat.

He slowly pulled away. "They're perfect."

She assessed them for a moment. He was right, but there was a familiarity to them as well. "These look like my wedding bouquet." Sadness rounded the edges of her voice. She dried her hands on her apron.

"I'm sorry. I tried to make them different enough. This bouquet doesn't have the white peonies your wedding bouquet had."

"Oh, no, it's okay. It's been twenty years. You'd think the triggers are gone. But I haven't had this flower in my house since, well, since my wedding. It's lovely. Thank you. I forgot how much I love them."

He stepped toward her. "It's time to remember things you love. To live for yourself." He cleared his throat. "You know, I recall you said that while Emily was home, you wouldn't get into a relationship." Maggie thought briefly about the dead private investigator and she didn't answer.

She turned from him. "I know. It's definitely something I'm looking forward to. Finding *my* happiness again. It's been far too long." The last time she considered dating somebody, the man ended up dead. Married, but also dead. "There is one thing I always wondered about. Can I ask you something? And you promise you'll give me an honest answer?"

"You can ask me anything." Paul took a small step toward her and set the flowers on the counter.

Maggie said, "It was a long time ago, but you and Chris. You used to be so close. But, right before he passed away, something happened. I have our last dinner periodically on replay in my mind. You fought, and things were so tense in the end for a few months. I asked him about it for a while, but he wouldn't answer."

Paul bristled. "That isn't a question." He turned to chop the onion more vigorously. Maggie rounded to him and settled her hand over his, and he stopped chopping.

"You know my question," Maggie said.

He stared at the onion. "Please don't ask it. I beg of you. Don't ruin right now."

The answer wasn't worth it for now. She released his hand and put it on his cheek, forcing his eyes to meet hers. His cheek was wet from the onion or tears she didn't know. "I won't ask you again tonight. But it doesn't mean I won't ask ever. One day you will tell me."

He nodded. "One day I will."

Maggie took a half step toward him, raised herself on her toes to reach his lips, and the familiar ding of a text shattered the moment. Before her lips reached his, she looked down at her phone.

Emily: *Mom we'll be at the station in 15 min*

"Oh damn," Maggie said.

"What, what is it?" Paul said, looking at her phone in alarm.

"I'm sorry. I forgot to tell you, Emily and her roommate are coming by for dinner before a concert," Maggie said.

Maggie texted her daughter back.

Maggie: *Ok. I'll be at the kiss and ride.*

Emily 'liked' her mother's response.

"Oh?" Paul said. She noticed his shoulders slumped the tiniest bit, and he breathed in a quick breath. The lustful energy dissolved and was replaced with a smile, lifting the sides of his eyes. They revealed a shadow of crow's feet. "It'll be nice to see her and meet her new roommate." She felt exactly how he looked.

"They aren't staying the night here, though." What was she trying to tell him? Did she want to take this a step further tonight? Was eighteen years enough to grieve a husband? Was a few nights enough to settle into her single life without a daughter to look after every day? Paul returned to chopping the onion.

Maggie stirred the sauce once more before glancing at her watch. "Can you keep an eye on the sauce while I run to get them?" she asked.

"Of course," Paul answered, and took the wooden spoon from her. His hand felt warm on hers. She kept her hand on the spoon for a beat longer than necessary. She wanted nothing more than to stay with him.

"Drive carefully," Paul said.

"Thanks. When I get back, we can start the meatballs."

She headed toward the door. "Wait," Paul said, and came toward her and wrapped his arms around her waist.

She leaned forward and half-shut her eyes, hardly daring to breathe. Finally, she felt him incredibly close and a sharp tingle ran through every bit of her body. Then she felt the heat of his hands leave her waist. Paul glanced at her, blushing, and said, "Your apron was still on." He held the strings he untied in his hands before her.

"Oh, right, thanks." Heat ran up her neck. She grabbed the apron and slipped it over her head. He held it in his hands as she turned from him and nearly ran out the door.

nineteen

. . .

MAGGIE SLAMMED her hands on the steering wheel in embarrassment. Her daughter and friend would be a pleasant distraction. She hadn't been in the car since her daughter's drop-off a few days ago. Emily left a hydro flask on the passenger floorboard that she hadn't noticed before. It rolled to the front of the floorboard as she pulled out of the driveway.

Twelve minutes later, she waited at the kiss and ride for the girls. She bent over and fished the water bottle off the floor. She looked up and the two girls were making their way to the car. They appeared nothing like their Instagram filtered photos. Emily wore her black backpack, which was likely full of all the things needed to make them social media perfected. For now, though, they both wore sweatpants, JMU sweatshirts, and their hair was in high buns with no makeup. The two could have been copy and paste versions of each other. Maggie preferred her daughter and friends in their natural state. Jenna's sweatshirt had a bleach stain Maggie recognized. The two were becoming one, sharing everything, including their wardrobe and families. Though envious, Maggie looked forward to meeting Jenna's parents, saving the world. How did they have the same twenty-four hours in a day and accomplish so much more than she?

Emily opened the front door and popped in. "Hi, Mom. Thanks for getting us. I missed you so much," she said with sarcasm.

"It's been so long." Maggie smiled back.

Jenna opened the back door and climbed into the seat behind Maggie.

"Hi, Ms. Becker."

Maggie glanced at Jenna through the rearview mirror. She was stunning, but they all were. "Oh, please call me Maggie. You live with Emily, you're practically family."

"Thank you so much for letting us come over. When my parents come back from Africa, we can all get together. I can't wait for you to meet my mother. She's a great cook. You would love her."

"She sounds lovely. I look forward to it." Maggie met eyes with Jenna through the rearview window and smiled. She felt a pang of regret for the Prego sauce dinner. While it was Emily's favorite, it wasn't exactly a gourmet meal or one worth traveling hours to have before a concert. Why hadn't she done the Beef Wellington for all of them?

Her mind wandered. Did Emily describe her as flattering as Jenna did her mother? Probably not.

"Speaking of family," Emily said, "Jenna and I are hoping we get picked for the same sorority during rush. So we'll be real sisters!"

"Oh, how exciting," Maggie said with feigned enthusiasm. It was thousands of extra dollars she didn't have, but what could she say? Sorry, we have a stalker, so we can't afford it. No, Emily would have her sorority if Maggie took a second job when this was all over. Though Maggie didn't understand the allure of the Greek secret clubs and sisterhood, she certainly wouldn't ruin it for her daughter. "I didn't realize you knew which one you wanted to join yet."

"I know, you just aren't into that stuff," Emily said. The words stung Maggie. Though it was true, she wanted to know what her daughter was doing and what she found important. She left it, as she left most things.

Maggie did as she always did when her daughter said something insensitive. She changed the subject. "Uncle Paul is already at the house. We're still making the meatballs, so dinner won't be ready for about another hour."

Maggie glanced over at Emily, whose eyes lit up. "Oh, that's awesome. Jenna, you'll love Uncle Paul!"

Jenna nodded and smiled. She stared out the window, looking lost in her own thoughts. Emily didn't notice Jenna's melancholy or else she was used to it, and rattled on.

"He's my uncle, but really was like a dad to me," Emily said.

Maggie smiled to herself. Maybe if she pursued whatever it was between her and Paul, Emily would be okay with it. If he was a 'dad' to her, then it only made sense he'd be with her mom. Maggie wouldn't have to change her name. She was getting ahead of herself, but the empty nester freedoms opened before her, deliciously tempting her back to happiness.

Emily streamed her phone through her mother's radio and turned up the sound. The sheer noise pounded Maggie's eardrums, and she felt the bass in her feet. But the girls knew and sang the words to the auto-tuned band whose voices were processed to the point of sounding like androgynous robots.

They pulled into the driveway. Jenna broke her silence. "Ms. Becker, your house is beautiful."

"Thank you," she replied automatically. Maggie surveyed her home, and it appeared anything but beautiful to her. The rain canceled the lawn service, so the grass shagged up and showed several shades of green from when she tried to fertilize it herself. The lawn service was another service she would probably have to cancel when the stalker got his money. On the bright side, she would love to admire Paul mowing the grass while they waited for the house to be sold. Maybe she would buy a tiny condo somewhere and the money from the house would fund the rest of Emily's college. She could start again with retirement. She was young enough. Besides, two incomes were better than one, maybe Paul... She blushed.

Emily grabbed Jenna's hand and pushed past her mom to the door. "C'mon, I'll show you my room."

Jenna half-jogged behind her and asked, "Can you show me where the bathroom is first?"

Emily blushed. "Shoot, yes, yes, I forgot you had to go since Union Station."

They opened the door and went inside. Maggie came in behind them and the scent of cooking onions and garlic greeted her. Paul ate the Sunday night meal so many times he, too, could have cooked it in his sleep. Maggie didn't like the meal, but it was Emily's favorite. How many more Sundays would she be home from college, anyway?

The girls vanished to the recesses of the house to do what teenage girls do. Before she reached the kitchen, she heard a text come in. *Oh God*, she thought. He knows she's here.

Maggie looked at the glowing screen.

Nate PI*: I see your daughter is in town. And you have company. Remember, this is between us. Don't consider not sending her back.*

Maggie*: Of course, I remember.*

Nate*: Good, you wouldn't want anything to happen to her or the girl she's with.*

Now Maggie needed nothing more than to put eyes on her daughter. She had to see her and Jenna after the text. She walked up the stairs to her daughter's room and knocked.

"Yeah?" Emily's voice replied with a hint of irritation.

"Can you open the door? I don't want to yell through it," Maggie said.

Emily didn't respond but opened the door. Jenna met Maggie in the hall coming out of the bathroom. "Yeah?" Emily asked, looking at her mother.

"Oh, I wanted to check with Jenna if she had any food allergies?" Maggie turned to Jenna.

The girl smiled back at her. "No, I'm grateful to be here for dinner. Thank you, Ms. B... err, Maggie." Jenna slipped past Maggie to join Emily in her room.

Emily turned to Jenna. "Okay, it's all powered up and logged in."

"Thanks," Jenna replied and jumped on her computer.

"Whatcha' guys doing?" Maggie asked, hoping for a few more moments to watch them.

"Jenna needs to finish her registration," Emily said.

"Yeah, I only need a few minutes. I forgot it was due today."

Emily said, "So unreasonable. I mean, you would think

your parents would have done it before." She rolled her eyes on Jenna's behalf.

"Great, well, dinner will be ready in about forty-five minutes," Maggie said, backing out of the room. While Jenna was on Emily's computer, her daughter retreated into the light on her phone. Again in the land of make-believe with a real world, and a real friend right beside her.

"Thanks, Mom," Emily replied, not glancing up from the phone but walking toward the door. She shut the door on her mother, still standing in front of the door.

Another battle Maggie refused to pick. She waited for the door to shut, staring at the girls as long as she was allowed. They were safe for now. Then she turned away to return to Paul in the kitchen. She wished equally for her daughter to have not come home and to have her safe under her roof.

Maggie retreated to the kitchen to find Paul had poured two glasses of wine and rolled the last meatball, placing it on the pan. He glanced at her and smiled. "They're ready for the oven. Can you put soap on my hands and turn the faucet on?"

As he washed his hands, she noticed he did not have the same manicured nails Nate did. His were rough in spots, from years of hard work in the plumbing industry. She much preferred his hands. She handed him the gray dishtowel and grabbed both glasses of wine. After he dried his hands, she handed his wine to him.

He held his wineglass to hers and said, "To new beginnings."

"To new beginnings," she agreed, and their glasses clanked before she took her first velvety sip.

Paul placed the meatballs in the preheated oven, shut off the sauce, and followed Maggie to the living room. As they sat a little closer than usual, she slid him her phone and he read the message. Maggie sighed from exhaustion and took another small sip of wine. "I don't know how he is in two places at once. And now he's looking at Jenna, too. Could it be more than one person? This is getting out of hand. I can't bring another girl into this."

Paul put his arm around her. "It's okay. We're going to figure this out. No one is going to get hurt."

"Except Nate."

She felt Paul stiffen. "No one *else* is going to get hurt," he corrected. They drank in silence.

After twenty minutes, Maggie got up. "I need to make the salad and start the noodles."

"Oh, let me help you," Paul said.

"No, no, you've done enough. Actually, if you want to do something, the guest bathroom faucet had a drip, and my tub is clogged. Is there any way you can help with those things?" Maggie asked.

"Of course," he replied. In the kitchen, she re-donned the apron he'd draped over the chair. She enjoyed the solitude of the kitchen. She put the sauce back on simmer, checked the meatballs, and started the water for the noodles. It was a tight galley kitchen, and with two people, it became crowded. Besides, she wanted to sneak a small snack as the wine traveled to her head, dizzying her.

Emily and Jenna started the home tour, and Maggie heard them going down the basement stairs. The basement door usually closed, but Emily didn't like to close it behind her. No matter what Maggie did with the room, Emily didn't like it. The girls' voices traveled. Maggie moved her salad fixings to the counter closest to the door. She remained quiet and leaned into Emily and Jenna's chatter. It reminded her of all the times she used to take her daughter around and get to spend time with all the girls and Josh. Those days ended years ago when Emily got her license. Despite trying to make her house the place where kids hung out, there was always a cooler and better place to be. So, their family home remained empty most of the time.

"Oh my God, what are those?" Jenna asked. Maggie knew they likely stumbled on the gun cabinet.

"Oh, these belonged to my dad's dad," Emily said.

"You mean your grandpa?" Jenna asked.

Emily chuckled. "Yeah, my grandpa. I never knew him. He left them for my dad, but they're both gone now."

"Oh, I'm sorry," Jenna replied.

"Don't be. They both died before I was born. I think they were hunters together or something. My mom knows nothing about guns, so she just left them here. I guess Uncle Papa, I mean my Uncle Paul, will probably take them someday. She probably kind of forgot about them. I did. I don't come down here really at all. It's so creepy, dark, and cold for no reason. Mom tried to make it a fun movie room, but meh, it's not a vibe."

Maggie could hear the clinking of keys and a laughter she didn't recognize, Jenna. She startled and looked through the door, seeing Emily twirling the keys to the cabinet. Emily's smarter than that, Maggie thought in alarm. She wouldn't access the cabinet, but if Maggie went down there, Emily would know she had been listening. Maggie stepped back but kept listening.

Emily's voice, rich in sarcasm, said, "Good thing they're all locked up, huh?"

Both of the girls laughed. Then Jenna said, "Wow, has it always been like that? My parents would have totally freaked having a gun cabinet with the keys next to it."

"I guess my mom didn't really think about it," Emily

said. Maggie listened to the keyring clink back on the hanger by the cabinet and breathed a sigh of relief.

Maggie needed to do something with those keys. Or better yet, give those guns to someone responsible enough to use them like Paul. Before Chris died, the brothers shot a couple times a year, and she'd completely forgotten about it. Paul had never asked for them back.

"Soooo... are we going to meet the infamous Josh?" Jenna asked. Maggie's ears perked up.

"Ugh, I mean, I probably should reach out to him. He's going to see me on Instagram going to the concert and everyone who is anyone is going."

"Girl, of course! I can't wait to see this joker. He's been such a stalker," Jenna said.

"He's not stalking. He just texts, FaceTimes, and calls... a lot."

"That's kind of the definition, isn't it?" Jenna laughed.

Emily chuckled and said, "I haven't figured out how to end it, but he's so sweet. You'll see. I'll text him to see if he can come to dinner. Oh look, I have sixteen unread messages from him."

"Sheesh, that is obsessive," Jenna said.

"I know, right?"

Maggie put the noodles in the boiling water. A few moments later Jenna said, "I'm going to get changed really quick."

"K, I'll meet you upstairs in a minute," Emily replied.

Emily came into the kitchen. "Hey Mom, Josh is around. Do you mind if he comes over for dinner?"

"Not at all. Sounds great. Dinner is ready in ten minutes. How's he doing?" Maggie said.

Emily shrugged. "I don't know, fine I guess. We haven't really talked much."

That poor boy, thought Maggie. No wonder he'd been driving past the house. He used to be her everything, knowing each other since kinder care, and now he was a joke to her. Maggie understood his feelings. As a mother, she also felt unceremoniously discarded.

twenty

. . .

EMILY WALKED out of the kitchen, and Maggie heard
Paul's voice as he came out of the bathroom after fixing the
faucet. "Is that my Emily?" Paul asked.

Maggie felt the smile rise in her cheeks. She walked out
of the kitchen to gaze at their reunion.

"Uncle Papa, I didn't know you were here already,"
Emily said. For a moment, the entire scene revolved around
the two. She ran to him and hugged him tightly. He swung
her in a hug before gently placing her feet back on the
ground.

"How's college been?" he asked.

"It's only been a few days... But they've been the best of
my life," she said, giving him a sly look. Paul shot an eye
over at Maggie and winked, betraying nothing of what he
knew.

Maggie took another sip of her wine as she leaned
against the doorjamb, watching them; a casual observer
from the outside looking in. Was this how mothers felt
when they watched their children bond with their real

fathers? She'd never know. She was a meteorite in someone else's orbit.

Jenna peeked out of the door of Emily's room and looked down the stairs at the commotion. Maggie spotted a shadow of jealousy cross her face, too. *It must be hard for her to see families when hers was so far away*, she thought.

Maggie met eyes with Jenna and beckoned her down the stairs. The girl came down, and Maggie cleared her throat to get her family's attention.

As Jenna stepped on the last stair, Paul turned toward her. Maggie said, "Paul, this is Jenna."

His eyes brightened and walked toward Jenna and held out his hand. She placed her hand in his, and her eyes turned up in a smile.

"I'm Paul, Emily's uncle. It's so good to meet you."

"Jenna, I'm glad to make your acquaintance, Mr. Becker."

He nodded. "You can call me Paul. We're pretty casual here."

She answered with a smile.

Emily pivoted to go back up the stairs with Jenna. She turned to her mother. "Can you call when Josh comes?"

"Yes, of course." Maggie retreated into the kitchen.

Paul followed Maggie, his hand at the small of her back when he met her in the kitchen. "Why do you let her treat you like that?"

"Like what?" she asked, but she knew exactly what he meant.

"Like you're her cook and maid," Paul said.

"Because it isn't worth the fight."

He nodded, and she tucked her embarrassment behind a weak smile. "Well, what can I do for you?" Paul asked.

"Set the table, please."

Maggie went to the noodles and took the cover off. The billowy starch steam blew back toward her as she poured them into the colander. She shut off the stove and did a last stirring of the sauce. She felt his hand at the small of her waist again and electricity pulsed through her. He leaned over her shoulder and said, "Mmmm, smells good." He almost sounded like Chris and felt like him.

She shut off the stove and spun toward him. Their noses were close enough to touch, and neither moved toward nor away. Maggie almost closed her eyes again before seeing in her peripheral vision the silhouette of Josh's truck pulling in. She pulled away from Paul and straightened her apron. His headlights shone through the house as he pulled into the drive. She shaded her eyes from the brightness until his truck rumbled to stop. He'd be at the door any minute. Again, the moment slipped through their fingers.

Maggie stepped to the door and opened it before he could knock. His hand poised at the door, he unfurled his fist for knocking and waved shyly at Maggie. Then, let his hand drop to his side.

"Hi, Josh. It's good to see you," Maggie said.

"Hi, Ms. Becker. Emily said to come over?" He wore a plaid shirt, dark jeans, dirty tennis shoes, and neatly combed hair.

"Yes, of course. I'll get her." She opened the door wider to make way for him as he passed. The smell of Axe body spray slapped her hard in the face.

Paul emerged from the kitchen to look at Josh. The boy straightened and took a small step back. Maggie shot Paul a 'not now' stare, and Paul smiled at the boy.

"Hi, Mr. Becker." He put his hands in his pockets and glanced first at Paul, then at the floor.

Paul's voice fell an octave. "Hi, Josh. It's good to see you again. I'll get another setting on the table."

Maggie eyed Paul over Josh's shoulder and mouthed, "thank you." She walked up the stairs to Emily's room and cracked open the door. The girls' faces were glowing with their phone screens. Their world, beyond reality, stuck in the highlight reels of others. "Hey hon, Josh's here."

"Oh, okay, tell him I'm coming." She ran a brush through her hair and reached for her lip gloss. Maggie wished she would either let Josh go or give him another chance. The in-between maybe stuff could drive anyone crazy. But sixteen unread messages, she conceded, was extreme.

Maggie walked through the living room where Paul and Josh sat. Josh's arms were crossed and his rosacea climbed up his neck. He pushed his glasses up on the freckled bridge of his nose. Maggie removed her apron and headed to the kitchen to plate the dinner. She heard Emily and Jenna's footsteps coming down the stairs.

"Josh, this is Jenna, my roommate. Jenna, this is Josh, my... friend."

An awkward silence followed, and Maggie heard Jenna's voice. "Hi Josh, it's nice to meet you."

"Nice to meet you too," he said. Sadness threaded in his voice.

They scooted the chairs out against the wood floors and guests settled into their places. Maggie brought the plates out. It was the first time in eighteen years that someone sat in Chris's seat. Jenna was now sitting in it, but no one had the heart to tell her. Emily looked over Jenna's shoulder at her mother and gave her a micro shrug and grimace. Maggie shook her head imperceptibly, reassuring Emily that it was okay. The placemat was always out for Chris's spot, but it didn't have the glass of water or any silverware. Paul set the table with care. He knew where the ghost of Chris sat.

Paul passed Maggie to get to the kitchen and brought the rest of the plated dishes out. She settled into her spot at the table and he brought her a fresh glass of wine, and she took another dark lovely sip.

A silence fell on the table while everyone assessed their dinner. Jenna took a bite and said, "This might be the best spaghetti I've ever eaten."

Maggie blushed and straightened in her chair. "Thank you."

Emily said, "It's just Prego. She puts a few other things in." And she took a bite.

Maggie shrank a little in her seat and took another sip of her wine.

Paul patted Maggie's leg beneath the table. He spoke to Jenna. "So, Jenna, what is your major?"

"Computer science. It's where the future is. When I was a kid, my dad bought me a computer, and he wasn't like normal dads who limit screen time. I played games, and it was so fun to build and rebuild over and over again. Ever since then, I was hooked." She shrugged.

Paul cleared his throat. "Your dad was ahead of his time. Computers are where the future is." He peered down at his calloused hands and said, "I probably should have spent more time inside and on computers."

Maggie admired his tan skin, and his dark hair, and his rough hands. She absolutely did not think he should spend more time inside with computers.

Emily smiled at Jenna and twirled a bite of spaghetti. "My mom had all the rules for screen time for me. Didn't you, Mom?" She rolled her eyes and took another bite.

Maggie nodded and gave a thin smile. She tensed her fork and spun her own noodles. Paul squeezed Maggie's arm gently and gave her a small wink.

Jenna turned to Josh. "So, Josh, where do you go to school?"

Emily shot a severe look at Jenna. Jenna smiled reassuringly back. Maggie knew the girls discussed where he went to school.

Josh shifted in his seat. "Well, I'm at NOVA Community College now, but I plan to transfer to JMU in a couple of years." He wiped his mouth and put the napkin back on his lap.

There was silence for a beat, and Jenna spoke up again. She said with genuine interest. "That's so great. It's a smart way to do it."

Josh breathed out and his shoulders relaxed for the first time. "Thanks. It's what my family can do right now. In the end, I get the same degree as everyone else, just save a little money."

Jenna said, "I understand. You should come visit us at JMU. I, I mean we, can give you a tour."

"I'd like that a lot," he said, and smiled at her.

Maggie looked at Emily, who stabbed at her salad. Emily said, "Yeah, Josh and I already planned to hang out at JMU. When we arrange it, maybe we can do coffee or something with you, Jenna."

Jenna nodded and said, "I'd like that." And she took another bite of spaghetti and chewed.

After dinner was finished, it was time to clear the dishes, Emily's job. Emily checked her phone and said, "Oh, Mom, I would help, but we've got to head out to the concert in like fifteen minutes. I need to get my stuff together."

Josh stood up and said, "I have to get going, anyway. I've got plans tonight."

Emily looked at Josh with surprise but said nothing. He looked at Jenna. "It was nice to meet you." Then he walked to Emily and wrapped his arms around her in an awkward hug. "I'll talk to you later." He turned and headed toward the door. "Thank you for dinner, Ms. Becker." He walked out and closed the door behind him. Jenna and Emily climbed the stairs giggling going back to her room.

Paul helped Maggie clear the dinner settings and turned the water on to do the dishes. Maggie placed her hand over Paul's. "No, not tonight." He turned the water off and swiveled toward her. She could feel she'd had too much to drink and fifteen minutes for her child to go to the concert felt like an eternity. Maggie couldn't decide if she wanted to go to sleep, sleep with Paul, or find a nice hole to get away from all of her worldly worries. One thing she was sure of, she didn't have the energy to fight with Emily and the dishes would wait until morning.

After thirty minutes, the girls emerged from Emily's room, appearing exactly as she expected them to.

"Okay, we're ready," Emily said. Her pink crop top showed almost the bottom half of her black lace bra. She wore black leather pants and white platform sneakers. Her heavy-handed makeup made her face a shade darker than her neck, making her face look a burnt orange. Her fake-lashed eyes framed her red-painted lips, and the apples of her round cheeks were far too rouged. She wore her hair down with a cascade of blonde curls that tumbled down her back. Jenna came out behind Emily, almost a clone. Black pants, crop top, platform shoes. Their hair was the sole discernible difference. Jenna wore hers in a tight high ponytail and stick straight. It seemed to pull on the edges of her temples and almost gave her a *middle-aged woman-who-overdid-the-Botox* look.

Maggie swallowed hard. "You both look great."

Paul smiled at both of them and said nothing.

Emily grabbed her purse and said, "Thanks. But we're ready. Are you going to get the keys?"

"Keys for what?" Maggie asked.

"I told you we were spending the night at Andrea's, but we still needed a ride to the concert." Emily shifted on her foot, put her hand on her hip, and checked her phone.

twenty-one

. . .

MAGGIE FELT the heat surge down into stomach. "Hon, I didn't realize you needed a ride. To be honest, I've had a couple glasses of wine and I'm not comfortable driving." She was a grown woman allowed to drink. Emily did not ask for the ride, and she was sure of it. Still, Maggie chastised herself for not staying sober enough to drive the girls, especially when Emily had company.

Emily rolled her eyes and shifted her weight to the other side. Jenna stared awkwardly at her phone. Maggie felt a twinge of anger building in the back of her throat. Paul interrupted, "Girls, I'll get you an Uber. It'll be easier, and we can clean up the kitchen and relax."

Emily smiled at Paul and hugged him. "Thanks, Uncle Papa, you're the best."

He hugged her back, and Maggie heard him say to her quietly. "Go hug your mom. She worked hard on dinner tonight." Emily nodded and went to her mother.

Maggie didn't want a sympathy hug, but here she was. Of course, she'd accept it. Emily opened her arms and

The Watcher · 153

Maggie walked inside of them. "Thanks for dinner, Mom. It was great, really."

"Yes, Ms. Becker, thanks for dinner." Jenna smiled at her from the door.

"Your Uber is around the corner. Do you girls want a coat? It's supposed to be cold," Paul said.

Emily laughed, but for him it was a good-natured laugh. She kissed him on his cheek. "We'll be fine." She glanced over at her mother. "On the way back to school tomorrow, we'll stop and get our bags. Not sure when we'll be by."

"Sounds good. If I'm not here, the hide-a-key is where it always is. Can you text when you get to Andrea's for the night?" Maggie asked.

"Yeah, yeah, under the secret and not at all plastic rock." She pointed to it as they headed down the drive to catch the Uber. Emily laughed, and the girls walked toward the white sedan with their arms interlocked. Maggie watched them as they climbed into the Uber and drove away.

As soon as Jenna and Emily left the house, it felt vast and too quiet. No more distractions from whatever blossomed between her and Paul and the constant worry of the man watching them. The quietness was a regular thing since Emily got her license, but it still sent eerie shudders down her spine. Maybe the Watcher was the actual source of her fear. Tired, Maggie rubbed one eye and looked over at Paul. "So, I got some apple pie for dessert. Hungry?"

"There's always room for apple pie," Paul said.

They walked to the kitchen, and he had their two empty glasses of wine. There was a bit of the wine left in the bottle and he poured an equal amount in both.

She eyed the wine, and her head was already dizzy. "I shouldn't."

"Okay. I'll just set it right here." He put it on the counter next to her and served the store-bought pie. He took his slice and grabbed two forks, his plate, and wine. She took her plate and grabbed the wine glass, following him to the table.

She sat in her normal spot, and Paul sat beside her. Chris's spot was once again vacant, across from them both. He took a bite of the pie and looked at her. "Will you have the money?"

Her mind sobered through the wine fog with his question. "Yes, the liquidation of my savings hit my account yesterday. I've got all but the $50,000."

"Don't worry, I have that now. So, what's next?" Paul asked.

"I don't know. He hasn't told me. We have a week left." Suddenly she wasn't hungry for pie anymore. She pushed it away and drained the rest of her wine. "Should I call the police? Why did I let her go to a concert?"

"I don't know. I think he knows where Emily is, even now. A concert is probably the safest place she could be. Many people, and Jenna and she, were connected at the hip. He could hurt her or you before they get a police officer to her. Plus, you don't want to scare Emily if we can make this go away behind the scenes. You saw what he did to the private investigator. Maybe he was jealous of the investigator's interest in you." He paused and took the last bite of his pie and finished the wine. Paul picked up both plates and took them to the pile of dishes already forming a mountain of work in the sink. She wandered to the couch and collapsed into it.

Under her breath, she said, "Nate. Nate was his name. He had a wife and three children." Paul couldn't hear her from the kitchen. But she needed to say his name out loud. The next morning was already decided for her by her daughter's lack of chores again. Like Humpty Dumpty, she would put the house back together again. She heard the faucet running. "No, Paul." The faucet shut off, and he came back to her. He sat so close to her on the couch she could smell the hint of his cologne. Maggie couldn't bring herself to pull away, nor did he move from her. She leaned her head on his shoulder and put her hand on his chest. His heart felt fast through his shirt. "When will it end? What would stop this guy from asking for more? I won't have any more after this. Maybe I can report Mr. Murphy to the police?" Maggie contemplated out loud.

"But are you sure it's him?" Paul asked. He rubbed her arm.

"I'm almost sure. Who else could it be? I don't understand why the background check I ran looked nothing like him. Nate, the private investigator, said he had something, but he was killed before he could share it with me."

"Are you, 'I bet my daughter's life on it,' sure?"

"No," she conceded. She wanted another glass of wine, to pass out and let everything turn black for a while.

"Let me poke around a little, see if we can find anything more out about Mr. Murphy," Paul said.

She startled out of her fogged mind and turned to him on the couch. "No, that's what Nate did. He's dead. I don't know what I'd do if I lost you. Please. No."

"Okay, it's okay," Paul said. And he excused himself to the bathroom. She sat alone on the couch and looked at her empty wineglass. Then a text chimed in.

Nate PI: *If you tell anyone, Emily is as good as dead. Do you have my money?*

She gasped. Paul came back from the bathroom. "What is it?" He asked. With a trembling hand, she gave him the phone. He studied the text and typed a response.

Maggie: *I have the money and I'm not telling anyone.*

Maggie felt tears welling in her eyes.

"It's okay, we're going to navigate this together," Paul said. She felt his fingers running through her hair.

She turned to him and said, "Make me forget about my life right now."

Before she could finish the request, he leaned into her. She pulled him in for a kiss. Paul startled, before leaning in and opening his mouth to her, and their teeth crunched together before he pulled away, blushing. "Sorry. It's just I've waited a really long time for that. I'll do better next time."

"It's okay, let's try again. You stay put, and I'll come to you." Maggie leaned into him and gently put her lips on his. He tasted like apple pie and cabernet. She wanted more. She pulled back and licked her lips.

He looked down at her, his green eyes watery, and tucked her hair behind her ear. "I don't deserve you."

"The last time I heard you say that, it was about Chris. The night he died. Why?" Maggie asked.

Paul straightened, and his mouth formed a straight line. "Because he didn't."

"Why?" Maggie asked.

"Mags, can we *not* talk about this tonight? Please? You said you wouldn't ask tonight." She nodded, and he leaned in for another kiss. Her lips parted to him like it was the most natural thing in the world.

"Should we get more... comfortable?" she said and rose from the couch. She grabbed his hand, and he followed her up the stairs. They crossed the threshold, and she had her fingers halfway through the buttons on his shirt, she felt his body stiffen and he placed his hands over hers, fumbling with his buttons. Maggie stared at him, confused, then around the room from his vantage point. He had never been in her bedroom, and it was still a shrine to his brother.

The large portrait of his brother and them feeding each other cake hung over the bed. Paul was in the picture's background, looking longingly at the couple. She hadn't noticed his face in the picture before now.

Maggie turned to face him, tears rolled down his face. She said, "I'm sorry. I wasn't expecting this."

"I know, it's okay." He buttoned his shirt.

"No, I mean, I wasn't expecting this yet. I've thought about it a lot. With you. I've spent eighteen years living with a ghost, and I well, I haven't..." She trailed off.

"You don't owe me an explanation." His hands moved down her neck, sending electricity through her. They traced the end of the necklace where her wedding rings clanged together, and he touched them like it burned. "After all this time, he's still everywhere." He glanced around the room. "I should go."

He turned away from her. "Wait," she said. "You've had too much wine. You can't leave."

He nodded. "I'll make myself a bed on the couch, like when Emily was small." He tucked her hair behind her ear. "You're not ready for this. Not yet. But when you are, I'll be here. Waiting. Like always." He kissed her cheek and walked away from her and down the stairs. She did not follow. What could she do? Her room was a shrine to the life taken from her. The ghost of Chris stood between her and any happiness she sought for herself.

Right before she drifted off to her wine-induced slumber, she received a text.

Emily: *At Andrea's - J said she saw Josh at concert weird I didn't see him c ya tmrw*

twenty-two

. . .

THE NEXT MORNING, she woke to the light shining brightly through her curtains. She checked her watch; it was nearly eight. Her head pounded a grim reminder of the night's wine. She rose and glanced around her room with fresh eyes. She'd need to do something about the ghost of Chris if she hoped for a future with his brother. She padded to the bathroom to assess the damage; an absolute mess. No longer in her twenties or thirties, a night of drinking took a much harder toll on her morning. Was Paul still there? She took three Advil, swiped her eyes with makeup remover disposing of the mascara and sleep, and brushed her hair and teeth before going downstairs to find out.

She started down the stairs, and she saw the back of his head, sitting on the couch. He typed on his computer, a bag from Einstein's Bagels on the coffee table with a mug of coffee half-finished.

He peeked over his shoulder. "Well, good morning sunshine." He smiled brightly at her.

"Ugh." She rubbed her head.

"Looks like you've got to get to the grocery store, so I

ran out for some bagel sandwiches and brewed the coffee. I waited on the sandwiches, but coffee was another story."

Maggie yawned and stretched. "I don't blame you. Thanks for doing that." She reached for his coffee cup to refill it while grabbing a cup of her own. Her stomach growled as she leaned over him.

He laughed. "I guess someone's hungry."

"Yeah, yeah." She grinned.

She came back with both mugs and set them on the coffee table, sat beside him, and rummaged through the Einstein's bag. Inside was the jalapeño bagel sandwich, her favorite. She took a large bite and chewed the now rubbery but still delicious egg.

"Whatcha doin'?" she said, looking over his shoulder at his computer.

"Well, after you went to sleep last night, I did a little research." He unwrapped his sandwich and took a large bite of his identical sandwich.

"Yeah? On what?" Maggie asked.

"Well, why the janitor doesn't look like your background check on Mr. Murphy."

Her stomach twisted, and she put down the bagel. She washed it down with the black coffee and leaned toward his screen, giving it her full attention. It was the picture of the Roy Murphy she had found, too. "Yeah, he doesn't look like the school janitor. But he has the same name, and he was the only one with that in the county."

"That confused me at first, too," he replied.

"And what did you find?"

"Well, the man here in this picture, he died six years ago. So, I found his obituary online. When I read it, it said his wife, Laura Murphy, and their son, Raymond 'Roy' Murphy, survive him."

"Oh, he goes by another name? The yearbook and school site used his chosen name."

"Yep, it seems like he goes by his middle name or nickname, which he shared with his father."

Maggie studied the photo and said, "Not to point out the obvious, but he's Black. The janitor Murphy isn't."

"I noticed that too. So, I ended up finding the Black Murphy's widow on Facebook. I checked her profile, and it wasn't locked down at all. Her son Raymond is hers, and her husband adopted him. Looks like they got together while she was pregnant."

"Um, that is an awful lot of personal information. How would you get that through her Facebook account?" Maggie asked.

Paul shrugged. "When Roy Sr. died, she wrote a whole thing about him adopting her son. They met when she was pregnant. She thanked him for loving her family when he didn't have to. She's an open book on Facebook. I can show you her profile?"

Maggie took another bite of the sandwich. "No, that's okay. But it was six years ago?"

"Yes, and I was prepared to scroll and scroll to learn about both Roys. But it turned out I didn't have to. She not only is an open book on Facebook, she re-shares all of her yearly memories every year. So each subsequent year is more and more cluttered. Though it didn't take long to find. She posts about her husband a lot."

Maggie considered this and took a couple of sips of her coffee. The Advil and bagel sandwich worked their magic, as she no longer felt her brain trying to claw its way out of her head. She picked up her phone and tracked her daughter to make sure she was still at Andrea's house and set the phone back down. No missed texts, which was a good thing.

Paul cleared his throat. "I found something else, too. She mentioned her son Roy's burns. It's quite sad, actually. About eighteen years ago, he was married, with a wife and child. His wife and baby were in a house fire. He was across the street at the neighbor's. He ran inside the burning house and saved his baby. Sadly, his wife died of smoke inhalation. He was badly burned saving his child. His mother had a newspaper article on her page. Young Roy went to the hospital, but the child was unharmed."

"Oh my God, how terrible," Maggie said.

Paul turned to her. "Mags, all of this explains his name, his job, and his burns. Someone who leaps into a burning house to save his baby doesn't sound like a killer or a stalker."

Maggie nodded her head and sipped her coffee. Paul was right. But something still felt off about him. "What about all the pictures and Nate's death?"

"I know you want answers to all of this, and to know who it is so you can call the police. But think about it, Emily wouldn't be the only one who coincided with the janitor changing jobs. Maybe if she went across five counties and he always tagged along? This really could be coincidence. I'm just saying you can't be certain it is him. I've got my doubts."

She swallowed the last bit of her bagel. "You're right. What would any of that have to do with me or Emily? But the private investigator, Nate, and the calls and the asking for money, and his murder. Who the hell could it be?"

"That's the real question. We have more questions than answers, but it's a start. It's enough to say we shouldn't go to the police because we don't have any actual evidence yet."

She drank the last of her coffee and considered his words but decided that she would think about what he had said later. Right now, Maggie wanted to address the elephant in the room. She began. "About last night—"

He cut her off. "We don't have to talk about or explain anything. You've got a lot going on right now. I came on too strong and quick." He shifted uncomfortably in his seat and took another bite of the cold bagel sandwich.

Maggie shot a melancholy smile at him. "No, no, you didn't. You've been right by my side for eighteen years. I wouldn't say you've been quick moving at all. Sloths move quicker."

His eyes darted to the floor, and he chuckled and swallowed, his cheeks flushed.

She grabbed his hand. "Don't look away from me. When this is over, let's figure out what we are. I want to be more than we were."

"We'll be however much you'll let me be. I've always loved you, Mags. But I think you've known."

She did. "You and Emily have been my family forever. I'm frozen with fear that if anything happens with this... If I screw this up, then I lose everything. I have so much to lose because of how big a part of my life you are."

He embraced her as they sat on the couch together. She felt safe in the radiating heat of his arms. She tilted her head up at him to get a better view of the man who had loved her forever. He gave her a small peck on the cheek. "I'd rather die than let anything happen to hurt you. You know that," Paul said.

"I do. And I know you've been patient. I'm going to ask you to be patient for a little while longer. Until we solve this current situation. Then, I'd really like to explore what we are," Maggie said.

He nodded and hugged her. "Absolutely, I can't wait." She could feel his heart racing as she leaned into him. "Let me refill our coffees," Paul said. He got up and went to the kitchen.

Then the familiar text dinged in. Please let it be Emily, she hoped.

Nate PI: *Are you ready for transfer instruction?*

Her stomach flipped, and she texted back.

Maggie: Yes.

Nate PI: *You will transfer my money to a Bitcoin. When we meet on Wednesday, you'll transfer the Bitcoin to me.*

Paul returned to the room with both steaming mugs and a relaxed smile across his features. She looked at him and traded him her coffee for the phone. "Read this," she said, shoving the phone in his free hand.

He studied the texts. "Okay. Bitcoin, that makes sense."

"How does this make sense? I know nothing about Bitcoin."

"I don't know much about it either, but I think it is untraceable. But did he say when we meet on Wednesday? He wants to meet you?" Paul asked.

"Yeah, I guess he does. I'll ask," and Maggie typed out a text and sent.

Maggie: *You want to meet in person?*

But there was no answer. The two stared at the phone, sipping their coffees for five minutes.

"Maybe I pressed too hard," Maggie said to Paul and the phone sitting silently between them both.

"Okay, don't text him anymore. Let him come to you and tell you what he wants," Paul said.

She set the phone aside, and another text came. This time it was from Emily.

Emily: *OMW to get our stuff*

Paul stood up. "I think I'd better go. I don't want Emily to see me in the same clothes I wore yesterday. She might get the wrong idea." He winked at Maggie.

"Wouldn't want her to get the wrong idea." Maggie smiled at him.

"I'll do research on how to buy the Bitcoin today to figure that part out. Then we'll be ready for Wednesday," Paul said.

"It's only a couple of days away. Paul, I'm scared to meet him."

"It's going to be okay. We're going to get through this. Together. Mags, let me help you with this. Don't shut me out. Promise?"

"Promise. Thank you for everything. You're always here. I'll make it up to you."

He kissed her on the cheek and walked out the door. Maggie got up from the couch. She had to move and be productive to keep her mind off the murderer watching her and her daughter. It could be Mr. Murphy, but then again, maybe not. And if it wasn't him, then who? Clearly, the police wouldn't be able to figure it out before he could get to Emily.

Then a text came back.

Nate PI: *Of course I want to meet. Don't you want to meet me? I've been waiting for you for a long time.*

twenty-three

. . .

MAGGIE DROPPED the phone as if it had burned her hand.

She walked to the laundry room and plucked the clothes out of the dryer. They had been there since yesterday and were a little wrinkled, but she didn't care. She walked upstairs, plunked the laundry on her bed, and looked around the room. Everywhere in the room there were hints of Chris.

Today, she thought. *Today would be the day she began to move on.* She went to Emily's room and found four empty boxes that she hadn't needed for her college move. The cathartic snap of the tape roll awakened her energy. Finally, she would make progress in her room. She marked each box: *Giveaway, Trash, Emily,* and *Maggie.* Anything to keep her mind busy while she waited for the stalker to reveal himself.

Not the bed yet, though it lost the scent and shape of him many years before, but she could surely do the nightstand. Their engagement photo stared back at her nightly across the valley of where he once slept. She looked at it and spoke to Chris. She hadn't spoken to him in years. "I've missed you so long, but now I'm just empty. We've been apart longer than you were here. Forgive me, but I need to move on." She gazed at the picture, his arms wrapped tightly around her waist, spinning her in a sunflower field the photographer picked that they never visited again. Her back arched and her mouth wide open in a wide laugh, eyes closed. She hated that picture, but Chris loved it. Her reaction was guttural the moment the photographer showed them. Her mouth was so far agape it looked like she had a double-chin. He loved it so much he insisted on it staring back at her from his nightstand and after he died, it seemed wrong to get rid of something he enjoyed so much. Even if at her expense. Yet, the years did not soften her feelings toward that picture. Today it would go. She opened the back of the frame. She still liked the frame with the gold scrolled sides. It would be perfect for Emily's senior picture she still had not framed. But the laughing hyena, double-chin picture, would absolutely go to the trash. When she removed the picture, a yellow crinkled note floated to the floor. It looked like old legal pad paper. She opened it and read.

Chris, We belong together. You'll see.

Her hands trembled. The handwriting belonged to a woman. The bubbly letters, the curled g in 'belong', gave her away. She turned the frame in her hands and at the bottom was a one-dollar price tag. She'd nearly forgotten they bought the frame years ago at a thrift store on their honeymoon at the Outerbanks. Could it be the note didn't belong to Chris? Why had he hidden it behind their engagement photo?

Had all the late nights at the office been a ruse? Their marriage, a lie? Worst of all, did she really waste eighteen years of her life yearning for someone who loved someone else? She changed her mind about the frame, tossed it in the giveaway pile, and slipped the note in her pocket. She would find out why he had it.

After the picture, she peeked in the nightstand drawer. Was there anything else worth investigating? Did she want to find anything else? It was mostly barren except for a couple of hotel receipts from work trips of years past. She left them to deal with another day. "No more nightstand for the day. I can't do any more secrets, Chris," she said out loud. She opened his side of the closet, and a musty smell greeted her. How much time would it take to clear her husband from her room, her life? It was a deed she delayed and dreaded for eighteen years.

His suits hung in the closet so long they went out of style and were back in again. The tops of the hangers creased the suits permanently. She'd give them away but wasn't sure a dry cleaning would salvage the shoulders. The cleaners would need magic to press the age and grief out of the clothes.

She looked up at the top shelf. There was a lockbox there, and she never found the key. In reality, she never bothered searching for it. Now, though, her curiosity grew about what might be in it. She put her hand back in her pocket to feel the note fueling her questions. Where would he have put the key? Could she take the lockbox to a lock-smith and have it opened? Would she want an audience to watch her as she discovered what other secrets he might have had?

She heard the door open downstairs and her daughter's voice. "Mom, we're here."

Maggie was startled back to reality and turned away from the closet. She felt that she had been caught snooping.

She left the bedroom and shut the door behind her. It didn't matter, though; the girls didn't notice her as they came in and ran past her, still wearing their concert clothes. She overheard them giggling and packing their things. Twenty minutes later, they were ready for a ride to Union Station. This time, Maggie was not too drunk to give it to them.

twenty-four

. . .

IN THE CAR, Maggie looked at the girls. Their mascara smudged, hair up in messy buns, the college sweats were on and ready for the two-hour train ride back to school. Emily flipped through her playlist until she settled on a song Maggie never heard with a voice auto-tuned out of the human register. She pulled into the kiss and ride and the girls still had twenty minutes to grab lunch and board their train. Both girls got out of the car, and Emily leaned in through the window. "Thanks, Mom. See you in a couple of weeks."

Maggie shot her a tired smile. "Sounds great."

Another text came in. Her stomach dropped. She looked down and breathed a sigh of relief. It was Paul.

Paul: *I figured out how to buy Bitcoin. We'll work on it tonight.*

Maggie: *Great. Dropped kids at the train station. Dinner?*

Paul: *Sounds good.*

Maggie did the dishes from the previous night. After, she had just enough time for a nap and a shower, before she needed to get ready. It would not be a good night to try the

Beef Wellington recipe. They'd order pizza. Emily was lactose intolerant, so pizza had been a rarity in the house for eighteen years.

She crawled back into bed.

Disoriented, she woke with another text. She couldn't tell if she'd been asleep for a couple of minutes, hours, or days. Her watch showed Paul would be there in about thirty minutes. *Please let it be Paul*, she thought.

It was another news article from her stalker. She read it.

Local private investigator, Nathaniel Dunn, died four days ago from a robbery. Due to several leads, police recovered a mask and hooded sweatshirt believed to be related to the crime in a nearby dumpster. No suspects have been apprehended. Investigation is ongoing. Police ask anyone with information to contact the Arlington Police Department. Do not approach the assailant. Due to the nature of the crime and the condition of the victim, the suspect is considered armed and dangerous.

Nate PI: Hmmm, they still haven't figured out who done it. Such a shame. I saw you that night you know.

Maggie gulped in terror.

Nate PI: You called another man to pick you up. Were you on a date with our investigator?

Maggie: No. He never showed, so I called a friend to get me.

Nate PI: It looked like you were on a date. You wore a blouse I've never seen you in. Seems Nate was a naughty boy. He paid the price though, didn't he?

A chill ran up her spine. She never wore the blouse before, but how long had he been watching her to know?

Maggie: I didn't know he was married.

It was all she could reply. He sent her another text, this time Nate's obituary. Maggie read how he would be memorialized.

Nathaniel Phillip Dunn, age 43, of Arlington, Virginia, died after a robbery in a parking garage in Arlington, Virginia. Nate was born in Sacramento, California to Bill and Eve Dunn. He was an only child. He graduated from Jefferson High school and served in the armed forces for twenty years.

In 2015, Dunn retired from the United States Army and turned his attention to law. He became a private investigator in Northern Virginia. He conducted investigations into fraud, infidelities, and violent crimes.

His wife Kathleen Dunn, sons Alex and Jordan, and daughter Jasmine, his parents, Bill and Eve Dunn, and a host of nieces, nephews, and cousins survive him. Memorial contributions can be made to the GoFundMe account in the comments. The proceeds will go directly to his children.

Maggie hovered over the link to the GoFundMe account for his children. What if the authorities were watching, who clicks the GoFundMe? Was it safe to use an incognito tab for an ongoing investigation? Finding out if the kids were donated enough money to pay for losing their father wasn't worth the risk.

Nate PI: *Do you have the Bitcoin?*

Maggie: *Tonight.*

Nate PI: *Good. I'll give you further instructions closer to our meeting time. Don't get any bright ideas. Remember, I'm watching Emily.*

Maggie: *I understand.*

Maggie's stomach twirled and twisted like a kite caught in a hurricane. If nothing else, fewer words might agitate him less.

She reached into her pocket and touched the note. Tonight, after they figured out the Bitcoin, she would ask Paul again. No more tiptoeing around the things in her bedroom to appease a ghost. The note must have something to do with the falling out Chris and Paul had before his death, and maybe something to do with what was happening now. After all, Mr. Murphy didn't appear in her life until Chris died.

twenty-five

. . .

MAGGIE WATCHED through the window as the pizza and Paul arrived at the same time. He took the pizza from the boy, slipped him a few bucks, and headed to the door. He knocked and entered. Tonight he came straight from work, still in his jeans, work boots, and Henley shirt.

"I see we're having pizza tonight." He smiled at her while walking past her to the kitchen with the pizza.

She got up from the couch and followed him in. "I just woke up from a nap not too long ago. After the dishes, I didn't have the energy for anything more in the kitchen. You're lucky I don't pull out the paper plates tonight."

He shrugged and went to where the paper plates were stored above the sink and opened the cupboard. "I don't mind. The pizza tastes the same on a paper plate."

"No, I'm not a heathen." She laughed.

They sat with their pizza and uncorked the second bottle of wine she'd picked up, pouring two healthy glasses. He handed her pizza, and they went to the table and ate in silence. She handed him the phone with the texts from the killer and leaned back in her chair and took a sip of wine.

She glanced at the flowers he gave her at their last dinner. The baby's breath was still sturdy, but the lilies wilted. It probably had a day or two left before it died completely, maybe Wednesday.

She watched him scan the articles with disinterest, and he returned the phone to her. "We'll get the Bitcoin handled tonight. Then we have one less thing to worry about," he said nothing about the articles.

She nodded and slipped the phone into her back jeans pocket. It would be good to put the money in the right account. "I wonder why Bitcoin and not a bag of cash or something?"

"I thought about it. Too many questions with a bag of cash, I think. The cash can be marked or traced. I researched Bitcoin, and it looks like you can transfer money without the normal identifying information you would need for any other bank transfer and the transactions cannot be reversed."

The transaction would not be reversible or traceable. A definite advantage for a criminal. Especially if he killed her and Emily. Maggie took another long sip of wine. "When we give him the money, what will stop him from killing Emily and me?"

Paul sipped his wine and said, "I won't let anything happen to you, or Emily."

After dinner, they sat on the couch with her laptop, and they bought Bitcoin. She felt a sickening pit in her stomach as she threw away her whole life's savings, her daughter's college, and $50,000 of his money, all gone with a few clicks of the mouse. "It's just 1s and 0s in a bank account," she said to Paul.

"Exactly, and money can always be remade. Together…" Paul said.

A cool sweat formed on her hands. "What if we lose the private key information? Or someone else gets ahold of it?"

He swallowed hard. She knew the answer. Paul said, "That cannot happen. We cannot allow that to happen. There isn't a good way to recover these types of currencies."

She nodded her head and put her hand in her pocket to pull out the note, wadded and wet with sweat in her hand. "Now that is done. I really want to talk to you about something."

He shifted uncomfortably and took a sip of wine and put down his glass next to hers. "Okay."

She unfurled her hand, and the note lay crumpled between them. "I found this." She unfolded it. The writing had smudged from her touching it in her pocket throughout the day. But it was still legible. "Today, I started to clear out my bedroom. Finally, make it my own. I started at the nightstand. I popped the sunflower picture out of the frame, and I found this note." His eyes darted to the note in her hand, then back to her face. Maggie continued, "I did not write this note. The frame was from Goodwill, so maybe it isn't his note either. But I want you to look me in the eye and tell me that this is not his note." She put the note in his hands.

He looked down at the yellowed scrap of paper between them, and back up at her. "I can't do that, Mags." His eyes turned away from her, fueling her anger. He leaned in and tried to put his arm around her, but she shrugged him away. He flinched from her dismissal but laid his hand limply at his side.

"What is this? Did you know about this?" she spat.

The red blossomed in his neck, his anger renewed, not at her, or the killer, but at his brother. "Yes, that note belongs to Chris. I don't know how to tell you why I know that it's his."

"If you have any care for me, you'll tell me exactly what this is, and why he had it," Maggie pleaded. "I need to know if I've wasted my life mourning a marriage I didn't have." Her voice cracked as the words tumbled out.

"Mags, can we talk about this once we've gotten you safe? Emily safe? This was a long time ago."

"He died a long time ago, too. No more delays. Please, tell me. If I have to move past this or through this, I need to know," Maggie said.

"Chris said something happened, and I wouldn't understand. And he was right because, how can somebody who has someone like you... do something like this?"

"What exactly happened, Paul?" Maggie asked.

"Honestly, I don't know. Chris told me he got tangled up in something with a woman. He would not specify, but he said I wouldn't understand, and it wasn't his fault. That was the day he wasn't my brother anymore. The day he betrayed you. He lived the life I always wanted, and pissed it away," Paul said. His chest heaved with a renewed anger, and he took a sip of his wine and did not raise his eyes to her.

"You were so angry with Chris that last night. I replay it over and over. Was there something I could have said that made him stay? Or was I too harsh when I pretended not to see him lean in for a kiss, to make him speed up and off the bridge? Did I make him careless? You know, they said speed was a factor in the crash," Maggie said.

"Mags, you can't blame yourself for what happened. It wasn't your fault. None of it."

She kept her eyes trained on her lap. Paul held the bottom of her chin and tilted it up to her. "I'm serious."

"I know, I know. You can't help thinking, what if? You know. I mean, when I was putting together this book for Em, I saw the newspaper article of his death again. I don't know why I read it, or why I saved it, but I did. For the first time, I realized, he wasn't heading to the office. I didn't have any idea. Then he knew I hated that picture on the nightstand, and he insisted on keeping it. At our bedside. And now, I find that he had another woman's note behind it." Her eyes stung with hot, bitter tears. She wasted years of her life mourning an unfaithful man. This woman whose note sat behind an ugly picture of herself. She snatched the note from Paul and crumpled it in her hand.

Paul put his hand around her fist and unfurled it. He took the note from her and shook it between them. "This changes nothing. You have been the most loyal wife and mother. The only thing it does is release you."

"You knew. This whole time." Her sadness gave way to anger. Paul knew Chris played her for a fool, and even after his death, said nothing.

"I promised him I wouldn't say anything. But I will not lie to you," Paul replied.

"We were all so young," she said. Feeling grief for the years she had wasted being faithful to a memory.

"You excuse his behavior even now," Paul said with anger hinged toward her.

"I know, I know I do. But it's so hard to be angry when you know there's no way we can talk it out and overcome it. It is impossible to be angry at a ghost. But you are right here, alive and well, and you knew." She took the note back from him and shoved it in her pocket. She crossed her arms over her chest. Which box would the note go to? *Trash* or *Maggie* as a reminder of how stupid she'd been.

Paul said, "I understand your anger. Even at his

funeral, I was angry with him. Angry that we couldn't move on and find closure. We both loved the same woman. He got her and completely messed up. I kept his secret, which felt and feels like a betrayal to you. I would have done nothing to hurt you. Even when we were kids, I watched in awe of all he had. And he threw it all away. And now, he's dead. Honestly, I'm glad you found the note."

She flinched as if he slapped her.

He enveloped her in his arms and said, "I shouldn't have said that. I'm sorry."

She pulled away from him and used her fingers to comb her hair. Then she used her shirt to wipe away the tear streaks from her face. Though makeup would have helped her look less tired, now she was grateful her face was bare. The only thing worse than a crying vulnerable face would be one stained and streaked with makeup, her mask to the world melting off.

"I think you should go."

It was his turn to appear struck in the face. She stared straight ahead. His shoulders rounded in resignation. "Okay. Call me as soon as you hear anything, please? We'll work through this together."

He left, and she went up to her room. Their room. The marks of him were everywhere. The only thing she could bring herself to do was wash the sheets and dust. Though his pillows had stopped carrying his scent years ago, she couldn't strip them naked to wash. Somehow, in her scientific mind, she knew some part of him was still there, lingering in the material where he once rested his head.

How did she miss every sign that Chris had been having an affair? He always seemed so glad to come home and looked forward to the birth of his daughter. How could she trust anything anymore? She was wrong about Chris and then Nate. Who else could she be wrong about?

Every memory she could conjure of Chris was a joyful one. Yes, she grew up with him and loved him. But his death brought amnesia to her. The troubles and trials of a young couple trying to make it work with a growing family. All the late nights at work evaporated from her memories the night he died. Until it was time to clean him out of her bedroom so she could move on. Then the less savory remembrances flooded back to her psyche. He worked a lot and loved his job. The business trips put a strain on the marriage and they were only in their twenties. She spent a lot of her married years alone.

Paul would have likely been a better fit than Chris, but he was born three years too late. Too exhausted to think anymore, she laid down in her marital bed and went to sleep dreaming of her husband's brother.

twenty-six

. . .

MAGGIE SLEPT LONG AND HARD. She tossed and turned, waking, crying, and sleeping with starts throughout the night. She didn't get out of bed until eleven. There had not been one day in her life since becoming a mother that she slept more than eight hours. The only reason she woke was a FaceTime call from Emily.

"Hello," Maggie answered, her voice groggy. She didn't realize it was a FaceTime when she answered, and the phone projected her full morning self to her daughter on the screen. Her old Metallica T-shirt had a coffee stain on it.

Jenna perched next to Emily on the call. When Maggie answered, Emily's jaw dropped open. "Oh my God, Mom, are you okay? I'm sorry, but you look like shit." Jenna bowed out of the frame and Maggie spotted Emily grimacing at her from off-screen.

Maggie rubbed her eyes. They were puffy from tears. "I'm a little under the weather." It wasn't exactly a lie. She didn't feel herself.

"Are you okay? I can call Uncle Papa to see if he can bring chicken soup."

Maggie rubbed her face and sat up. "Thanks, honey, for your concern. Really, it's okay, maybe a virus or something." She forgot how she left things with Paul until Emily mentioned him. She'd need to deal with all that later. Too tired to lie anymore, Maggie pivoted the conversation to Emily's favorite subject. "You look pretty. What are you doing today?"

Emily ran her fingers through her long, blonde hair. Her loose curls grazed the top of her slender shoulders. She wore a pale pink blouse and a white skirt. "Oh, thanks. Today is 'bid day' so we find out which sorority we're in." Jenna popped back into the frame. They looked like twins. She wore a powder blue blouse with a white skirt. She waved and smiled at Maggie. Both girls looked like they were headed to church. Save for the length of their skirts.

"Have a great time." Maggie yawned and stretched.

"Thanks, Mom. Are you sure you're okay?"

"Yes, hon, don't worry about me. I'm going to get moving and get errands done. We can chat later, okay?"

"Okay." She gave her mother a kissy face in the frame, and Jenna waved goodbye in the background before they hung up.

After they hung up, Maggie's stomach growled at her to get up for the day. It was time to have coffee and eat. The coffee supply was dwindling. She would need to add the grocery store to her errands. It was the one staple she could not be out of, no matter how she felt.

There were no texts from Paul or Nate. It was better not to hear from either of them right now. After she made the coffee, she went outside, still in her sweatpants and t-shirt. She watered her plants. Gardening was her meditation. Gardening, hiking, and reading helped her, but most of the time, she learned to live with her wandering thoughts. Her meditation counselor (who called himself a guru) called it her 'monkey mind.' Trying to calm her monkey mind usually incited a riot in her mental zoo.

Uneasiness crept into her mind, and she realized that for many years she had often felt watched. Now, she knew it wasn't paranoia or her monkey mind. It was the gut she should have listened to the entire time.

A text chimed in.

Paul: *Good morning*

She saw it on the screen and didn't open it. Responding to Paul would take more energy than she could muster. Maggie turned the hose back on and watered the side of spent hostas. Another text chimed in. Irritated, she glanced down to tell Paul she'd call him later.

It wasn't Paul. Nate's number sent a picture of her daughter. The picture was of her daughter in the pale pink top and tennis skirt. She stood on campus among a gaggle of girls, all in pastel tops and white short tennis skirts. None of them played tennis. The shot caught Emily mid-laugh. It would be a picture her daughter hated, but she loved. Like the one that stared back at her from her night-stand. It captured her essence. How could he get so close and take pictures of her unnoticed?

Maggie: *I have your money. I bought the Bitcoin. Please leave my daughter alone.*

Nate PI: *I will. Once I get my money. This is a reminder to you not to try anything stupid.*

Maggie breathed hard and texted.

Maggie: *How do I know you won't ask for more or hurt us, anyway? This is all I have.*

She immediately regretted sending the message.

Nate PI: *You don't. But I won't. I want only what you owe.*

Unless she planned to drown the plants, she could

water no more. Maggie went inside to take her last cup of coffee and clean up for the day, thinking about who she owed money to. Eager for a distraction today, she would finish tackling the nightstand. Staying busy was key as she waited for the killer's next set of directions. Staying busy kept her sane while she waited on a killer's direction.

After her coffee and shower, her eyes appeared less puffy, and her hair was slicked tight to her head. Blow-drying it seemed a useless delay tactic for the bedroom, so she left her hair wet and dripping down her back. She went to Chris's nightstand, now devoid of the dreaded picture, and opened the drawer again. The scraps of paper were the detritus of a busy professional. There were several hotel receipts from Domber Inn, now curled on the edges with age. He had always saved every shred of paperwork for taxes. She never dealt with the taxes, but the Domber hotel receipts were dated over a year before he died. If he used those for taxes, they would have been in the tax file in the office, not his nightstand drawer. Curious, she plugged the address of the hotel into her map. It was close to the bridge he had died on. It was exactly on the way. Not the office, which was in the opposite direction. Why, after eighteen years, did she just now discover he had been driving in the wrong direction?

After he died, she didn't do the taxes, handle the life insurance, or the budget. Paul took over all of Chris's duties and she never asked. He handled her expenses for a full year until she could get her arms around trying to remember how to breathe.

If she could examine the ledger from eighteen years ago, she might get an idea of what was going on. What would that fix? Maybe she should let it go like water under the bridge that Chris drove off.

Maggie took the receipts and threw them in the trash box. She slipped on jeans and a cardigan sweater and pulled her wet hair back into a ponytail to start her errands. Glancing in the mirror, she noted she appeared stronger today than yesterday. Tomorrow she would be stronger still. She should have moved on from Chris a long time ago. For her errands, she would do the grocery store first. She checked the map again. It would only be a slight detour to get to the address where Chris had spent all of those nights. She needed to pay this place a brief visit.

twenty-seven

. . .

ON THE WAY TO COSTCO, Maggie turned right
and headed toward the address on the receipts. Her unconscious desire to see the hotel and get closure turned the
steering wheel to cross the bridge. As she felt the grates
rattle the car beneath her, she peered down at the unfor-
giving black water. Anxiety crawled into her chest. How
easy would it be to just drive over? If anything happened to
Emily, that's exactly what she'd do.

She came across a derelict long-abandoned mom-and-
pop hotel. Plywood covered the windows and spray paint
adorned the side. The adobe chipped walls wore the sign
"For Lease" with a phone number beneath it. The
surrounding town had the markings of long ago charm but
was now in disrepair. A couple of blocks over, new condos
cropped up from the rubble, and the gentrification would
make its way to this area, too.

Maggie couldn't recall what this neighborhood would
have been like eighteen years ago. Chris had never taken
her here or talked about this part of town. Why had she
driven here? Why had she really made this detour? Did she

think she'd go inside and ask the people who worked there if they remembered a young man coming here almost twenty years ago? The one who died on the bridge returning home from a tryst to his pregnant wife. Did this mystery have something to do with Roy Murphy Jr., the man watching her? She slammed her hands on the steering wheel, turned her car around, and headed to Costco.

After Maggie hauled the last Costco box to the kitchen to unload it, her phone chimed in. Another photo. This one was more unflattering than the last. His fascination with her daughter escalated. Emily was clearly drunk, and her top was almost off as she was passed out on the ground. A boy with a brown mop of hair lay next to her, with a chiseled body but no shirt, and what appeared to be crocodile boxer shorts. He was definitely her type. Save for his enviably sharp jawline, she could not make out his face because his hair covered it. His arms were around her waist, and they both slept on the lawn. College kids were carelessly drinking in the background. Maggie spotted a couple of bare feet in the frame's corner where it looked like another girl passed out on the grass. Maybe Jenna? While it was night, the area was well lit with solid white orbs of artificial light she recognized from the school's quad on their tour.

Maggie's heart plummeted to her feet. This couldn't be happening.

Maggie: *Please, leave her alone. I'll do anything.*

He didn't respond.

She went upstairs to her room to get under the covers. The covers made her feel safe, and she called Paul; he picked up, and she didn't say hello. "He texted again. I don't know what to do. I'm so scared. It was a picture of Emily. What if I just get her right now? Pull her out of school and hide?" She cried.

Paul's voice came through the line, calming. The voice of reason. "You know you can't do that. By the time you arrive at the school, someone could already have hurt her. You don't know how he's tracking her or you."

"I know. How can he be in so many places at once? If he hurts her, I will kill him myself." She growled. Maggie thought of the black water beneath the bridge, beckoning her car off the bridge. Would it hurt to die of hypothermia? Drowning?

"I'm leaving work and I'm on my way," Paul said.

"Thank you," she said and hung up.

Nate PI: In case you try to do anything crazy like take your daughter and hide, I want you to know she'd be dead before you got here. Don't play with me.

How did he read her mind?

Maggie: I won't. I promise.

Nate PI: If you go to the police or the media, I'll slit her throat. If you try to come here and pick her up, you won't be able to find her. I will send you pictures of what I do to her.

Maggie: Please, please. Stop. I'll do anything. Please, just leave her alone.

Nate PI: Good. Now that I have your attention. I'll send you meet up instructions tomorrow. Act normal and I won't hurt her.

She gulped down the taste of bile. There was no way out, no way she could ensure Emily's safety.

Maggie went back downstairs to wait for Paul to come to her. Before he got there, she felt someone peering in her window. Maggie looked back, thinking it might be Paul walking up to the door. It was dusk, but not too dark yet when the boogie men came out. In her peripheral, there was a shadowy figure walking quickly by. He wore a hoodie, sunglasses, and gloves and she recognized a hilt in his gait.

She retreated to the kitchen and sat at the kitchen island. Her head in her hands.

A few minutes later, Paul knocked and walked through her front door. She peered up from her head in her hands as he walked past her and filled her brass kettle with water and put it on the stove. Once the water boiled, he took two cups to the couch and sat down. She followed and took her red fading to pink paisley cup from him. The chamomile bag bobbed to the surface, with the empty promise of relaxation. They sat close to one another. The heat of his thigh against hers permeated her jeans.

She turned to him and took a sip of her tea. "I went by the Domber Inn today. Have you heard of it?" she asked, trying to keep her voice steady.

His eyebrows turned up in slow recognition, and he took a sip of his tea. "It sounds familiar."

"I don't want to think about this stalker or killer right now. There is nothing I can do. I'll think of literally anything else. Right now, what I'm trying to unravel is why my marriage may have been crumbling before Chris died. I didn't know it, had absolutely no suspicion. So, I'm going to ask you again, since you handled my taxes and expenses for the year following Chris's death. Have you heard of the Domber Inn?"

He shifted in his seat and set down his cup. "Yes. Chris frequented the hotel, but it was never on his expense reports. That's all I know."

Maggie sighed. "He was a mystery. I thought his love for me was real." She finished her cup of tea and put it next to his on the table. "Thank you for always being there for me." She kissed his cheek.

He turned to her and leaned in, and this time, their lips met. There was no clashing of teeth. Just the soft feeling of their lips moving together as one. He fumbled with the top buttons of her shirt. His brother's wedding ring popped out and grazed his fingers. He pulled his fingers from her, almost like his hands had been scalded on a hot stove. She looked down at the two rings laying under where her second button was. Maggie buttoned her shirt.

"You aren't ready for this," Paul said, turning away from her.

"Maybe not yet, but I'm getting closer. I promise." She would have done it. Anything to keep her mind off the most awful things her mind could conjure.

He stood and straightened his shirt. He picked up the teacups and took them to the kitchen. She heard him pick up his keys from the kitchen island. He walked to the living room. "Good night, Mags."

He turned to go, and she sat speechless. He had almost slipped out the door before she eked out, "Paul, wait."

Paul faced her, his eyes sad. "Of course, that's what I've been doing since I've known you. I'll wait as long as it takes."

"That's not what I meant. I mean, can we talk about this…"

"No, not tonight. I already know. I'm sure his closet is still the same, and you're still wearing your wedding rings, for God's sake. You told me you cleared the nightstand. And well, it's a start. But that's the first thing you've done to move on in eighteen years. I hope it doesn't take another eighteen years. But if it does, I'll wait. I don't want to be your distraction from what is happening right now. I want you to want to be with me for me."

She didn't respond, because he was right, and she didn't have the energy tonight. She went to him and put her arms around him. He slipped his arms around her waist.

Under his breath in her ear, he said, "I'm tired of being the little brother, Mags."

"I know you're tired of it. Believe me, I see you as more than Chris's little brother. I know things have been wonky right now," Maggie said.

"It's okay."

"Wait, I have to tell you something. Promise you won't call the police? I can't risk Emily," Maggie said.

"Of course. What is it?"

She told him about the man peering in her window.

"Mags, you need to tell me about everything that happens so we can be a team on this," Paul said.

"What? Like you were a team with Chris?" Her voice grew hard with anger. She regretted the accusation instantly. "I'm sorry, I shouldn't have said that."

"It's fine." But she saw it was not fine. He put down his keys. "I'm staying."

Paul went to the closet where the spare blankets were to make his place on the couch. He laid the weighted flannel blanket down and put his pillow in place. "Goodnight, Mags."

Maggie went upstairs and changed into her pajamas, ripped up t-shirt and ragged sweats. She peered down at him from her bedroom. He sat, shoulders slumped. It would be another uncomfortable night on a couch just to make her more comfortable. She went toward him.

"Paul?" she said from halfway down the stairs.

He looked over his shoulder at her. "Yes? Do you need something?"

"I do. But I hope you won't be uncomfortable with it. You can tell me no."

"Okay, what is it?" Her nerves tingled.

"Will you lay with me? Nothing more. I'm scared and

exhausted. I want to sleep so badly, but there's so much happening..." Her voice trailed off.

He said nothing but grabbed his weighted blanket and pillow and went up the stairs to her. She crawled under the covers, and he tucked her in like the many times she had tucked Emily in. He circled the other side of the bed and stood there for a moment. He hesitated, and she barely breathed for fear of scaring him off. His breathing slowed, and she felt him moving Chris's pillows and placing them gently on the floor. Then the weight of him dipped his brother's side of the empty bed. He laid on top of the comforter with his own pillow and blanket.

She turned to him, kicked off her blankets and put the weighted blanket over her body too. Her head rested in the crook of his arm, and then there was nothing but sweet sleep. It was the first night she slept solidly in months. Maybe years. Finally, she felt safe.

twenty-eight

. . .

A FACETIME JOLTED MAGGIE AWAKE. She glanced around the room orienting herself. It was daybreak and Chris's, or was it Paul's, side of the bed, was empty. The scent of coffee filled the air.

She answered the FaceTime. "Hi, sweetie."

"Hi, Mom," Emily said. There were heavy bags under her eyes and what looked to be yesterday's makeup still thick on her face. Not at all like the confident girl she sent off to school. More like an unruly toddler who desperately needed a nap.

Her daughter said nothing about her mother still being in bed. Maggie's gut grew uneasy. She sat up against her pillows. "What is it, honey?"

"Mom, I wanna come home," she said. Her eyes were red-rimmed and glassy.

"What, honey? What happened? Are you okay? Did anyone hurt you?" Maggie asked, looking in the frame for any more context or clues to what upset her daughter. Emily's miserable face was the only thing filling the frame.

"Yeah, yeah I'm okay. It's just, I'm tired. I want to be home. I miss you, my friends, and I miss Josh," Emily said.

"Mostly Josh?" Maggie breathed a sigh of relief. Boy problems last week may have sent her mama's heart into anxious overdrive, but today it was the best unsolvable problem to have.

"Yeah, mostly Josh," Emily conceded, her voice thick with regret.

"I know, he has been a big part of your life." Maggie rubbed the sleep from her eyes and spotted her own last night's makeup as Emily came in to focus.

"I want to come to see him for the weekend. Do you think I can get money for the bus today?" Emily asked.

Maggie recalled the text from last night. If Emily came home, or tried to come home, it could mean something awful for either of them. The killer would be here, focusing on Maggie, collecting his money. "Okay, I can come pick you up on Thursday. I can make a day trip of it and we can have brunch together. I can bring you home for the weekend. This is a part of growing up. You are probably just tired. Too much partying. Can you hold out until then?" Maggie asked.

"Why not now?" her daughter whined. Maggie got up from her bed and went downstairs, following the scent of the coffee.

"It's too soon. You'll have to start the separation process all over again. This is a part of the college journey, hon. You need to make friends where you are," Maggie said.

"I am making friends, Mom. It's normal to be homesick." Her whining intensified.

Maggie was too tired to fight but needed to win this battle for all of their sakes. Maggie would give anything to go to her and hug her. But the risk was too great. She entered the kitchen.

There, Paul, with hair wet and freshly showered but in yesterday's clothes, sipped his coffee and read the news on his phone. Maggie spun quickly around to leave the kitchen.

"Uncle Papa?" Emily asked.

Paul came up behind Maggie and looked into the phone. "Oh hi, sweetie," he replied, and a smile eased on to his face. Maggie's face froze in place. Paul turned to her and said, "I got the faucet fixed before I headed out to work. Call me if you find it's dripping again and I'll stop by after if it gives you any problems. I didn't want to wake you, so I just came in. Coffee is ready." Then he looked at Emily. "Hope you're having a great day at school. I've gotta run."

"Thanks, Paul. I appreciate it," Maggie said.

"Of course." And he headed out of the frame. Maggie lowered the camera and mouthed, "Thank you." Paul nodded and slipped out the door, shutting it quietly behind him.

"What would you do without him?" Emily asked.

"I honestly don't even know," Maggie replied, and she meant it. "So, what's your plan for the day?"

"I have English class today, but it ends at three. After, I might go out with Jessica, since you won't let me come home," Emily said.

"Oh, who's Jessica?" Maggie asked, changing the subject.

"She's super nice. I met her at a party the other night."

"Is Jenna coming?" Maggie asked.

"Honestly, I need some space from her. She's kind of been on my nerves lately. Last weekend, she left and hung out with some guys. Didn't even tell me she left. Then she's always around. We're in the same sorority, almost the same classes. Except for her computer science ones."

"Even the best of roomies will get on your nerves. I remember your godmother Jasmine would drive me crazy with her snoring." Maggie laughed.

"Yeah, I guess." Emily sighed. "I just miss being home, Josh, you, Uncle Papa. All of it. Everything started out so perfect at college. It's just getting kind of old now."

Maggie smiled at her. She recalled this time in her life. "That's called the honeymoon phase. You've been there less than a week. After the initial shine wears off, you notice the tarnish. It happens to everyone. You realize this is your new reality, and it isn't just a visit anymore. It's okay sweetie, it means you're adjusting."

Maggie blew out a sigh of relief. A normal conversation with her daughter, filled with the regular angst. A week ago, this same conversation would have filled her with anxiety and dread for her daughter. But today it was the best problem to have.

"Did it happen to you and Dad?" Emily asked.

Maggie didn't mention the parade of men Jasmine brought into their room. It was like a revolving door, and sometimes Maggie got jealous of Jasmine's freedoms. Sometimes, if she really thought about it, she felt shackled to Chris. She didn't regret meeting Chris, but wished they got together a little later. Maggie needed to stall her daughter. "It did. Honey, it happens to everyone. I promise. I'll tell you what, give it a couple of days. If you still want to come home, I'll pick you up on Thursday." After she resolved the issue with the Watcher on Wednesday she'd get eyes on her daughter on Thursday.

Emily nodded her head and rubbed her eye like a child. Maggie decided against asking about her partying or school grades. She saw the pictures, and if there were things her daughter didn't want to share, then Maggie didn't want to know.

The killer didn't have his money. Hurting either of them would not make sense yet. Not until the money was exchanged.

"Okay, but Thursday you promise to get me? I want to come home," Emily said.

"Deal. I love you," Maggie said.

"Love you, too, Mom." Emily disconnected the call.

Maggie breathed a sigh of relief. Thursday couldn't come soon enough for either of them. She wanted more than anything to get eyes on Emily. She appeared healthy enough, but was clearly struggling with the transition. Mothers sniffed out their children's troubles. Even if they did not know what was going on with their husbands behind their own bedroom doors.

Maggie went upstairs, got ready and straightened her bed, and put away the weighted blanket and pillow. It felt right to have Paul on the other side of the bed with her. She hadn't slept that well in years. If she could free herself of this man stalking her she would sleep in Paul's arms forever if he'd have her.

A few hours later, another FaceTime request came in from her daughter. Two in one day. She accepted the call.

twenty-nine

. . .

EMILY'S HAIR was piled high in her blonde messy bun, her eyes were red and swollen from tears, and her nose ran. She dabbed at her eyes with a tissue. Before Maggie said a word, Emily choked out, "He, he, broke up with me."

Maggie's mouth dropped open. "What do you mean? Josh? Why?"

Emily wailed and cried. Saying the words out loud reinvigorated her tears. Maggie couldn't decipher her words through the choking heaves and sobs.

Maggie's heart pinched for her daughter's aching heart. "Slow down, sweetie. I don't understand what you're saying. Smell the flowers and blow out the candles. C'mon, do it with me."

The two breathed in and out for a few breaths. Emily's ragged breathing slowed, and she blew out her candle again. Just like when her daughter was a toddler and tried to climb out of her rage-filled tantrums, they breathed together over and over. Until her daughter's shoulders stopped shaking and she regained enough composure to speak.

"Okay, so, I was, um, at a party and we were outside. Hanging out with some guys and stuff. I mean, it was nothing. Anyway, so someone sent pictures to Josh. It's an open campus, I know, but it's not like we saw anybody creepy hanging out. I mean, I know what to look for with creepers," Emily rambled.

Maggie knew in an instant what photo she was talking about. Gingerly she asked, "Were you drinking?"

"Yeah, I actually completely blacked out. Josh sent a picture and a video back to me. I mean, I know it's me. It's clearly me, but I don't remember it. I don't even remember much of the night. He called me crying and stuff," Emily said.

Being blacked out should not be part of the college experience, but Maggie bit her tongue. A conversation for another day. "I'm sorry, hon."

"I just had too much to drink. So, I obviously am not coming back today. I just can't be there and see him," Emily said. Another tear ran down her face and landed on her shirt.

"Okay, let's decide closer to the day. I can come to you, or you can stay. Decide nothing right now. Wait, I was picking you up on Thursday. You weren't coming home today," Maggie said.

Emily rolled her eyes. "I was going to surprise you. Josh paid for my train ticket to come home and I thought it would be fun. Also, I didn't want you to say no. But I'm not doing it anymore, so it doesn't matter. Tonight I'm going out with Jenna. She's been awesome through this. Going to do some lunch and retail therapy. I need to be off-campus for a while. Think I can have a little money?" Emily asked.

"Sure, I'll transfer some into your account. Get coffee and do a little shopping. Call me if you need anything."

"I will, I love you, Mom," Emily said.

"I love you, too."

A few minutes later, a knock at the door startled Maggie. She checked the deadbolt from the stair landing; it was unlocked. Maggie walked softly to the peephole and looked. She could tell by the top of his head it was Josh. He didn't look up at her. He knocked again, harder.

She opened the door, and his face was strained with tears of his own. "Come on in."

Josh walked in and plopped on the couch. "You heard, huh?"

"I did," Maggie said. "I'm going to put on some tea." Maggie walked to the kitchen and put the tea kettle on. How could she comfort this boy? Fate was not destined for these kids, but it didn't need to end this way, so painfully. She walked back to the living room and sat next to him.

"I, I know I shouldn't be here," Josh said.

"It's fine. Do you want to talk about it?" Maggie asked.

"No. I mean, yeah, but not really. Look, just look at what I got."

He handed the phone to her as if it was a hot potato, and it was as she suspected. The exact picture she received. She looked at the text, an unfamiliar number to him. The number burned into her memory. He also received a video.

She pushed play. It was Emily earlier in the night. She danced with the boy in the alligator boxer shorts. He had not stripped down to them yet, but Maggie recognized the brown mop swishing back and forth. Emily's crop top was still firmly in place, and he wore jeans and a t-shirt. Emily leaned into him and kissed him, and he kissed her back. Concentrating on the video, it looked almost as if the boy was holding her up. Emily must have drunk a lot. Josh's face shriveled to a grimace, watching the kiss. He must have seen this video hundreds of times.

The angle of the camera looked like it was from a way off. No one would notice because there were dozens of college kids outside partying. Then it zoomed in on the pair. The boy took off his shirt and swung it in a circle around his head. He tried to take off his pants and stumbled to the ground, finally kicking them off. Emily tumbled to the ground beside him, both of them giggling.

He shut off the phone and put it back in his pocket. "See, it's like she forgot everything. Who is she?"

Maggie asked herself the same question more than once. The Emily that went to college was careless with all she held dear, including Josh.

The tea kettle whistled, beckoning her back into the kitchen. The timing was perfect. She, too, needed to catch her breath. "Smell the flowers, blow out the candles," she said to herself as she poured the tea. Before she returned to Josh, she texted the killer.

Maggie: *Please, leave my daughter alone. I'll get you the money.*

Nate PI: *He deserves to know what kind of person she is.*

Maggie: *How do you know I'm talking about Josh?*

Nate PI: *I know everything.*

Her hands trembled, but she picked up the teacups and peered out the window. She half expected to see the loping figure who peered in her window before, but it was a bright day. Nothing suspicious, just a broken-hearted boy crying on her couch. She walked back into the room, and Josh quickly shut his phone and stuck it under his leg. But there was another phone, the one with the pictures he showed her sitting on the coffee table.

Maggie handed the cup of tea to Josh. "Here, drink this. Tea always makes me feel better. Blow it first, it's hot."

He calmed and took the teacup from her. "Thank you, Ms. Becker."

"What's the other phone you have?" Maggie's eyes glanced at his leg and where the phone sat.

"Oh, it's my work phone. The boss just gave it to me. My phone is getting turned off at the end of this month, because money is tight at home. I was supposed to be there fifteen minutes ago, I called out. I can't go to work like this." He shifted uncomfortably in his seat.

She owed a response to the killer. "Give me one second. I have a message I have to reply to," she said.

Maggie: *I understand.*

A simple message and she waited. Ding. Josh's phone under his leg made a noise. Her eyes peered down at his leg, and he fidgeted.

"Did you get a message, Josh? Your phone is making noise and glowing," Maggie said.

He glanced down. "Uh yeah, it's probably just my boss replying. I'll read it later. I should go. Thanks for listening." Josh didn't finish his tea and walked out the door.

Maggie took the teacups back to the kitchen and watched Josh from the window. He looked down at his message and read. She looked at her own phone, but the read receipts weren't on, so how sure could she be that Josh had something to do with it? As Paul would say, was she *risking-her-daughter's-life-sure*? No, but she was getting closer to certainty.

thirty

. . .

JOSH HAD BEEN a constant part of the family since they got together four years ago. Why now? Jealousy over Emily's college experience? The boy she danced with? How would he be able to see her, unless he was driving there and watching, then texted himself on the second phone and came over to Maggie's to check on her? Show her the evidence and lose her from his trail? The plan seemed beyond what Josh could conjure up. If he spent half of that energy on his own life, then he would have had the scholarship and been alongside Emily at JMU. It made little sense, and she scrubbed it from her mind.

Tackling her dead husband's side of the closet was too much today. Maybe the pictures would be enough to distract her or give her a definite clue of who watched her family. There was nothing else to do except worry, and she'd done enough of that.

She caught her reflection in the mirror in the hall and stopped and turned to herself. How long had it been since she found the janitor watching her? Hired the private detective who got killed? Became a victim of a ransom request? It felt like years, but really, had it been just a week, less? She couldn't remember. The constant state of anxiety taxed her physically. She now understood why periods of extreme stress aged people in fast forward. During a trip to D.C. once, she viewed pictures of Abraham Lincoln at the National Portrait Gallery throughout the civil war and it ravaged his body long before he fell to a bullet at Ford's Theater. When she assessed herself in the mirror, she understood why. She didn't recognize the bags under her eyes. They were contrasted with the extreme alertness of her features. Her eyes were wide, like a doe protecting her fawn, alert and scared. A walking image of worry.

She turned away from the haggard woman watching her and went back to her home office. Reentering the place where she had first unveiled her danger felt surreal. The room appeared neat enough, but inside the computer sat evidence of years of darkness swimming beneath the surface. Her fingers trembled as she hovered over the photos folder. She navigated back to the pictures of the janitor.

There her daughter was, in fifth grade. Emily beamed at her mother and gave her a flower for Mother's Day brunch at the school. Maggie had so few pictures of herself, and she'd forgotten the teacher snapped this one. Maggie looked into her own eyes. They were sad, but full of love for the little girl giving her the red carnation. At the corner of the frame, she eyed Mr. Murphy again. This time, she noticed something different. It wasn't her family he watched. It was her, not Emily. But why? It couldn't be. Chris was her first and last. Save for Nate, she had never been on another date. And she wasn't sure Nate's date wasn't just a slimy business dealing.

Maggie went back to the hundreds of pictures where his

face was picked up on the software. Over and over, his eyes were not on Emily at all. They were on the photographer. Sweat formed on the back of her neck. So many times she ignored the feeling someone watched her and she failed to see past the subject of her photo. Maggie captured moments, but also the stalker watching her. She opened Instagram and looked back at the picture of Emily playing soccer. The angle of the shot was clear. His eyes are in the stands. The far left side of the stands. Exactly where Maggie sat, every time.

How did she not feel him watching? Too many times to be coincidence. She felt his constant presence since Chris's death. She knew that now. Her friends discussed the feeling of being watched walking alone in a parking lot or going on a run, and Maggie was no different. But if she reported it as often as she felt it, she would be the boy who cried wolf. However, there was now a wolf lying in wait and watching. But why now? And why her?

Buried in her research, she forgot she made plans for Paul to come over. He came daily now to check on her and be with her. She heard him let himself in.

"Mags? I'm here," Paul said from the doorway.

"Upstairs in the office." Her voice cracked.

His footsteps hastened and were as familiar as Emily's or her own. He opened the office door, and she spun in her chair, her mind still reeling and lips trembling.

"I don't know what to think anymore. I think I'm going crazy," Maggie said.

He crossed the room and circled her in his arm within a heartbeat. "You aren't going crazy. I'm here."

"The stalker, he has Josh's number, or he is Josh. I don't know anymore. And this guy, whoever he is, killer, stalker, or maybe just the janitor with a weird crush, is only looking at me. Look at these photos. Every one of them."

Paul scrolled through the photos, and his chest rose in anger.

Maggie said, "I don't think it can be Josh. But he had a second phone I didn't recognize. And he has been so angry and jealous since Emily went to college. I got texts from Nate when I was out of the room. I came back, and he was slipping a phone under his leg, a second phone. He said his boss gave him the phone. He came over because he was sad that Emily and he broke up. He showed me a video and picture. I had the picture, but I had not seen the video. I don't know if I should call the police." Her words rushed out and she couldn't stop.

"You don't think Josh might have a fascination with you? While Emily has been gone, he's been here an awful lot. And he showed you unflattering pictures of Emily. Could he be painting her as a villain?" Paul asked.

Maggie considered his theory and shook her head. "I think it's too sophisticated. This boy has loved Emily forever. None of it makes sense. And how would it relate to the janitor in all the photos?"

"I don't know, Mags, but I'm going to find out." His chest heaved.

She stood and put her hand on his chest. She felt his heart thumping through his shirt. The janitor was a lot more dangerous than a school kid could ever be. "Please, don't do anything that can put Emily or yourself in danger."

His eyes widened at her. "You know me better than that. Don't you?"

Maggie saw his face distorted with anger once before. It was the night he and Chris had a heated disagreement. And Chris never came back alive. "I know you better. I'm sorry, but I just don't think you should help anymore," she said in a small voice.

"I know what you're doing, Mags. You're trying to create distance to protect me, Emily, and everyone else. You are always the one behind the camera, trying to be the protector, the one looking on. But, you know what, you need to stop and join the land of the living. You didn't die when Chris did, so stop acting like it. I'll be back tonight. I'm going to stay with you until this is all over. Like it or not. After that, you can decide what you want for us."

The words slapped Maggie hard across the face. He stormed down the stairs and out the door before she could respond. There was nothing for her to do but lock her door and wait.

thirty-one

. . .

PAST TEN, and three kettles of tea later; there was a knock on her door, but it didn't sound like Paul. She peered through the peephole, and he looked back at her through an eye actively swelling shut. "Oh my God," she said as her fingers fumbled for the lock to open the door.

Paul limped through the entry, holding his side. She circled around him to support his weight and they limped to the couch together. Maggie set him down gingerly and sat across from him on the coffee table, assessing his face.

"Paul, what happened?" she asked.

He smiled at her weakly, bearing a chipped front tooth. "I went to Mr. Murphy's house and knocked on his door. I intended to scare him into leaving you alone. Nobody answered. As I walked away, the next thing I know, I'm splayed on the ground. And someone stole my keys and phone. When I woke up, I looked everywhere for them, and they were just gone."

She looked at his nearly shut eye, with dried blood crusted on the corners of it.

"How did you get here?" Maggie asked.

"Walked."

"In your condition?"

"Yeah. I didn't have a phone to call you or an Uber. It was a few miles," he replied.

Her hands grazed his face, and he flinched. Then he touched her face in return. Maggie's face was wet with tears. "I'm so sorry, Paul. I think we should get you to the hospital."

The gash above his eye bore the shape of a moon. If it was an inch lower, he likely would have lost his eye. "No. It's okay. We're going to see this through. I'll definitely go to the dentist when this is all over," he said with a weak smile.

She cleared her throat. "You should go to the doctor. Get checked in, and be where you can be safe. I'd never forgive myself if something happened to you."

"No, this is exactly why I'm going to stay. You need me here. But I am going to get some protection. It won't go down like this again." He winced as he moved back to a standing position and headed to the basement door. Maggie retreated to the kitchen to put on a fourth kettle of tea. She knew that he was going to the gun cabinet.

"Mags?" he called from the basement.

"Yes?" She hadn't been to the basement in months. Emily wasn't the only one creeped out by it.

"Can you come down here?"

The tea had a few minutes, so she made her way down to him. His face was ashen, and the one good eye looked at her with concern.

"There's a gun missing," he said.

"What? That can't be."

"It is. Right there, that is where the 9mm was. When was the last time you saw it?" Paul asked.

Maggie shook her head. She didn't know how many guns were in the case at all, let alone if one was missing. She shrugged. "I don't know. Maybe that gun never made it here? I really cannot remember."

"It was here. Chris and I went shooting twice after Dad died, and that was the one I shot. Every time."

"Chris had a lockbox. It's in the closet. I never looked for or found any keys to it, but maybe it's in there? I don't know where the key is. Frankly, I haven't really looked for the key." She gazed up at his face and changed the subject. "Let's get you cleaned up."

Paul nodded. "It's plausible that he'd have a gun in the lockbox closer to his bedroom. That's where I'd keep it. I'll take the.45, but Mags, we need to find out what happened with this other gun, for sure. You don't think Emily feels stalked too, and maybe she took it?"

"I don't. She's never shot a gun before. And she'd tell me if she was in real trouble," Maggie said.

"Would she? Have you told her what's going on? Or would she do everything she could to protect you?"

The kettle whistled, beckoning her back to the safety of the kitchen. While she poured the tea, she opened her daughter's Snapchat. Maggie could not contact her at this hour without raising suspicions, but she had to know if Paul's attempt to help put her daughter in any sort of danger. A deep resentment and anger built at the back of her throat. He shouldn't have tried to take matters into his own hands. This wasn't his problem, and she specifically asked him to back off. Her daughter had a Snapchat story posted fifteen minutes ago. Maggie opened it. Emily danced with a guy who was not the alligator shorts guy. Maggie recognized it instantly, a story to make Josh jealous.

Paul returned to the couch, the.45 beside him. "The ammunition for all the guns is gone. Except this one, which was loaded with a single bullet. Quite irresponsible to store it that way. I don't know if the ammunition was gone before or if Chris did it when he stored the guns, knowing you had a baby on the way. It wouldn't be smart to store them together, especially with the keys next to the gun cabinet."

"Wouldn't the bullets have gone bad by now?" Maggie asked.

"No, ammunition isn't perishable. It would be helpful if we can find out where Chris kept the bullets. If not, we'll need to buy more."

"When Chris died, I never went down there and properly stored the guns. When this is over, I'm getting rid of all of them. How can I not know how many guns there are and if any are missing?" Maggie asked. She smacked her palm against her head.

"It's okay," Paul said. "I should have taken them back when Chris died. I knew you didn't want them. Which makes me just as responsible."

Maggie handed Paul his tea and said, "I can't wait for this to be over." She went to the kitchen and got an ice pack and handed it to Paul.

He placed it over his eye and winced with the pressure. "Soon, Mags. Soon. It has to be."

"C'mon, let's get you cleaned up and go to bed," Maggie said.

Like an obedient child, he followed her up the stairs, tea in hand. He sat on the closed toilet lid while she opened her First Aid kit. Maggie took a wipe and swiped away the dried blood. The moon-shaped cut was smaller than she thought. The worst of his injuries were his swollen eye, which blackened, and the tooth and one rib that had him doubled over with pain, probably broken.

She sighed and finished cleaning him the best she could. "You really should go to a hospital."

He held her wrist over his face and kissed the inside of it. The electricity shot through her arm and dissipated her anxiety in a flash. Her body responded in an instant. She wanted him. After this was over, she would have him.

"Where do you want me to sleep?" he asked. Glancing up at her, his brow a question.

"With me." She meant it in every sense of the word, but tonight it would be sleep.

"I don't have any pajamas, and these clothes are covered in blood and dirt."

She agreed. His clothes were filthy. They were in no condition to sleep in. "I've got clothes you can use. Wait here." Maggie hadn't opened Chris's side of the dresser in eighteen years. Even the laundry she did for him, she kept in a small pile on his side of the closet. Her stomach weakened, and she opened the drawer. She plucked out Chris's flannel pajama pants and a vee neck white t-shirt. When she went inside his underwear drawer, her hands skimmed the bottom for the newest, least worn pair. Her fingers fumbled with a small object at the bottom of the drawer. She fished out a pair of plain powder blue boxers that looked new. Maggie retreated to the bathroom and handed Paul the clothes, and walked away, closing the bathroom door behind her.

A short while later, he came out. He looked exactly how Chris might have had he lived. They were both too tired for pleasantries and collapsed on the bed, under Chris's covers, on Chris's pillow, and in his pajamas. Maggie nestled into his arms, beckoning for sleep.

Her mind was programmed to wake for her phone. It had been since Emily got her license. Today was no different. A call came in from Emily's phone.

"Hello?" Maggie answered groggily. Paul popped up beside her and listened.

"Hi, this is Jenna. It's about Emily," Jenna's voice shook.

"Oh my God, what happened?" Maggie shot up completely awake.

"There was an accident. We're at INOVA. I'm with her. Her leg is pretty messed up. I can't see her yet, but they're going to call you. Please come." Jenna sounded desperate.

"Oh my God, thank you, Jenna. Please stay with her. I'm on my way."

Paul was already up, his eye swelled shut and back in his dirty, blood-stained jeans.

thirty-two

. . .

MAGGIE SLIPPED a pair of jeans on, and Chris's Virginia Beach sweatshirt over her pajama tee and got in the car. Paul drove her the two hours in near silence. Sleep and his injuries were long forgotten. Her arms were crossed tightly over her chest. She peered out the window and prayed to a God she didn't believe in that Emily would be okay.

Paul dropped Maggie off at the front of the hospital and she ran in without a word to him. The artificial light stabbed at her corneas as her eyes adjusted and she found the front desk. The large woman nurse picked her teeth at the front.

"Hi, my daughter is here. Can you help me?"

"Name please." She did not look up from her computer.

"Mine or the patient?"

The large woman rolled her eyes and glared at her. "The patient."

"Her name is Emily. Emily Becker."

The woman's fingers worked to find her daughter. Maggie texted her daughter's number at the same time.

Maggie: I'm here. What room?

"She's in room 2447," the woman replied and lazily returned to picking her teeth.

Emily: 2447

The text came in at the same time. The placard to the right of the nurse's head showed 2447 was located down the hall.

Maggie breathed deep, the scent of antiseptic and sickness mingling into a sickening waltz in her nose. She hurried down the pale, sterile corridor and entered the room. Her daughter's blonde locks were greasy, her makeup had melted down her face, and they had hoisted her foot in a boot. She looked equally like a domestic violence victim and a little kid shrunken in her bed. Her eyes were closed.

Jenna stroked her hair. Maggie pushed away a twinge of regret that she wasn't there for her daughter, but her roommate was. She brushed it off and rushed to her daughter, replacing her hand with her own, and Jenna stepped back. "I'm here baby. I'm here." She kissed her daughter's head. Maggie looked over her shoulder at Jenna. She still wore what Maggie assumed to be her party outfit. Her top looked like a black lingerie piece from Victoria's Secret fall collection. Her shorts were cherry red and shiny, and her converse shoes were red to match her shorts. She looked younger than her years with her makeup mostly gone.

Jenna said, "I've been here the whole time. We told them I was her sister. I didn't specify sorority sister. I couldn't have her be alone." A tear rolled down her cheek.

"Thank you, Jenna." Maggie hugged her tight.

Emily's eyes fluttered open. "Mommy?" She hadn't called her that in fifteen years.

"Yes, baby. Are you okay? What happened?" Jenna stood back and sat in the visitor chair against the wall.

Emily's voice was small and weak. "I, I don't know. This is where I just woke up. I don't remember anything, and now they say my leg is broken." Her bottom lip trembled.

Jenna got up and went to Emily, putting her hand on her good leg. "After Josh, she went to a party with me. I wasn't watching her close enough. She drank a lot and fell down some stairs in the parking garage. It was pretty bad. We called an ambulance, and they brought her here. I didn't know what else to do." She rubbed Emily's good leg.

Emily looked at Jenna and back at her mother. "I don't know what would have happened if she wasn't there. I don't remember."

Jenna looked at Maggie and Emily. "I'm sorry I didn't watch closer. I'm so sorry."

Maggie turned to Jenna. "Oh, honey, it's not your fault. Thank you so much for taking care of her." She squeezed her shoulder tight.

Jenna said, "I don't know how much Emily remembers, she's been in and out. But, the last time the doctor was here, they said her leg would eventually be fine, but she's probably going to need to be wheeled around for like six weeks."

An Indian woman in a white coat entered the room. "Did someone say, doctor?"

"Hi again," Jenna said. "I'm going to excuse myself. This is Ms. Becker, Emily's mom." And she walked out the door.

"Hi Ms. Becker, I'm Dr. Patel." She held out her slim tanned hand, and Maggie took it in hers. Maggie was suddenly self-conscious about her sweaty hand.

"Emily," Dr. Patel turned to her patient. "Your blood results came back, and we have a few things to discuss. Do you approve of me discussing your medical information with your mother in the room?"

Emily reached for her mother and took her hand, squeezing it. "Please, I'd like my mom here."

"Very well then." Dr. Patel's kind eyes glanced over at Maggie and back at Emily. "First, how are you feeling?"

"Never better," Emily said.

"I see your sense of humor is still intact." Dr. Patel smiled.

"There is a small amount of flunitrazepam in your system."

Emily's eyes widened. "What does that mean? I drank, but that's it. I promise, Mom, I don't do drugs."

Maggie gasped. "No Emily, I think that's the long name for the roofie drug, right?"

Dr. Patel looked at Maggie and nodded. She put her hand on Emily's good knee and said, "I'm afraid so."

"Impossible," Emily said.

Dr. Patel said, "Unfortunately, that is what the toxicology reports say. It happens more than you think. We see it often being so close to a college campus. Would you like us to do a full examination?"

"Do you mean a rape kit?" Emily asked. Maggie's stomach seized. How could this be?

Dr. Patel answered in a soft voice, "Yes, that's what I mean. I can send a nurse in here if you would like?"

"No, I was at this party and Jenna was with me the whole time. I just fell down some stairs. I was only out of her eyesight for a moment," Emily said.

Maggie nodded in agreement. She saw the Snapchat story of her dancing, which must have been just a little while before she broke her leg. Perhaps this leg break saved her from something more violating, less easy to heal from.

"You are lucky to have your sister. She hasn't left your side since this began," Dr. Patel replied. "Ms. Becker, I'd like to examine her leg a little, and I'm going to ask you to give us a few minutes."

"Of course." Maggie patted her daughter's leg and said, "Emily, I'll be right outside." Maggie walked back into the cool, sterile halls and saw Jenna braced against a wall. Her head bobbed as she tried to stay awake. It stabbed at Maggie's heart to ask, but she had to. "Jenna, they found she had been roofied. Is there any reason we should look closer at a rape kit?"

"Roofied? That isn't possible. She was literally out of my reach for a couple of seconds and tumbled down the stairs. This is a crazy accident, but I guess now we know why she lost her balance so easily." Jenna put her head in her hands. "I should have watched her closer. I didn't realize someone drugged her. My God, what gross frat guy could have done this?"

The back of Maggie's hair prickled. "Do you know anyone who might do this? Who might wish her harm?"

"Oh my God, she's literally loved by everyone," Jenna said.

"Thank you so much for taking care of her. You are an amazing friend." Maggie draped her arm around Jenna. Jenna rested her head briefly on Maggie's shoulder.

Dr. Patel exited the room. She patted the side of Maggie's arm. "Emily is going to be okay. She's asking for you both. You can come for a few minutes, but really, she needs to get some rest. We'll be able to release her tomorrow."

"Thank you, doctor," Maggie said and slipped past her into the room. Jenna followed.

Maggie moved to the head of her daughter's bed and patted her oily hair. It hadn't appeared greasy on the

Snapchat story. "Em, want to come home while you heal?" The stalker could go to hell for telling her that her daughter could not come home. She would take them both and hide forever. She'd liquidated all the accounts and had her own Bitcoin at this point. What would stop her? Her heart broke looking at her daughter lying helpless in a hospital.

Emily sighed. "Mom, I'll get so behind. I promise I'll be more careful."

Jenna said, "I can totally wheel her around. I promise I'll take better care of her."

Emily smiled at Jenna. "It isn't your job to take care of me. I'm sorry you have a roomie who's such a mess."

"No way, you're my favorite roomie ever," Jenna said.

"I'm your only roomie." The girls laughed. She turned to her mom. "Mom, I want to stay. But can I come home this weekend?"

Jenna interrupted, "We have the big sister reveal this weekend."

"Oh shoot, that's right. Next weekend?"

Maggie nodded. "You girls can come home whenever you want." She leaned in and kissed Emily's head.

Jenna squeezed her daughter's hand and smiled. "I'm going to Uber back. I need to clean up."

Maggie peeled her sweatshirt off and gave it to the girl. The oversized shirt covered her red booty shorts, as well. Now it looked like Jenna wore no pants, but it was still an improvement. "I'll take you back to the dorms. I can't thank you enough for how kind you've been. She's had such a hard time with Josh." Maggie kissed her daughter, and Jenna patted Emily's knee. The two women walked back out into the hall and to the waiting room. Maggie knew Paul would be there.

In the hall, Jenna said, "She was so upset about Josh, you know. Why are boys so awful?"

Maggie winced, remembering the photos and videos and the crying boy in her living room. She said, "Relationships are complicated."

Jenna stared straight ahead. "Yeah. They are."

Maggie saw Paul fidgeting in his chair. His face was pale. The time must have been unbearable for him. He loved Emily as his own. Why hadn't she texted him, tell him how Emily was? She couldn't have saved him a few moments of agony? He stood to greet them both.

Jenna stared at Paul. "What happened to you? It seems like you should be in here too?"

His hand reflexively went to his eye. "I was in a minor car accident. It's nothing."

"But your tooth, too? Are you okay?" Jenna asked.

"Yeah, it's fine, really. Thanks for your concern. I didn't want Emily to see me like this. No need to upset her anymore."

Maggie said, "I appreciate it. She's going to be okay, though."

"I know she is." Paul looked at Maggie over Jenna's head.

Paul and Maggie dropped Jenna at the front of her dorm. The last time Maggie had been there, she said goodbye to her daughter while the stalker watched and took pictures.

Jenna got out of the car. Before shutting the door, she said, "Thanks for the sweatshirt, Ms. Becker. I'll wash it and give it back to you."

"No rush. Emily can bring it back whenever. I'd let you have it, but it was her father's."

Jenna nodded and got out of the car. A couple of girls wearing Greek lettering on their shirts waved at her, and she waved back and ran beside them to enter the dorm. From the back, she looked just like Emily.

thirty-three

· · ·

AFTER THE NEAR silent ride home, Paul dropped Maggie off at the house. "I'm going to get some clothes and the second set of keys to my car so I can pick it up from the janitor's neighborhood later. If it's still there. I think I should stay until this is over, and I don't want to wear my brother's things."

"I get that," Maggie said, and he pulled out of the driveway and slowly headed toward the end of the cul-de-sac. Daybreak was a half-hour off, so there was no use getting sleep at this point.

She sat on the couch, anticipating Paul's return. She felt the hair prickle on the back of her neck again when she heard a slight noise at her door. Trust it this time, she said to herself. Instead of drawing the curtains closed, she went to them. Opened them wide and saw someone walking away from her door in the dusk. She opened her door and nearly tripped over keys and a phone. A dark figure with a loping gait she recognized slipped around the corner. Before she could think, she ran after him.

She heard him panting, trying to create distance from her.

"I see you over there. I have a gun," she lied.

He turned and stood under the streetlight. Twilight began and soon the early morning joggers and people heading to the office would be out, too. He bowed his head and walked toward her slowly. With a little over six feet between them, she anchored her legs to prevent them from crumpling beneath her. Maggie tucked her hand in her pocket for her 'gun.' "That's close enough," she said, her voice cracking.

He stopped and said, "Uh, hi. I was just walking in the neighborhood."

Mr. Murphy looked older than what she thought, though in the pictures he appeared to be about the same age as her. His legs fidgeted beneath him, leaning on his good leg.

"You're Mr. Murphy, right?" Maggie asked.

He blushed. "Yeah, I am."

"Do you live in this neighborhood?" An answer she already knew.

"No, I'm just visiting friends," he said.

"Oh, who? This is a cul-de-sac. We all know each other pretty well. I can help you find who you're looking for."

"It was just a walk." He turned to retreat.

She yelled, loud enough for a jogger or passerby to hear, "Why are you following me?"

He turned to her, his eyes widening. "What?"

"You're following me. Why?" Her courage built. It was him. He was the root of all of it. If she had a gun in her pocket, she would have used it and ended the nightmare.

He looked at her, puzzled, and took a step nearer to her. "I haven't followed you. I've been looking out for you.

Maybe admiring from afar, but I meant no harm." He showed his palms to her in defeat and helplessness. The intense crimsons and purples were now faded to silvery white lines on his damaged hand.

She took a slight step backward, to create more distance between herself and him. "Why me?" she asked. "And why did you attack Paul?" Her voice rose.

He looked at his feet. "Is that what he told you? I never attacked him." He shoved his injured hand in his pocket and kicked the ground.

"Then what happened?" Maggie asked.

"He came to my door, pounding and screaming. He said crazy things. Saying I stalked you, and that if I so much as laid a finger on your or Emily's head, he'd kill me. He told me he had a gun and wasn't afraid to blow my brains out. I didn't answer the door, but I had to defend myself," he said.

"What do you mean, defend yourself?" She studied the hand tucked in his pocket. "Take your hand out of your pocket," she said. He removed his empty hand from his pocket and placed it limply at his side. She kept her hand in her pocket on her fake gun. How quickly could he brandish a knife and get to her? Would she have time to escape?

His mud-brown eyes looked back at her. "Let me explain," he said. "I don't get around great, and he challenged me to a fight. A crippled man. He accused me of unspeakable things. Another man a few days before, one I didn't recognize, did the same. I couldn't take it. I, I just waited for him to leave. But, Paul kept screaming at the neighborhood about what a criminal I am. I'm not a criminal. I went out the back, grabbed my old cane on the porch, and I cracked him in the ribs, and pushed him down. My neighbors, what would they think? What was I supposed to do? Can I not defend myself? I didn't want him thinking he could come back."

"And you just left him there? You broke his tooth and cut his face," she growled at him.

"I admit he landed hard, but the concrete did that. I hid and waited for him to leave. He said he had a gun. I didn't know who or what he'd come back with. When he didn't get up for a minute, I checked on him. Just to make sure he was breathing, you know? He was out cold but breathing, so I searched for his gun, and he lied. I saw his keys and phone on the ground. Look, I wanted to make it difficult for him, but not to kill him. I picked those up, but left him lying there. I didn't want him calling the police to make false accusations. But I kept watching, just to make sure he got up. Then I saw him get up, look around, and wander off, looking dazed. But the yelling stopped. I didn't want him to come back into my house and hurt me. He scared me. I didn't even want to stay home. But my puppy, Greta, needed me, so I had to. I stayed up all night, waiting for him to kill me. I shut the phone off so he wouldn't trace me, and I thought I could leave it at your door so you'd get it back to him. But, he needs to leave me alone."

He halved the space between them, and she stepped back. "Stay where you are. What about Nate?"

"Nate?" Roy shrugged. "Is that the other man who came to my home? Nate? He came to my door. I answered, and he told me to stop skulking around you. To leave you alone or you'd press charges. I denied it. I was embarrassed. He showed me pictures and evidence and I tried to explain myself. Finally, I shut the door in his face. What would you do if someone like him came to your door and accused you of things? He wouldn't listen to what I had to say."

Her anger boiled over. "So you killed him?" she yelled.

His three children were without a father because Roy did not want to be embarrassed.

His eyes widened with surprise. "What? What are you talking about?"

"You know," she spat.

"I don't know. He's dead? I didn't lay a hand on him. Yeah, Paul, I pushed him down with a cane, and I wasn't sad he fell. But the other guy didn't come over screaming. He told me some things. He was quiet about his visit."

"What things did he tell you?" Maggie asked.

"He said he knew who I was and that I should leave you alone."

"And who are you?"

"I'm a widower," Mr. Murphy said.

"I'm sorry for your loss." The words fell out of her mouth so automatically before she remembered whom she had spoken them to. She had been on the receiving end of that awful sentence too many times to count.

"Thank you. I know you're a widow, and I'm sorry for your loss, too."

She cleared her throat. "How did you know I was a widow?"

"I know more than you think," he said.

"What is that supposed to mean?" she asked. Her gut twisted with anxiety.

"Let's sit down, and I'll tell you what I know." There was no way for Maggie to reach Paul. His phone sat on her front step with his keys. She wasn't sure if the phone was charged, and neither of them had a home phone. *How stupid to come after him,* she thought. She kept her distance while they walked to the corner park and sat on opposite ends of a bench in view of her neighbor Martha's windows. Maggie kept her eyes on his hands. She hoped he still believed she had a gun. She counted on Martha being able to hear her if she screamed.

He watched Maggie assess her surroundings. "I won't hurt you. That's the last thing I would think of doing to you." He began, "Vivian, my wife. She was a difficult woman." He paused and sighed. "We were together a long time. Matter of fact, in high school, she got pregnant. Her father, an overbearing man, wanted us to get married. I was never happier. But she cried and cried. Eventually, we lost the baby. He was a boy."

"I'm sorry." Her response was automatic.

He cleared his throat. "That's not the point and has nothing to do with you, but I wanted you to understand where she was coming from. Anyway, we stayed married, only God knows why. I hung on for dear life, and she let go. It was a constant push and pull, the way some marriages are, I guess. Anyway, she met someone else."

He sat silent; she sat silent. The spark of understanding dawned on her.

"She loved another man very much. But he was already married, and he and his wife were trying to have a baby. My wife met him at work."

"Where did your wife work?" Maggie's stomach lurched forward.

"I think you know."

"May I ask what happened?" Maggie asked gently. She stopped, watching his hands.

He began the story Paul had already told her. "Yes, she died in a fire. Our house was on fire. I was across the street with neighbors, and the house burned orange and yellow and red with a lot of white. The white was the hottest part. I ran across the street, and my daughter screamed at the opposite end of the house. I had to make

a choice. Right or wrong, my daughter, was my choice."
He looked down at his lap, his good hand caressing the
burned one.

She nodded. Her choice would have been the same. As a
mother, she could not override the primal instinct to
protect her young, no matter the cost. It was the right
choice.

"I'm so sorry about your unspeakable choice. But what
does this have to do with Chris?" Maggie asked. She feared
she knew the answer.

"They were sleeping together. I found out, and she was
going to leave me for him. After they died, I watched you.
To make sure you were okay. Then, I don't know, I never
stopped." Roy shrugged.

"Is that how you knew who Paul was? And where to
return his things?"

"Yes," Roy answered. He took his good hand and
reached for his pocket.

"No," she yelled.

"It's okay. I'm just going to show you a picture of my
Vivian."

"Here, look at her." He handed the crackled picture of
his wife to her. The ends curled with age. "She was
gorgeous and far out of my league."

Maggie touched the soft edges of the picture and shook
her head. Vivian was a beautiful young woman. Objectively,
she was beautiful, but even in the picture there was a look
of madness in her eyes.

He continued, "It's okay. We both knew she was far out
of my league."

"There are no leagues in marriage. It's a union," Maggie
replied. But she gazed at the picture of his stunning young
wife smiling at the camera, her arms wrapped around the

homely janitor. In her arms was a ball of blankets, with their daughter tucked inside.

He put out his hand, and she dropped the photo back into it. She didn't want to touch him or be too close to have him grab her. He smiled sadly and tucked the photo back in his pocket.

"I just wanted to protect you and be there for you. You look so much like my Vivian," he said.

"Where is your daughter now?"

"My Marie is in Barcelona as an exchange student in college," he replied.

"You must be so proud," Maggie said.

"I am. She's a lot like her mother was."

"I see a lot of my husband in my daughter, too. It's awful and wonderful that his genes were strong." Maggie's admission lay bare between them. She didn't recognize the truth of it until it exited her lips.

How could he be the one hurting her daughter if he was here pushing Paul down instead of a hundred miles away roofing her baby? Now, she was glad she didn't have the gun, because she might have used it moments ago. But it didn't mean he was not in on the scheme for money. He knew too much about her. Maggie thought about the picture that started it all. The one where Marie looked at the balloons, and she and Emily were on vacation.

"Sixteen years ago, you were in Florida at the same time as us. Was that a coincidence?" Maggie asked.

He blushed and didn't meet her eyes. "No. You were such a good mom. I thought maybe I could be the parent you were, or try to. I was screwing it all up, but you did everything right."

Her toes curled. She was right. He followed them to Florida. "How did you know we'd be on vacation?"

He laughed and cleared his throat. "Emily told anyone who would listen at the daycare. She was so excited. I wanted my Marie excited, too. My girl is more melancholy than yours, I guess, from her mother. And it must be hard to be a girl raised without a mother. You were the model parent and knew exactly what you were doing."

"None of us know what we're doing, Roy. We're all winging it," she replied.

"You never looked lost, or scared. I've watched Emily her whole life. You have given her a great life," Roy said.

Maggie said, "Things aren't always what they appear. But I need you to stop following me. It's important."

"I know, and I'm sorry I scared you. I only wanted to help and be like you. And somehow, during it all, I fell in love with you," Roy said.

Maggie felt an anxious shiver jolt in her stomach. She blurted out, "You're frightening me."

"I'm sorry, the last thing I wanted to do was scare you. I'll leave you be." His lip trembled, and his eyes watered. He turned from her before she could see the first tear fall and shuffled away.

Paul texted her. He found his phone, which meant he was home waiting for her. A flush of relief flooded through her body.

Paul: *Mags where are you? I'm worried.*

Maggie: *I'm on my way.*

She rushed home, looking over her shoulder the entire way.

thirty-four

. . .

SHE SPOTTED Paul sitting on her front stoop, scanning the road. He wore his familiar stone-washed jeans, sneakers, and his Nike windbreaker. His hand poised on his temple, rubbing it next to his eye, the swelling subsiding, but still a deep purple. She observed him before he made eye contact with her. The color was drained from his face. Then he saw her, and the mask of relief washed over him as he rushed to her, halving the distance between them.

"My God. When I saw the phone... I didn't know what happened to you. I shouldn't have left you for a second," he said.

"I'm so sorry. I didn't think about what you would think if you saw it. I was in such a hurry," Maggie replied.

"It's okay. I'm glad you're okay. If anything happened to you..." He didn't finish.

"I know, I know." She hugged him tight and wished she could stay in his embrace.

He pulled away and lifted the phone to her. "How did

my phone and keys? How?" His hands clenched around his phone, and he shoved it in his back pocket.

"Let's go inside, and I'll explain." They walked across the front yard, and he followed her through the door. Maggie said, "Can you put some tea on? I'm going to get my computer so we can do a bit of research."

They settled on the couch, armed with cups of tea and a laptop. She told him everything about Roy. Maggie said, "He seemed helpless, almost pathetic. His daughter is in Spain, and he has no one. Well, you were right about one thing. I was not 'bet my daughter's life sure' that it was him. He's creepy and sad, but I don't think he did this. Though, I don't know for sure if he isn't somehow a part of it. You should have seen his face. Plus, the killer said he'd hurt my daughter. How could he get close enough to her? Even if she was roofied the college kids would know immediately he didn't belong."

Paul said, "Then who could it be?"

"I don't know. Do you think, maybe Josh?" Maggie conceded.

Paul scratched the stubble on his chin. "Maybe, but even that I'm not sure of."

"Paul, did you know about the affair between Vivian and Chris?" Maggie asked.

"I didn't. Like I said, I knew there was something. He said I wouldn't understand. But I wouldn't have kept that from you, especially now."

"She was beautiful, you know," Maggie said and her shoulders slumped. She leaned her head against Paul's shoulder.

Paul patted her head. "I'm so sorry. I wish there was something more I could say."

She shut the computer, and her phone buzzed. A Face-

Time from Emily. She answered the phone. The pink in Emily's cheeks made relief surge into Maggie's heart. She wore two braids which made her look like a grade schooler. "Hi Em, I like your hair."

Emily smiled and lifted a braid with one hand. "Hi, Mom. Thanks. Jenna did it." She tilted the phone to put Jenna in the frame. Maggie saw the glowing racetrack of fluorescent lighting in the hospital corridor behind Jenna.

Jenna smiled and waved with one hand at Maggie. "Hi, Ms. Becker." Jenna's other hand was on the handle of a wheelchair.

"Are you in a wheelchair, Em?" Maggie asked.

"Ugh, yes. Some policy that I can't leave on crutches. It has to be a wheelchair." Emily pointed the camera down to show the crutches laid across her lap. They created a barricade wherever the wheelchair went, blocking the entire hallway. "We're heading back to the dorm. The doc said I'm all good and just need to come back in a couple of weeks to make sure it's healing right."

"Does it hurt?" Maggie asked, her brow turned up in concern.

"No, not too much. A little achy, but the doc said it was a pretty clean break. I have Advil in case. Don't worry," Emily said.

"I know, but it's my job to worry."

"You're good at it." Emily grinned. "Hey, is that Uncle Papa I see?" Maggie almost forgot he was there. His hand rested on her shoulder. She tilted the phone toward him to add him to the call. "Hi, Uncle Papa."

"Hey Em, how you doing?" Paul asked.

"Never better," she said, a wry smile on her lips. Then she looked at him with concern. "Jenna told me you got into a car accident. Are you okay? Your eye looks pretty bad."

He touched his eye and smiled at her, showing off his chipped tooth. "I'm okay. You should see the other guy," he said.

"Oh, and your tooth." Emily grimaced.

Jenna's voice chimed in. "We're almost at the front and the Uber says it'll be here in two minutes."

Emily said, "Okay guys, my chauffeur awaits. Love you." And she hung up.

"Love you too," Maggie said to the disconnected line.

Paul held her shoulder tighter. "Are you okay?"

"Yes, no. I don't know. It's Wednesday. Today is the day he said he wanted his money. We haven't heard from him. But I'm ready," Maggie said and gulped down air.

"So, we wait," Paul replied.

"I know a way to pass the time, but I could use your help," Maggie said.

thirty-five

. . .

SHE FELT Paul's shoulders stiffen beneath her. "I'll help you with anything. What do you need?"

"To clean his side of the closet. I don't want to do it alone. It's so overwhelming. I know it isn't fair to ask of you, but my room is so full of Chris. A man who apparently didn't love me the same way I did him. There's nothing else to do but wait for the person stalking me to give me direction. I've wasted eighteen years. I don't want to squander another minute." The confession spilled out like dandelion seeds in the wind.

He hugged her tight against him. The mahogany scent of his cologne filled her nostrils, and her breathing slowed to normal. "You have wasted no time. You've built a beautiful life for yourself, Emily, and me. I'll be by your side every step of the way." He let her go and stood, holding out his hand to her.

He led her up the stairs and stood back as she walked in. Four boxes stood sentry in front of the closet, waiting to be filled: *Trash, Giveaway, Emily, Maggie.* She breathed in deep

236 • Ava Page

and opened his side of the closet. Paul sat on the bed and looked on.

She pulled out his five suits and laid them on the bed beside Paul. Maggie felt the material through her fingers, searching for moth holes or damage. "You know, these are still in style. Or back in style. Would they fit you?"

"I don't want to wear my dead brother's clothes, Mags. Besides, they won't fit. The flannel pajama pants and boxers you let me sleep in the other night were tight. He was in his twenties when he died," Paul said.

"Fair enough." Her fingers poked inside a hole where the pocket met the seat. "Think this can be fixed?"

Paul held the pants up to the light. "No, that rip isn't on a seam."

Maggie removed the hanger from the damaged suit and placed it in the *Trash* box. After inspecting the others, she folded the other four and placed them in the box marked *Giveaway*.

The laundry basket of folded clothes sat on top of the shoes. Maggie had folded the laundry eighteen years ago and did not have the heart to throw them away. Today was the day. Maggie pulled the basket out and spilled its contents onto the bed beside Paul.

A tangle of shirts unfolded and tumbled on the bed, a few boxers, socks paired up, and one lonely black sock followed. She never found the twin. At the bottom of the laundry basket was the answering machine she stowed away long ago, and it fell on top of the socks on the bed.

Maggie could have forgotten Chris's voice had it not been for Paul. They sounded like twins. The only recordings she kept of Chris's voice were on the answering machine. He used to leave notes and messages to her. She couldn't bear to listen to them after the police shattered her universe that cold night in January. But, knowing his voice was in that tiny device, she couldn't bear to throw it away either. Soon, it didn't matter because technology dethroned the clunky gatekeepers sitting on every kitchen counter. She remembered recording their greeting for the unlucky caller: "Hi, you've reached the Becker residence. If you got this message, it means we're probably out or we're avoiding your call. Leave a message and maybe we'll get back to you."

His laughter at the end, and Maggie's voice saying, "Chris, it's not true——just leave the message." And the two giggling before the beep cut them off.

After he died, she unplugged the blinking reminder of him and wrapped it tightly in one of his work shirts. She couldn't bear to record over it and returning condolence calls became a burden too weighty to bear after his death, anyway. Well-wishers called, sent flowers, and food for weeks, until they forgot about her and lurched forward into the next tragedy. For eighteen years she hadn't touched his things, even to smell the musky wood scent he wore. On his last Christmas, Maggie splurged on the bottle of Givenchy Pour Homme that now stood half full on his nightstand. It dropped a few millimeters from evaporation with time.

Maggie tossed the basket and held the black machine in her hands. "I forgot this was in here. Should we plug it in?"

"If you want to, sure." Paul shrugged.

"I never checked it after I went to the hospital and it was already full. It will be a bunch of condolence messages, I'm sure. I couldn't bring myself to listen. So, there's probably a lot on here." Her fingers fumbled to remove her charger from the plug behind the bed. She plugged in the machine. *Smell the flowers, blow out the candles*, she thought.

Her finger trembled over the play button. She squinted her eyes shut and pressed the play arrow button.

She heard his voice "Babe," and pushed stop. Maggie looked over at Paul.

"I haven't heard this message before." Eighteen years since she heard this voice, and it still pierced a place in her where she didn't know she could hurt. She'd forgotten that he had a cell phone. His company issued him the Nokia 1100 the previous month, before cell phones were commonplace. It was never recovered, and she thought nothing of it. She pressed play again. "I'm in an accident. There's water everywhere. My God, the car is filling. I need to tell you something. I want to tell you, I love you. We are having a baby together, and I'm so happy. And, God, I'm so sorry. I've messed up. If you get this and I'm gone, please forgive me. I don't know what happened, or how I lost track of who I was. I blacked out a couple of years ago and I strayed. Mags, I'm sorry. If I survive this, if I make it home, I want to make us right." He choked up and continued. In the background, she heard him banging against the door. He shouted, "Shit shit—I can't get out." Then back to her. A resigned sound in his voice. "I'm so sorry. I've tried to end it over and over again, but she had pictures and threats. She promised she'd tell you. I didn't want you hurt. Forgive me, I love you." Then the sound of what Maggie assumed was water gushing into the car, and the line went dead.

Maggie now knew how the story ended. It ended with the police at her door in the early morning hours saying they found a body with his identification on it, dead of hypothermia. And that she needed to make a positive identification. She never did. Her water broke first. Paul identified his brother after he sat with her through the birth of Emily. Paul never mentioned the identification. She stared at the black box, Chris's last words that would have set her free so long ago. Tucked away in a closet hiding beneath his altar of clothing. Paul reached for her hand, and his fingers intertwined with hers.

Her other hand trembled over the stop button, but then the next message started, a new message with an unfamiliar female voice. A baby cried in the background. The woman's voice filled with passion, grief, and rage. Maggie knew it had to be Vivian. "He loved me. We had something you would never understand. We were soulmates and meant for each other." Vivian ranted at the machine, pouring her grief into the little black box. Then she sounded like she spoke to someone else. "What are you doing here? You're a loser. I never loved you, you piece of shit. Get away from me. You disgust me." Then the insults were muffled, and the message ran out of space. Maggie sank to her knees in front of the machine.

Paul pushed the stop button and went to the floor and sat in front of Maggie, putting her hands in his.

thirty-six

. . .

PAUL'S HANDS around her waist were the only thing tethering her to reality.

Maggie said, "That was Vivian and Roy on the second call." She couldn't think about Chris's message, not yet.

"I think you may be right. When did the call come in?" Paul asked.

"We didn't have a smart machine. I know it's before all the other condolence ones. So..."

"She must have known he was in trouble on the bridge before the police did. Which means..." Paul said, completing her thought.

"He called her first. It sounded like his phone died on my message." Maggie completed his sentence. "Based on the direction he went at the time of the crash, I think he was on his way back from the Domber hotel. Vivian's house was close to the hotel."

Paul's hand was slick with sweat, and she pulled her hand out of his. He looked at her. "But why? It makes little sense. Why would he do this with her?" He raked his fingers through his dark hair.

"Well, she was beautiful," Maggie admitted.

"As are you. But you're beautiful inside and out," Paul said.

"Thank you, but when I was pregnant, I was snippy, and we were young, so young. Maybe he wanted to see what was out there. I guess sometimes I wished we met later. Maybe he would have come back to me, or it wouldn't have worked out. Or, I just was never enough. We'll never know now," Maggie said.

Paul put his hand on both of her shoulders and turned her body toward him. "He said he had been seeing her a couple of years, not just during your pregnancy. And you've always been more than enough." His green eyes locked on hers and he did not let her turn from him.

Maggie cleared her throat and looked up at the back corner of the closet. "While we're here, we should know everything. Rip it off like a Band-Aid. Maybe something can save Emily and me. I need to know what's in that." She pointed accusingly at the lockbox. "I have to find that damn key." She went to Chris's dresser drawers and poured the contents of each one on the bed. In the last drawer, the underwear drawer where she had fished around to find the blue powder boxers just a day ago, a key tumbled out.

"Okay," Paul said, and he rose on his toes and grabbed the lockbox at the back of the closet and set it before Maggie on the floor. He placed the key in her hand. She felt the cold metal and twisted it through her fingers.

"Maybe the missing gun is in there. I admit, that would make me feel a lot better," Paul said.

"It's crazy. A missing gun would be the least of my problems right now."

"I know, Mags. Me too. He was my big brother, and I looked up to him. He duped all of us. I'm right here with you." Paul settled in beside her. The warmth of his shoulder radiated to her.

She put the key in, and the lock twisted easily. "He always told me these were 'important papers.' And I believed him." The weight of the fireproof lockbox lid was heavier than she imagined. From the distance on the shelf it looked like a cheap plastic box. Maggie lifted the lid. Papers, letters, and photos filled the box. But no gun.

Paul's shoulders tensed. "I wish the gun, or at least the bullets would have been in there," he said.

"It's not, but there's a lot of other stuff in here." Her hands trembled over the first photograph. A photo of a baby being held by Chris in a pink blanket. Chris wore fear on his face, his lips stretched in a grimace over his teeth. While she couldn't see the baby's face, she knew it couldn't be Emily. She was born the day after Chris died.

"Who is this?" Maggie asked. She picked up the photo and turned it in her hands. A woman's scrawl on the back, 'Like father, like daughter.' The handwriting was the same as the note he kept behind the nightstand picture. *It cannot be*, she thought and dropped the picture as if it burned her. "We still can't know for sure," Maggie said.

Paul picked up the picture and tucked it behind the other papers on the bed. He rubbed Maggie's back. "Are you sure you want to keep going?"

"I have to. I can't unknow any of this now, and I don't want to, but I need to know the truth," she choked out.

"Do you want me to look first and tell you?" Paul held her hand.

"No, no. You've done so much for me. I want to discover this with you. Just be here with me. Please." Beneath the baby photo was a letter. The linen paper contained specks of gold and felt soft in her hands. She held the letter to her nose. Could she still smell perfume on it? After all these years locked tight in this box. It smelled like roses and made her stomach turn. It was in the lockbox the whole time, sharing a room with her. She slept with his secrets for over eighteen years. She unfolded the letter and a Polaroid picture slipped to the ground. Paul put his hand over it and flipped it over before she could see what was in the picture.

"What is it?" She asked him.

"Please, no. I don't know how this will help anything. Chris isn't who any of us thought he was," Paul said.

Maggie put her hand over Paul's and moved it away from the photo. Her husband's face shone back up at her. His eyes closed in an ecstasy she recognized. His head resting on bland white hotel sheets, his back arched upward. A woman's hand with red manicured nails braced herself on his hairless chest. Her knee saddled up beside him bare. The picture taken from her vantage point, on top of him.

Maggie's stomach lurched forward as she choked back the bile building in the back of her throat. Paul flipped the picture and tucked it under the other documents on the bed. "I'm sorry, Mags," Paul said.

She nodded and pushed back tears and read the letter behind the photo.

Chris,

I am a letter person, but that doesn't mean I don't keep copies of everything we've done. Our baby will know when you finally leave your wife that her father loves her, and chose her, and chose us. This is the night, the moment we made her.

I won't be patient forever. This is one of a thousand other photos I have of us. Our beginning, our family in the moment of

*its creation. Just tell your wife and be done with it. So you can
come home to us.*

Love,

Vivian

A hot tear dropped on the word Vivian, creating a pool
of ink where her name was.

Maggie couldn't look at the picture or think of the letter
another moment. "I think Emily always knew she had a
sister," Maggie said

"She did always have her imaginary friend, Sissy," Paul
said.

"Yeah. When this is all over, I'll take her to Barcelona to
meet her. If nothing else, she'll have gained a sister."
Maggie rummaged through the remains of the box. It had
bills, their marriage certificate, his social security card, both
of their birth certificates, and random pictures of her and
him in their happier days. There were no more clues.
Maggie stacked the letter and pictures back in the box of
Chris's secrets. "I thought because he was such a great
husband, that he would have been a great dad, too."

Paul rubbed her back and said nothing.

"If he really loved me, why did he keep that note from
her behind the picture of me?" Maggie asked.

"I believe he loved you, Mags," Paul said.

"Me too, but I think he may have loved her, too. Or at
the very least, cared deeply for her. Why else would he have
all of this stuff saved?" Maggie asked.

"Maybe he was confused, but I believe with all my heart
that message he sent to you before he died was true. His
death brought clarity. It has always been you, Mags. It is
impossible that it would not be you," Paul said.

She reached behind her neck and unlatched the necklace that once held Jesus and now her rings. A weight she

didn't know she bore lifted. "I don't want to take who her father was from her. But I will not deny her a sister either," Maggie said.

She wrapped their wedding rings and necklace up and kept them tight in her palm. She felt the cutting of the diamond in her grip and slipped it in her pocket.

thirty-seven

. . .

PAUL AND MAGGIE finished sorting the piles of
clothing that she had piled on the bed from the empty
dresser. Most of his items were giveaway, but she saved a
few well-worn shirts for Emily and herself. The bed was
finally clean, and she put his side of the bed's pillows in the
Trash box. The room looked stripped clean and naked. Her
heart felt lighter, and she was right, this long-delayed task
passed the time easily. The hours hurried past as they
continued to scrub Chris from her room. It was dark now,
with no call or word from the stalker. Maggie stood on the
bed, trying to dislodge the wedding picture from the wall
when a knock on the door startled both Paul and Maggie
back to the present.

"Are you expecting anyone?" Paul asked.

"No," she said and hopped down from the bed with the
wedding picture in her arms.

Paul pulled his gun from his windbreaker pocket. How
could she have not seen that? "When did you start carrying
that?" she asked.

"After I found myself face first on concrete outside of

Roy's house. Stay here. I just have one bullet in the chamber. I haven't got ammunition yet." She heard the flick of the safety switched off, and he padded down the stairs. She moved to Emily's room next door. Maggie didn't want the wedding rings in her room anymore. She fished them from her pocket and placed them in Emily's jewelry box next to her bed. Then she stood at the doorjamb and listened.

She heard the door swing open.

"What are you doing here?" Paul asked. His voice lowered to nearly a growl.

"I, I just wanted to talk to Ms. Becker," Josh whined.

While Maggie eavesdropped from Emily's room, a green light caught her eye. Her daughter's computer was powered on. She crouched before the camera. Was the camera always lit like that? She wondered. She went down the stairs to Josh. "Josh, how are you?" she asked and shot Paul a 'calm down' look. Paul retreated to the couch. As he sat down, he kept his eyes on Josh and his hand in his windbreaker pocket.

"I'm okay," Josh said. He avoided eye contact with Paul, who continued to stare.

"What brings you by?" Maggie asked with feigned brightness.

"I, I haven't heard from Emily. I tried to text her and make up. But she told me to go to hell; I was a loser, and she never wanted to talk to me again. Then I think she blocked me. Ms. Becker, we've fought before and stuff, but she's never been so mean. It didn't sound like her, and I'm worried. Is she okay?"

"I'm sorry to hear that, Josh. She's okay. When did she text you?"

He checked his phone. "The day before yesterday."

Maggie shot a glance at Paul. It was the night she was

roofied. Paul stood from the couch and went to Maggie and settled behind her. Maggie asked, "Do you have the time?"

"Yeah, let me see. It was 10:59pm. Why?" Josh asked and put the phone in his back pocket.

Paul interrupted, "Because she was probably at a party. We aren't naïve, if she drank she may have said things she didn't mean. Give her time."

Josh nodded and looked at Maggie. "Ms. Becker, can you tell her I checked on her?" Then Josh's other back pocket rang. He pulled it out and looked at the screen. "One second, sorry," he said. "Hello?" A pause. "Yes, sir. I can cover that shift. If I leave now, I'll be ten minutes late. Is that okay? Alright." And he hung up. "Thanks, Ms. Becker, I've got to go. Someone called in for the graveyard shift, and I could use the cash." Josh half-jogged to his truck and backed out of the driveway, disappearing down the street. Paul took the gun out of his pocket, clicked the safety back on, and put it back in his pocket.

Maggie looked at Paul. "At 10:59, I think she was already roofied. Or nearly there. It's questionable."

"She could have sent the message right before," Paul said.

"Maybe. She blocked Josh once before, so it's not unheard of. One thing I noticed though..." Maggie paused in concentration.

"Yeah?" Paul asked.

"That second phone, it was his boss. It isn't Josh either," Maggie said.

"Maybe. Unless..." Paul said.

"Unless what?" Maggie asked.

"He wanted you to think that and he planned the call. Maybe he was here to check on you."

"You really give that kid more credit than he deserves. He's a kid dealing with his first heartbreak."

"One thing I understand, Mags, is heartbreak. It can drive anyone insane..." Paul said, his voice trailed off.

Maggie let the truth of his words tumble between them. There was no time to help him carry his emotional baggage right now. "I think I found something in Emily's room. Follow me." They went back up the stairs, and she pointed at her daughter's computer from the doorjamb. The light gave the room a greenish hue. She pointed to the computer and walked past Emily's room and beckoned him to the other side. She whispered, "I think he's been watching us the whole time." The color drained from Paul's face.

Paul wrote on his phone: *That's how he knows our next steps. We can't talk. Only text. Let's go back downstairs.*

She nodded, and they walked back down the stairs. *Smell the flowers, blow out the candles,* she said to herself. Just breathe. In and out. Keep breathing.

A text chimed in.

Nate PI: *You really think I would just have sound on? I saw you look at Emily's computer. Aren't you nosy? Too bad, I should cut off a finger for that.*

A photo followed. Her daughter sat in a wheelchair, a red handkerchief around her mouth, her eyes covered with her pink silk eye cover that Emily insisted she bring to college to sleep better. Her hands were bound in front of her. Maggie gasped and collapsed to the ground at the sight of her daughter. Emily's shoulders slumped against the restraints. The braids so lovingly put in by Jenna were a mess of flyaways. Her daughter was not conscious. Was she alive? A knife was at her throat, and a small trickle of blood showed where the point touched. Maggie stroked her daughter's face on the phone, her chin slumped against her chest. "Be alive, baby," she croaked. The only thing in the shot was the killer's arm at her throat. Maggie focused on the background. The room looked institutional, familiar somehow. The college?

Nate PI: *We're ready to meet you now.*

Maggie tamped down the rage building inside her and rebuilt it into a steely resolve. Maggie texted back.

Maggie: *Where? I have the money. Please don't hurt her.*

Nate PI: *I promised I wouldn't hurt your daughter and I won't. Emily won't feel a thing. She's taken a little something that's made her drowsy. Meet us at the Jensen High School gym in twenty minutes. And bring that boyfriend of yours. Write the Bitcoin address and bring it with you. Also, your phones. Leave them where I can see them in front of the computer. I don't want anyone to call the police. You won't know where I'll be, if I'll even be there, or there will be another phone when you get there. If I so much as smell a police officer, Emily's dead.*

Maggie looked up at Paul, who wrote on his phone: *He can hear us, see us, and probably knows I have a gun, too. But he may not know I only have one bullet. The school is ten minutes away. It doesn't give us enough time to get more ammo.*

Maggie's fingers felt numb. They wouldn't work to respond. Paul texted back on her phone.

Maggie: *We'll be there.*

Maggie's legs became noodles, and she pitched forward on the floor and puked. She had nothing but tea in her stomach. No amount of smelling the flowers or blowing out the candles would calm her.

Nate PI: *It would take just a flick of the knife. So tempting. Lights out.*

He taunted her now. There was nothing she could do but focus and not reply.

Maggie texted Paul: *Jenna. Oh my God, is she safe?*

She found Jenna's number and called.

"Hi Jenna, this is Maggie, Emily's mother. Have you seen her? She was supposed to call, and I never heard from her," she lied.

Jenna's voice sounded cheery. "No, not since this morning. A guy from one of her classes came and picked her up to wheel her to walk, well wheel her, to class. They were going on a date after. I think his name was Luke." She laughed a little and added, "He was super cute."

"Thanks, her phone is off, so if you see her, could you let me know?" Maggie asked with feigned lightness.

"Oh, shoot, looks like she forgot it, it's actually sitting right here on her desk. I think it's dead. Is everything okay?" Jenna asked.

"Oh yes, I just got a little concerned when she never called me back, but since her phone is there it makes sense. I was trying to connect to see if she was still planning to come this weekend," Maggie rambled. She knew the call didn't make sense coming at this hour, asking about Emily's weekend plans, but it was too late now.

"I think she planned to. We were coming together. If I hear from her, I'll let you know," Jenna said. College kids kept late hours, and she didn't seem to notice the odd time of Maggie's call.

"Thanks, bye," Maggie said, and disconnected the call.

A few minutes later, **Nate PI** sent a video text. Emily's voice, muffled from the handkerchief her eyes still covered. "Mommy, help." A fist came into the frame and punched her daughter in the face, her chin lolling back down to her chest.

Maggie let out a primal scream, spilling all the terror built from the weeks, months, and years. It felt eighteen years overdue. Paul pushed his hand over her mouth and she curled into him. He whispered, "We can't let anyone know. Your neighbors will call the police."

She pressed hard into his shoulder and screamed as loud as she could. Only a muffled moan could be heard, but the release expelled the energy, displacing it to make space for the calm resolve she'd need to execute this killer. She imagined him listening at Emily's computer, laughing.

Maggie would get the last laugh.

thirty-eight

. . .

PAUL TOOK both of their phones and ran upstairs. He came back down with a note in his palm with the Bitcoin address and grabbed her keys from the table at the door and tugged at Maggie's hand, leading her to the car. He didn't lock the house. *It didn't matter*, Maggie thought. The bad guy already got in. There was no one to keep out anymore. He climbed into the driver's seat beside her.

Paul said, "I don't think he can hear us in here."

"What are we going to do?" Maggie asked.

"We're going to save Emily. The gun is missing, and someone has been on the computer. So, we can assume he has the gun. I've got one bullet in the chamber for this." He pulled the gun from his pocket. "We don't have time to pick up more. Not at the risk of running late."

He drove the car to the school. A route familiar to them both, they never missed a game, assembly, or back-to-school night.

Maggie pointed to the two cars in the lot. "One of those is Kevin, the school officer. Maybe he can help? Should we park next to him?"

Paul shook his head. "We don't know how far this goes, or who's involved." He pulled the car in across the parking lot from them both. He opened the gun and checked for his single bullet again and clicked the safety off.

Maggie held his hand. There were a few minutes left. "Red you're dead," she said at the gun.

"Yep, Dad taught us that. If the safety is off, prepare to shoot."

Maggie leveled her eyes at him. "Don't miss."

He met her eyes and smiled. "I'm an excellent shot."

He appeared deranged with his missing tooth glaring back at her. "Right, but how long has it been since you've been shooting?" Maggie asked.

"About eighteen years..." he conceded.

"It's been about eighteen years since I've done a lot of things, too," Maggie said.

Paul looked at her and placed the gun next to his leg on the seat. He tucked her hair behind her ear. "I love you, you know."

"I know, and I love you, too. I was scared to live after Chris, but I'm not scared anymore," Maggie said.

He leaned into her and kissed her softly. A tear slid down her cheek. "We've got to go inside now," he said.

She swallowed hard. They opened their car doors and trudged into the inky darkness, making their way to the school door. "How will we get in?" Maggie asked.

Paul pointed to the door closest to the gym, propped open by a crutch. Maggie ran to the crutch, her mind no longer cautious. Paul chased after her and yanked her back hard by her arm. "Shhhhh," he said.

"But that's Emily's crutch. It was in the FaceTime when she left the hospital," she hissed, straining against his grip.

He pulled her back into the darkness. "You can't just

run in. Don't lead with your emotions. The only way we're getting out of this is if we think with our heads." His voice terse with her for the first time ever.

Her arm slacked against this restraint. "You're right, I'm sorry."

"It's okay, follow me." They crept to the door. Paul peered inside and turned to Maggie. "I don't see anyone," he whispered.

He pushed the door, and it responded with a loud creak. Maggie gasped at the noise. Paul wriggled in, and she followed. The school smelled like she remembered: old books, milk cartons, teenage sweat, and office supplies. She breathed in and listened. There was nothing. They kept their backs to the wall opposite the lockers and sidewinded toward the gym. *One more corner*, Maggie thought.

Then she spotted him. Kevin, the derpy school officer's back to them. He sat at his desk at the end of the hall. His office was propped open with cameras in front of him. She ran to him. He could call the police while they stalled the killer.

"Kevin," she whispered, and Paul pulled against her shoulder and stepped in front of her toward the security officer. She wiggled out of his grip. Kevin knew her. "Hey," she hissed.

He didn't turn around. She made out his silhouette from the glowing security cameras in front of him. His arm hung down, and the radio dangled absently at his side. He didn't move or respond. Could he be the reason she was here? He wore earbuds, and rumor was he didn't do his job well. Was he sleeping on the job? Listening to music? "Kevin?" she asked again. Paul drew his pistol from his pocket and Maggie approached him. Something was wrong.

She placed her hand on his shoulder and it felt hard and cold. His head lolled back to her, his eyes fixed ahead. Only then did she notice the blood spilled along the front, darkening his dark blue uniform to a black. His throat was slit almost all the way through, and her white sneakers were soaked with it. Too shocked to scream, Maggie put her hand over the deep slice and tilted his head back forward, but the slice was cold and clotted. "You're okay," she cried. "You're going to be okay."

"Mags." Paul tugged back on her arm. She drew her hand back. The blood didn't gush or drip from his neck. His cold, sticky blood clung to her hand. "He's been gone a while," Paul said.

Her head knew the words were true. His pimple pocked face was gray. Kevin, she'd known him for four years, a young kid in his first job. The security guard dead before he lived, before his complexion cleared. Paul pulled her in to him, and she heard the sickening stick from his blood on the bottoms of her shoes. She cried silently on Paul's shoulder.

Maggie whispered to him, "He doesn't mean for any of us to get out alive.

"If the rumors are true, Kevin's bosses check on him a lot," said Maggie. "Our only hope is to keep the killer busy long enough for them to check on us."

Paul's shoulders tensed as he drew Maggie in closer to his chest. "Don't look, but he's missing a couple of fingers," Paul said.

"What?" She twisted out of his grip and saw Kevin's ring and pinky finger were missing.

A booming voice she didn't recognize startled them both over the intercom. "Evening announcements. The game will begin in the gym in just a few minutes. Don't be late, you don't want to miss the main event."

Then, a voice she recognized. "Mommy, help!"

Maggie's knees buckled, and Paul held her by her elbows to keep her from collapsing in the drying pool of blood beneath her. She scanned the security cameras and the top left square marked 'main gym.' A person wore a mask holding a voice changer. Kevin's killer waved through the grayscale camera. Then he turned to Emily and hit her hard at the base of her skull. Her head jerked forward.

The blood drips and splatters traced a path through the second door, short-cutting to the gym. Paul led, and she followed it. They walked closer to the gym and urine filled Maggie's nostrils. A puddle of fluid mixed with the blood the rest of the way to the gym. The blood splatter continued. *So much blood*, she thought. She hoped it still belonged to Kevin's fingers. Her eyes darted nervously around the corner to glimpse the killer.

They entered the gym.

thirty-nine

. . .

EMILY SAT IN HER WHEELCHAIR, her arms tied behind her. Her one good leg tied tight to the chair. "Emily," Maggie yelled, her arms outstretched.

"No, no," the killer said back to her. His voice was clearly being modified by a voice changer. He applied the slightest pressure of the brown bloodied knife to Emily's throat. Was it Kevin's blood? Nate's too? Another tiny droplet of fresh blood dripped down her daughter's neck and disappeared under her JMU sweatshirt. Emily didn't respond.

Rage surged in Maggie's chest. She considered forcing herself across the room to kill this person with her bare hands. But she knew she wouldn't make it before the killer would slice her daughter's throat. Paul's arm wrapped around her waist, holding her tight at his side.

Maggie's eyes followed the knife up to the person in the pink mask. She assumed it was gray from the security cameras. The killer's stature appeared smaller than Maggie expected. And the figure straightened with the knife still at

Emily's throat. The killer pointed the tip dangerously close to her carotid artery. This person wore black leggings and a sage green Virginia Beach sweatshirt. The last time Maggie had seen that sweatshirt was when she gave it to Jenna at the hospital. But she had spoken to Jenna on the phone immediately before going to the school. Emily's head lolled forward, and the blindfold slipped below her right eye. Maggie couldn't tell if the killer bumped her wheelchair, or she was waking. Emily's eyes stayed closed.

"You're right on time," the voice changer shot back. But the killer was not talking to Maggie or Paul. Behind them, Roy shuffled in with his unbalanced gait.

Maggie turned to Roy, his pallor gray in the harsh light of the gym. Paul tugged Maggie's sleeve, moving her away from the door. "You two are a team?"

An anxious shiver ran down Maggie's spine. Her eyes returned to her daughter, sitting weakly in her wheelchair.

"Not exactly," the voice said, and the killer tossed the voice changer on the ground and removed the mask.

Maggie stared back at the girl. "Jenna?"

Jenna took her free hand and fished a gun out of her pocket. It looked like Chris's gun, and it didn't. It was longer than she recalled, almost like it wore a Maglite flashlight at its tip. She had a knife in one hand, and a gun in the other.

Paul breathed sharply. "A silencer."

Roy said, "Marie? What are you doing? I don't understand." He met eyes with Maggie and asked, "Who's Jenna?"

"Your precious Maggie or should I say—Ms. Becker—won't know, Dad," Jenna hissed. "You're an idiot, always have been. What is my middle name? Jennifer. But in my new life, everybody calls me Jenna. One of the few things I have left that my mother and I shared, our middle names. I go by Jenna Johnson here. Mom's original last name. I'm no Murphy," she spat.

Roy looked back at Jenna, the whites around his eyes visible. "Why? I thought you were in Barcelona? In college?"

She rolled her eyes. "Mom was right. You are so dumb. I never went overseas. You dropped me at the airport and never checked. You couldn't have cared less. Especially after what you did to my mother. When I worked to be this pretty, it was easy to get my money through alternative means... Matter of fact, I made so much in high school, that I was able to pay for my first year of college, so I could collect what is owed to me."

Emily's head bobbed back up, her one hazel eye stared at her mother. The other hidden behind her silk sleep mask. "Mommy, what's happening?"

Maggie's heart snapped at the sound of her daughter's plea. It was the first time Maggie was sure they were all going to die. How could she console her daughter? She couldn't save her, just like she hadn't been able to save Chris.

Jenna hitched her voice up a register and created a poor imitation of Emily's voice. "Mommy, what's happening? Shut up, Emily." Jenna's eyes shot back to Maggie. "You know, you irritate her, right? She doesn't love you like I would have loved my own mother." Emily shook her head 'no' at her mother, her visible eye pleading. Jenna lifted the butt end of the knife and struck her at the side of her temple. The one eye Maggie saw rolled backward. Maggie heard a voice ringing in her ears and only realized it was her screams as she reached for her daughter. Paul yanked her back and threw her to the ground.

"Paul?" Maggie looked up at him, shaken.

"If you take a step closer, she will kill Emily. Please, trust me," he whispered.

"No secrets here," Jenna yelled back. "Speaking of mothers... Father... It's time for the truth. Get on with it."

"Please, Marie. I can't," Roy said.

Jenna dropped the knife and it clanked to the ground. She aimed the gun at her father's feet and shot. Despite the silencer, the shot was louder than Maggie expected and she jerked. The bullet hit three feet from Roy and ricocheted into the wall between Paul and Roy. "Next time I will not miss. And I'll shoot Maggie first. So, Daddy dearest, I think you can."

Roy raised his hands in surrender. "Okay, okay. Where do you want me to start?"

"I know everything except how she died. Her diary gave me everything else."

"She kept a diary?" Roy sank to his knees and looked at the floor. "Where?"

"In all of her books you tossed in the garage. When you threw her life away," Jenna's voice cracked.

Roy looked at his daughter. "Then you know, ladybug. I packed her things in boxes. At least those that survived the fire. I meant to go through them. But any diary she kept wasn't meant for you. She was ill." He shook his head.

"She was my mother. Of course, she meant it for me. It's all I have left of her."

"I know what would be in that diary, Marie. It was not meant for you. I helped her through a lot, and when she was done with me, she threw me away like trash. She wasn't well, but you can be better. I can get you help." His back straightened, and he took a small step toward his daughter.

Without warning, Jenna shot toward Maggie. The bullet whizzed past her head and buried itself into the wall a few feet from the other. "Enough, Dad. Start talking."

forty

...

A TEAR ROLLED down Roy's cheek. His voice broke, and he started, "Your mother and I were high school sweethearts. She was so beautiful, like you, Marie." He grimaced and looked at her. "We got married right out of high school when she got pregnant. But she lost the baby. Over the years, she changed. I guess we changed. Anyway, she started seeing someone from work. I found out it was Chris. She became obsessed with him." Roy breathed in and looked at Jenna. "I'm sorry I wasn't more present with you, Marie. You remind me of her so much that maybe I pulled away. I shouldn't have done that..." He stopped.

Jenna pointed the gun at Maggie and shot again. This time, the bullet landed closer. "Finish the story. I didn't know it until the diary, but somehow I knew. You weren't my father."

"You're right, you weren't my daughter, by blood. I tried to do what was right by you, and I failed. I knew it from the day at the hospital they gave us your blood type. But, I thought maybe Viv and I could make it work. Be a real family. After she had you, she grew angrier. I finally told her

I knew, and I would still be your father. But it only made things worse. She started talking about how she wanted to be with the father of her baby, Chris. And that I was never good enough."

Jenna rolled her eyes. "Skip to how she died."

"I can't," Roy said.

She shot his good leg, and he buckled to the ground, yelling. Maggie screamed, "No." And reached for him. Paul rooted her tight to himself, and Emily didn't respond at all.

"Next I will shoot Maggie between the eyes," Jenna said.

And she swung the gun toward Maggie. "No, no," Roy replied, holding his hands up in defeat.

He wiped sweat from his brow, and the blood from his leg pooled. His pallor whitened under the fluorescent light. "This isn't about anyone else, just you and me. Please," he pleaded with his daughter.

"Talk." Jenna's eyes filled with fury narrowed at him.

He winced and shifted on his backside. He pulled his pant leg up, and the tiny hole produced by the bullet simmered over with blood. Maggie wiggled out of Paul's arms and scrambled to Roy. She sat beside him and placed pressure on his leg, if she could keep him alive maybe his daughter would change her mind. Maggie felt the beating of his heart through the pulsing wound in his leg. His blood, still warm, pooled on the gym floor beneath him. She glared up at Jenna. "This may be a major artery. Let me keep pressure on his leg. Your dad needs a doctor," Maggie yelled at Jenna.

Jenna laughed manically. "Fine, keep the pressure on his leg. No doctor, though. Talk, Dad."

Roy's eyes met Maggie's in an apology and looked back up toward his daughter. "I was getting ready for poker night with the neighbors. Her postpartum moods were worsening. She was on the phone and in a rage. She called me a loser, a piece of shit, and that I disgusted her. Those were the last words she said to me. She was smoking a cigarette and blew the smoke in my face. Then, she reminded me of what I already knew. You weren't mine. We weren't a real family. You belonged to the love of her life who she said was dying. Which I didn't understand until later when I saw in the news the car went off the bridge. She repeated, I'd never amount to anything. I just snapped." Maggie's breath caught.

He stopped talking. Jenna took a step forward, her gun aimed at Maggie's head. Maggie remained crouched over Roy, holding his leg, and stayed focused on his wound as the pulsing of his leg weakened. Jenna shooting the good leg would make walking a challenge if he survived.

Jenna stared at her father. "You're not done with the story. How did you snap, Dad?" she yelled.

He breathed in and began, "Understand, she was sick, mentally. She yelled at me, said unspeakable things. And I wanted quiet. Peace. I took the lamp from the bedroom and I hit her on the back of the head. I never raised my hand to her before that, ever," he cried. "She laid on the bed, and I swear she wasn't breathing. You weren't my daughter. She didn't want to be my wife. I felt unwanted. She called me a loser and said she never loved me. The cigarette tumbled out of her hand. The covers caught fire. It was so fast, I had to decide. She was gone already, you see? You understand?" Maggie remembered the voicemail, Vivian's last moments on her answering machine. The cruel words spoken to her husband right before she died. Or was killed.

He went silent. Jenna said, "No, Dad, the story isn't done. She died of smoke inhalation, not blunt force trauma."

Maggie yelled, "What more do you want? I have the money. Just tell me what you want so we can all go home."

Jenna said, "Tsk, tsk. Nobody was talking to you. I'll tell you when I'm ready to hear from you. Finish the story, Dad." She walked over to Emily and kicked the wheelchair over on its side. Emily's shoulder smacked hard against the gym floor and her head bobbed. Emily woke and cried out. Paul started toward Jenna, and she shot a bullet, narrowly missing his chest.

"Okay, okay." Maggie held her free hand up.

"Stop." Roy's voice cut the air. "I'll finish, I'll finish." He straightened his back and winced against the pain in his leg. "I saw the blankets catch fire, and I walked out. They would rule it an accident. So, I went to the neighbor's house for our planned poker night. I regret it, but that's what I did."

Maggie gasped but kept her eyes on his wound. She would not interrupt again.

Jenna's mouth opened into a smile. "Where was I Dad? When you went to poker night?"

He turned from her. The blood he had left in his body rose to his cheeks. "You were in your crib on the other side of the house."

"You left me there, sleeping. And she wasn't dead, was she?"

"I didn't know it, but she wasn't. I left you there, something I'm sorry for every day. The neighbors saw the house on fire, and we called the fire department. When I saw the house ablaze, I changed my mind. I ran for the house, went inside and I could hear you crying, and I could hear her banging on the door she was trapped behind. I heard your little coughs and cries, and I ran through the fire for you. I chose you. It was so hot, I felt my hair melting into my face and smelled my skin burning. But I got to you, and we jumped out of your bedroom window. You were so small. I didn't mean for her to die. I didn't mean for any of this."

Roy turned to Maggie. "I've always been at Emily's school to watch over my daughter's sister. My wife destroyed your family, but I felt like we were a family of our own. While I watched her and you, I fell in love with the family you are. I hoped one day to be a part of it."

Jenna screamed, "Dad, you sent me to a different school and went with Emily! It was always Emily and Maggie, and never me."

Roy said, "I'm sorry for everything. I made so many mistakes. Please, let everyone go. I'll take the blame for this. Please. I'm so sorry, I wasn't a better father. You always reminded me of your mother. Beautiful, independent, smart, but sick. So very sick."

"Shut up, Dad. You know what's unfortunate for you?"

"What?" He looked up at her, his eyes glistening with tears.

"I am smart, like my mother. I found your will and your life insurance. Too bad you only got a term life insurance. Your time has always been just about up."

"I'll get more, and I'll renew it," he pleaded.

"You won't. Go to hell." And Jenna shot him in the stomach.

The blood gurgled out, and Maggie took her other hand to apply pressure to his soft white belly. He looked like a fish hoisted out of the water as he gulped for air. Paul raced to her and put his hand on her shoulder to steady her. The warm blood bubbled beneath her hand. She couldn't will his soul to stay inside his body. His belly spilled his life on the floor in a dark crimson pool.

Roy put his hand on hers. "I'm so sorry for what I've

done, and who I created. Forgive me." He looked up at Jenna, his eyes surprised with the shocking finality of death hurdling toward him.

"It's okay, Roy. Rest now," Maggie whispered. She kissed him on his head, and a relaxed smile cut across his features. His eyes fluttered in the back of his head, and his shoulders rattled as the last life force left his body. Then she felt his shoulders relax as he succumbed to his fate.

forty-one

. . .

JENNA'S SMILE grew taut and wide. Her teeth gritted together in unnaturally white chiclets lined up in a neat row as she gazed upon her dying father. "Goodbye, Daddy." His face was no longer rosy with shame, now a grayed pallor. His hollow stare gazed up at the gym ceiling marred with brown water stains.

Jenna did not intend for anyone other than her to survive this night; Maggie saw that now. They bet their lives on Kevin's incompetence and that he would be checked on. How long would it take the police station to check on Kevin? All she needed was more time. *Keep her talking*, she thought.

Jenna looked at Maggie and said, "I listened, you know. Ever since the day you invited us to your home for dinner. Those concert tickets were worth it. You suspected just about everyone. Except poor, pitiful me. Is it because I reminded you so much of your perfect little girl?" She kicked the wheel on the chair and it spun absently in the air. Emily's eye remained closed. "Hmmm, I'm not ready for Emily to die just yet. Let's see if she's still alive. Shall we?"

Jenna kept the gun pointed at Maggie but lifted the knife from the ground. She ran the serrated edge across Emily's shoulder and let the knife clang back to the floor. Emily's blood-curdling wail pierced the air. A surge of white furious energy shot through Maggie. Before she could think or control her body, she lunged, and slipped in Roy's blood pooled on the floor. Something pulled her back. She looked down and Paul's arm was locked around her waist. He used all of his strength to drop her back to the ground on her bottom. She clawed at his arms to get free.

"Emily, baby." She yelled to her daughter, raising her hands marred with Roy's dried blood to her daughter. Then she tried scrambling free again, scratching Paul's skin as he held her tightly to the ground. His grip tightened as he cried in her hair. She looked up at Jenna. "I'll kill you." She growled. "Let me go," she pleaded to Paul.

"Shhhhh," Paul whispered in her ear. "We've got to keep us alive long enough to get help."

"That's right. Sit, like the dog you are," Jenna spat at her.

Emily looked at her mother, a small blackish-red puddle pooled beneath her shoulder. Her eyes were unfocused but drifted toward where Maggie sat, arms outstretched, crying to her. "Mommy?"

"It's okay, baby girl. It's okay." And Emily's eyes rolled to the back of her head.

The cut in her black sweatshirt turned blacker with her blood. Maggie couldn't see the color of it, just a wet pool of blackness soaking her sweatshirt.

Jenna turned to Maggie. "You raised a real whiner. Every time I turned around, she sniveled about you or Josh. Or going back home to visit that idiot. I programmed my face into her phone after I roofied her and blocked that crybaby, Josh. He was in my way. It saved his life, really. He should thank me." She shrugged and said, "Maybe after all of you are gone, I'll go to him for comfort." She slipped a smiling mask of innocence over her menacing face. "Oh, Josh, please comfort me with the loss of my best friend. I'm so scared and sad." She laughed and slashed the knife through the air.

Paul said, "But why Nate?" Maggie felt a gratitude toward Paul, his level head keeping her focused on stretching out the time.

"Who's Nate? Oh, the owner of this?" Jenna threw the phone toward Maggie's feet. It landed in a coagulating pool of Roy's blood. "Or maybe his fingers. If you're curious, his fingers were cut off, just like that teenage security officer. If you want to know where the investigator's fingers are, check your freezer, Maggie. Paul and Emily will lose their fingers, too. It's your choice if they lose them before or after they're dead. It all hinges on your behavior, Maggie. Looks like I've already made the choice for my dad." Her grin twisted into a sneer.

"What? Why? Fingers?" Maggie choked out.

"Nate was a scratcher. My DNA had to be removed. And you just can't be too careful. They took a nice bleached bath. Now, they are in a little Ziploc bag behind your chicken breakfast sausage. In the end, it was really you who killed the investigator, anyway. If you never hired him, he would still be alive." Jenna smiled at Maggie and shrugged. "You're a sick woman, Maggie. Turns out your guilt got the best of you and you called the police and told them you killed the investigator. I bet the cops are probably at your house right now, searching for your finger trophies. When they show up here, and find you all, they'll find these too." Jenna fished in her pocket and threw two pale appendages on the ground. Their blood drained. They looked like a Halloween prop.

Maggie's bottom lip quivered. "But why kill Nate?"

Jenna's eyes glistened. "He came to the door, said he knew Dad was following you. Of course, he was. Emily and I had just become roomies. I didn't have time for anyone to come in and ruin everything. Nate was collateral damage. He was an easy mark. While Dad defended himself, mumbling and apologizing and nearly fessing up to everything, I grabbed a knife, mask, and hoodie and went to the back of his car. I didn't know what he knew or didn't know. As soon as he pulled into the parking lot to have a date with you, he texted. I saw him unlock his phone, then I held the knife to his throat. He told me he knew nothing and promised not to tell. It was my luck he didn't keep his records on a computer." She shrugged, her dark beads of eyes studying Maggie's horror-stricken face. Then, a smile spread across her features and she continued, "And, because he was so scared, I knew he was telling the truth. That meant my secret would die with him. It was my first time. It took a couple of cuts, but he didn't die loud. He was good practice. The security guard died quicker." She paused, and added, "I did pop by and see his wife and kids, and you know what? His wife looked like she was doing fine without him. Enjoying his life insurance payout. Something I'll be enjoying soon."

Ahhh, there it was, Maggie thought. The life insurance money. She received $500,000 for Chris's death. Jenna wanted $250,000. "So, you want your half of Chris's life insurance?"

"He was my father. It's the least you can do," Jenna said.

Emily's eyes fluttered open. She said, "He may have been your father, but he wasn't your dad." Jenna kicked her hard in the face. One of Emily's perfectly aligned teeth skittered across the floor.

"He wasn't your dad, either. Your mom made sure of that. So, shut up already. You're lucky I haven't killed you yet," Jenna barked at her. "I already broke your leg... I needed to know where you were and wheel you around. God, you were so stupid to let me hold your drinks. You really have to be the biggest idiot of all."

Emily spit out blood. "I hate you."

"Emily, shhhh baby, trust me," Maggie said.

Jenna snickered. "Yeah, because you can see how well that's going. Your mother sent you right to me. Out of the hospital, right into my arms."

Jenna turned back to Maggie. "If I can't have parents, I'll take the life insurances and build my own life."

Maggie tried to muster up a sympathetic expression for Jenna. "I'm so sorry for what you've been through." She stood and took a tentative step toward her.

"Stay where you are."

She pointed her gun at Emily's head. "Don't pity me. It's because of you."

"What do you mean?" Maggie asked.

"You were the reason my dad died on the bridge. You killed the private investigator, but you also killed my dad. You are responsible for all of this. Blood is on your hands, too. Just look at them." She pointed her knife at Maggie's hands.

Maggie peered down at her own bloodied hands. Jenna seemed proud of her intricate plan and sought admiration for it. It was Jenna's arrogance that was keeping Maggie and her family alive. She had to keep her talking. "How did you match with Emily?"

Jenna laughed. "That was the easiest of all. These

college kids are carbon copies of one another. I've learned to blend in, be a chameleon. I researched her, and I made an Instagram and fashioned my life to be her perfect match. Freshman year, I decided my life would be different. So, I had four years to become someone your daughter wanted to be. She used to call me a 'sister from another mister,' ironic, isn't it?"

Maggie's shoulder tensed. "What are you going to do once you get the money?"

"I'm starting a new life. I'm going to begin again. You will die with my secrets. Maggie, I am saving you for last. You killed the life I could have had, so one by one you'll watch everybody you care for disappear. You're my living diary, but after you're buried, I'll be reborn. All motives will link back to you. Of course, you'll kill yourself with your dead husband's gun. How sad."

"What are you talking about?" Maggie asked. "I have no motives to kill anyone. No one will believe it."

"Well, you were pretty upset about Nate standing you up. Turns out, he was a pretty naughty boy. Slept around with a lot of women who used him for services. And I guess he picked the wrong woman. When you found out he had three children and a wife, you threw yourself into a jealous rage." A sly smile twisted Jenna's face up into an ugly grimace. "But that will not be what really sends you over the edge. What really sends you over the edge is Paul and Emily's affair."

forty-two

. . .

PAUL'S GRIP tightened around Maggie's waist. She felt him pivot forward and throw up on the linoleum gym floor. The splatting sound and the stench of his vomit made her stomach twist. The bile built at the back of her throat. Maggie looked at Emily. Her eyes stayed shut as she lay on the ground in her knocked-over wheelchair. Maggie turned to Paul. He wiped his mouth with this sleeve. "I would never," he whispered. "But we have to keep her talking." She smelled the rancid vomit on his breath as he breathed hotly toward her face.

Maggie looked at Jenna. "But how? Why would they do that? Paul is a father to Emily."

"Fathers sometimes do terrible things." She shrugged and showed her impossibly white teeth at Maggie like an apex predator. "Everyone will believe it when they find all the evidence."

"What evidence?" Paul shot back. Maggie sat stunned, her eyes still on her daughter, whose eyes fluttered open.

"No one will think I did anything to hurt Emily," Paul said.

Maggie looked at Emily and blinked twice. Emily blinked twice back and closed her eyes.

"Oh they will," Jenna growled. "I saw how you hugged and swung her around like she was your world at dinner. She gets two dads and I get none?" she spat.

Maggie said, "I'm sorry you didn't have anyone who cared about you. But how does hugging someone turn into an affair?"

"I said that was my inspiration. After Paul involved himself, I couldn't let him get away, too. He would spend the rest of his life avenging you both. You'll be in a jealous rage when you find your sweet daughter having an affair with the man you love. Maggie, you'll shoot them both dead with your husband's gun. You're an irresponsible firearms owner. When my poor father came into the gym and caught you both, he died because of it. He and that security officer killed because they were in the wrong place and wrong time. You were in a bloodthirsty rage, Maggie. Out to kill anything in your way."

"Why are you doing this to us?" Maggie cried. "We have your money. We can give you the information right now. You can have your piece of the life insurance. Please, just leave us alone. We promise we won't tell anyone." Her shoulders sagged against Paul.

"Because you had something that was mine. My dad, my life. I want a new beginning with no one who knows my past around. Call this... therapy." Jenna smiled wryly at Maggie.

"None of us knew," Maggie said.

"It doesn't matter anymore. Paul's key was conveniently in your hide-a-rock outside. Emily used the keys to get back into the house after the concert."

Paul's mouth fell open. "What evidence do you have?" he asked.

Jenna kept the gun aimed at Emily's head while she fished in her pocket. She threw the small piece of fabric across the floor toward Paul and Maggie.

"Underwear?" Maggie asked.

"Not just underwear. I went to Paul's house, and he had Kleenex at his bedside and I put the contents on this." Maggie turned to Paul, who crimsoned under her gaze. He turned away from her. Maggie leveled eyes with Jenna. Humiliated as she was for Paul, she needed to keep her talking.

"How did you arrange for everyone to meet at the school?" Maggie asked, changing the subject.

"Ha, easy. The senior prank shows Emily knew how to get into the school. I played a great Emily in the gym that day, right? It gives her opportunity. I knew how to get into your house since I got in and took her shirt, and her hat. When I entered the school I made sure just the right amount of hair showed, and I didn't face the camera. She couldn't prove it wasn't her, but everyone believed it was. Emily, such a lost and disturbed girl, having an affair with her uncle." Jenna laughed. "There are a lot of private places to do things here. Of course, it wouldn't have been me, the innocent janitor's daughter, from the wrong side of town, with access to the master key." She rolled her eyes. "Everyone underestimates me at every turn. Initially, Paul wasn't on the list to die. She was going to be having sex with my father. But Paul inserted himself into the narrative like an idiot. But, honestly, it's better now. There are no loose ends. I've given my plan room to grow and shape as you all played your roles. So Maggie, you killed Paul, too."

"You're sick." Maggie stated simply.

"I want what's mine," Jenna replied. "You are a loose end. My mother, she was with my real father. They loved each other. I found her diary, and it gave me everything I needed to know about them. They would have been together, if not for the people in this room."

Maggie lifted herself from the floor, and Paul stood with her. The knees on her jeans stiffened with Roy's blood. "Please don't do this," she pleaded, her hands in front of her palms facing Jenna.

Paul pulled his pistol from behind his belt and fired. The bullet missed its mark. His single bullet, a fail. Jenna's eyes gleamed with hatred and she aimed her pistol at Maggie and squeezed.

Paul jumped between Maggie and the gun, and the bullet hit him in the stomach with a thunk. He crumpled at Maggie's feet. She fell to the ground beside him and cradled his head in her arms. "I'm sorry, Mags." And his eyes flickered shut.

"No," Maggie screamed. Emily still lay in the wheelchair playing opossum, but Maggie saw her eyes squeeze hard and her lip quiver.

Jenna said, "Now, before I get ahead of myself, I'm going to need that Bitcoin transfer."

forty-three

. . .

MAGGIE'S HANDS trembled as she fished for the Bitcoin note from Paul's windbreaker pocket. He didn't respond, but she saw the shallow breaths from the tiny rises and falls in his chest. The only thing keeping them alive was Jenna's inability to access the Bitcoin.

"Stop wasting my time," Jenna said. She aimed the gun at Emily's head.

Maggie ran her finger over the ink of the Bitcoin key, smudging the last numbers."I got it, but the last numbers are smudged. If you kill me, you'll never know what they are." Maggie cried, holding up the note like a white flag of surrender.

"Bring it to me," Jenna said.

Maggie placed Paul's head gently on the ground and got up. She walked toward Jenna and looked at Emily. Emily's eyes popped opened, and she looked at her mother, and Paul dying on the ground. She nodded imperceptibly at Maggie.

Jenna said, "Close enough. Hand it over."

Maggie stretched her hand out with the scrap of paper

with blood on the corner. Maybe it was Roy's. Or Paul's. Or Kevin's.

Jenna looked down at the scrap of paper and licked her lips, placing her fingers around it to snatch from Maggie. Emily's cast leg kicked the back of Jenna's leg hard, and she landed on her tailbone with a bang. The gun dropped from her hands and skittered across the linoleum. Maggie lunged forward and grabbed the gun, the cold metal slipping in her bloodied hands. Her hands were covered in pieces of Kevin, Roy, and now the warm addition of Paul.

Jenna scrambled toward the knife and grabbed it.

Maggie said, "Please, Jenna or Marie, put the knife down. I don't want to hurt you. This has gone far enough."

"You don't have the guts." But her knife hesitated, and she stared back at Maggie.

"Please, you never had a mother, so you don't know what we'll do to protect our children. And I'm sorry you didn't have a mother. Please, we can get you help. Let me call the police and get help. You don't have to do this. We can save Paul, and maybe even your father." Maggie knew her father had long been dead, but Paul was still breathing.

Jenna glared at Maggie. "Why would you protect Emily, anyway? You know she's awful to you. You irritate her, and every time you text or call, she rolls her eyes. Why kill for her? Why die for her? She doesn't love you." Jenna said.

"You don't understand love. And I'm sorry for that, it's unfair. But part of growing up is letting go of your parents. You never got the chance to let go of something you never had. Please, put the knife down," Maggie pleaded.

Jenna's lip quivered, and she steeled herself again. "What have I done?" She asked, and looked at Maggie. Then she lunged for Emily with the knife. Maggie squeezed the trigger her finger slipped with the blood on her hands. The bullet whizzed past Jenna's head and buried itself into the wall. Jenna paused briefly, and her eyes widened in surprise as she stared at Maggie. She squeezed the trigger again. This time, the bullet did not miss its target. A dark crimson hole appeared between the girls brows. Jenna staggered back, and fell to the floor with a thunk, a blackish red puddle pooled around her head.

Maggie screamed and threw the gun out of her hand as if it was a branding iron. "Oh my God," Maggie cried. She ran to Jenna's body and kicked the knife crusty with blood out of the girl's hand. So much blood, Maggie knew the back of her head was gone. The girl stared blankly at the ceiling. Maggie shut the girl's eyes and ran to Emily.

Paul opened his eyes and croaked, "It's okay. It's over. She died of suicide. I'm sorry, Mags. Call the police."

Running footsteps filled the hall before she could get the phone from Jenna's body to call the police. Emily still lay on her side, her face contorted against the deep cut in her shoulder.

The doorjamb filled with a man and a woman both in Fairfax County Police uniforms. It reminded Maggie of the night eighteen years ago when two police officers had cast a shadow on her doorstep.

The woman police officer surveyed the room and aimed her pistol at Maggie. "Face down on the floor," she yelled.

The male police officer talked into his shoulder, asking for an ambulance. Maggie rested her head on the floor. It was over. She looked up at Paul from her place on the floor. "Stay with me, please," she cried to him. His consciousness slipped away. Emily screamed.

Maggie cried from her prone position on the floor to the police officers, "Please, help him, and help my daughter.

The girl who's dead next to my daughter did all of this. Please, help us."

Emily yelled to the police officers, "My mother saved us. Please, let her go."

"Please let me go to my daughter. You can take me to jail. I have done nothing, but please. I need to see her and Paul. Make sure they're okay," Maggie yelled to the police officer who was cinching the metal behind her back.

The female officer frisked Maggie and escorted her with her hands still cuffed together to her daughter. The male police officer turned Emily's chair upright and mercifully wheeled her away from the sight of Jenna's lifeless body sprawled on the gym floor.

Maggie, with bound hands, leaned in and put her head on her daughter's uninjured shoulder. Emily cried, "All those things she said, about me saying bad things about you..." She didn't finish her sentence.

Maggie nuzzled her hair. Under the sweat, grime, and blood, she recognized the musk of her daughter's head, the same head she smelled as a baby. "I know, I know, I know your heart."

"Mama, I'm sorry."

"It's okay my love, it's okay." Maggie felt the clumps of blood in her hair and hoped they were from the security guard.

The male police officer crouched over Paul and applied pressure to his stomach wound. "We need an ambulance right now," the officer said. Maggie felt the other officer's grip slacken, and she looked at her partner working on Paul.

"Please help him," Maggie cried. Emily's lip trembled, and she buried her head in her mother's neck. The female officer nodded and rushed to support her partner with Paul lying unconscious on the floor.

The minutes dragged on, but more footsteps followed, with two stretchers and paramedics rushing in the door. Maggie sank to her knees and rested her head in her daughter's lap. The paramedics first ran to Paul, their faces grim. "Save him," Maggie screamed in a hoarse voice into the cluster of people hovering over him. They hoisted Paul up, covering his face with an air mask, and wheeled him toward the door.

"Go with him," Emily said, and nudged her mother toward Paul.

Paul's eyes opened briefly. He removed his mask. "Stay with Emily. Please. For both of us."

Maggie nodded, her lip trembling. "Don't die on me. I love you, Paul."

"I love you too." And his eyes drifted shut. The crew shuttled him out the door. The other paramedics then loaded Emily onto a gurney. Maggie followed them and then climbed into the ambulance with her daughter. The roofy drugs were wearing off and as the reality of the day set in Emily turned white with shock. Maggie crouched over her, still in her handcuffs. "Just breathe, baby." And together they chanted, "Smell the flowers, blow out the candles."

forty-four

. . .

THE POLICE WERE EXECUTING a search warrant in Maggie's home at the same time the scene was playing out in the high school gym. The investigators found the fingers in her freezer where they expected to find them. Marie had called the police, saying she was Maggie, and confessed to everything she had done. But she would not tell them what her next moves were going to be. It was supposed to be her suicide note to the world. She spun the lies of Paul and Emily, but left out Roy, who was framed as a mistake, and Kevin, who unfortunately was a mistake.

Based on the evidence, police allowed Maggie to stay with Emily at the hospital. "Mama, I didn't suspect Jenna, or Marie, or whoever she was. She drugged me, pushed me down the stairs, sent awful things to my boyfriend, almost killed all of us. We still don't know about Uncle Papa. How could I have been so blind?" Emily asked.

Maggie winced, thinking of Paul. Since Maggie was not technically listed on any medical information, there was little the medical staff could share. No visitors were permitted yet. But based on the hallway snippets and hints from sympathetic hospital staff, it could go either way.

"We were all blind," Maggie finally answered.

"I don't want to visit two graves on Father's Day," Emily said, and tucked her head into the pillow.

"I know," Maggie said. She ran her fingers through her daughter's clean blonde locks with the dark roots forming.

"Want me to braid your hair, honey?"

"Sure." Emily sat up and leaned forward. Her mother nestled in behind her.

She wasn't armed with a brush or prepared at all for the request. She slipped her own hair out of its neatly tucked ponytail to have a fastener for her daughter. Maggie took Emily's yellowed strands of hair, they were silky and rich despite the bleach and weaved them through her fingers like when her daughter was small.

"I love you, Mama."

"I love you, too. I want to tell you something, so we can always be honest with one another."

"Okay," Emily said, her voice hitched with worry.

"The senior prank, the one I now know, was Marie... I didn't believe you. And I'm sorry for that."

"Good," Emily said, breathing out.

"Good? What do you mean?" Maggie asked.

"You aren't perfect. I made so many mess ups, and I'm glad you did something wrong. Sometimes it's hard to compare myself. I always come up short," Emily admitted.

Maggie squeezed her daughter, and she jumped with pain in her shoulder. "God, I'm sorry. I love you more than life itself."

"I know, Mama. I love you, too."

Maggie finished the braid in silence and slid back out of

the bed and nestled into her chair as her daughter leaned back.

"So, do you have any idea what you'll do about Josh? Do you think you'll contact him again?" asked Maggie.

"I don't know. I love him. Once I realized she blocked all of his calls, I unblocked him. He's messaged me a lot. I don't know what to do." She shrugged with her good shoulder. "While Jenna drugged me, even when I wasn't drugged, I was unkind." Emily stared down at her lap.

"Well, if you love him, maybe go for it?" Maggie asked.

"Honestly Mom, I haven't had a very good example of that." Emily's eyes turned to her, and she smirked.

"What do you mean?" Maggie asked.

"Uncle Papa," Emily answered quietly. "Mom, it's about time you found happiness. I couldn't have picked anyone better for you. I've always considered him my dad. So, really, the only person missing out on any love or pleasure was the two of you."

"I should have talked to you about it before now," Maggie said.

"Mom, I know you loved Dad and miss him. You've been so good at keeping him in my life, but you know, I never knew him. Uncle Papa, he's always been Dad to me."

"I know," Maggie said.

Then, a lithe, brunette female nurse popped into the room and glanced at Maggie. "He's asking for you."

Maggie looked at Emily, who grinned. Maggie turned to the nurse. "Can I go to him?"

"Of course, I'll take you now," the nurse said, and smiled.

Maggie's stomach clenched hard as she rose and followed her to Paul. "God let him live," she said out loud.

The nurse cracked open the door and Maggie followed

her inside. She did not prepare Maggie for his fragility as he lifted his arm to her. "Hey, stranger," he said.

The nurse bowed out of the room and said, "I'll leave you two for a bit. He can't visit long because he needs his rest."

Maggie nodded. She went to his bed and grabbed his hand. It was dry, and his hair peaked and spiked a thousand directions. "How is she?" he asked in barely a whisper.

"Good, she made it. Better than I thought. They say she can come home today and the laceration on her shoulder has a long-running suture, but remarkably mostly surface. No permanent damage except some scarring and the drugs are nearly out of her system. Her ankle was recast and she'll need it on for another six weeks."

He breathed out a sigh of relief. "I thought I might have lost you both." The pain shattered his face into such sadness she turned from him.

Maggie squeezed his hand and said, "I thought I lost you. And it would have killed me." The words ran out of her mouth before she could stop them.

He winced, grabbed her wrist, looked into her eyes, and said, "I love you, I loved you since, forever."

She leaned in to kiss him, and he brushed her hair from her neck. The necklace stayed gone. He pulled her in and kissed her hard. "God, I've waited way too many years for us."

"Me too, And I'm sorry about that," Maggie said.

"Never be sorry for taking your time. I know you're deliberate, and once you loved me back, we'll never part."

"Paul, I've always loved you back."

forty-five

. . .

A FEW WEEKS LATER, Emily decided she would
return to JMU. Jenna had taken too much from her, and she
wouldn't take her dream of JMU too. Emily and Maggie
came back to the dorm to move her in.

Maggie's skin squirmed as they studied Marie's side of
the room. No one cleaned it out yet, there was no one
left to.

As Emily settled in and with her things, they decided to
move all of Jenna's things to the top of her bed. Then,
they'd call the school to have them removed.

Maggie went to the photo of Marie's parents. She held it
up and turned it in her hands, unlatched the back, and
opened it. It was a picture of two models in a magazine. A
made-up life. She handed the magazine picture to Emily
and plopped next to her on Emily's bed.

"Want to know something?" Maggie asked.

"Sure."

"I was jealous of this. Her made-up life. I felt so inferior
to her illusion. I'm ashamed to admit it." Maggie's shoulders slumped.

Emily put her good arm around her mother's shoulder. "It's okay Mom, me too. I was jealous, too."

Emily rose and went to the bathroom to clear out Jenna's toiletries. Maggie perched on the bed and recalled the blue diary that tumbled out of Marie's desk the day they moved in. She moved the desk chair and opened the drawer. There it was. Emily returned from the bathroom holding her toiletry kit and a brush. "Mom, what are you doing?"

"I have to know," Maggie said. She ran her fingers along the worn leather spine.

"Are you sure?"

"I am." Maggie opened the diary from the back. She needed to read about Chris. The looping handwriting was the same as the note behind her picture on their bed stand and the note in the lockbox.

January 16, 2002

Dear Diary,

He came to me again. One day it won't be because of the pictures, the threats, or his daughter. One day it will be for me. Today, I put her in his arms gain. As soon as she laid there, she stopped crying. I told him I'll slice her throat if he doesn't raise her with me. A life wouldn't be worth living for either of us without him. He looked scared and begged me to stop saying things like that.

I don't know if I'll do it. Maybe. It wouldn't be the first time. At least he believes me enough to come back. He will raise this family with me. He brought her a necklace and a stupid Snoopy dog, thinking that would be enough to fill in for being here with her. It is not.

Love,

Viv

She didn't write often. Only when something big happened in her life. Chris was big. She flipped back several pages and scanned for Chris's name.

February 27, 2001

Dear Diary,

I just keep replaying the night in my head. It was so much better than I could have imagined.

We went to happy hour. Everyone had drinks, and after a few shots, we were feeling a little tipsy. The others wanted to dance, so Chris and I stayed at the table. I was flirting, making sure he knew what my intention was. It seemed like he was flirting back, so I kept going. I inched closer and closer to him, and he didn't back away, so I took that as another sign.

When I got close to him, I leaned in and kissed him when no one was looking, but he pushed me away, and I got embarrassed. He said, "I love my wife." I knew this was a lie, but it still stung.

I said, "I'm sorry." But I wasn't.

I put the pill in his drink when he went to the restroom. When he came back, I kept a close eye on him as he sipped the drink. When I saw him getting dizzy (I'm so glad those pills didn't expire), I guided him back to the hotel across the street and brought him up to my room.

I got him on the bed, and he was mumbling words. I swear, at one point, he even mumbled, "I love you." As he laid there on the bed, I couldn't help myself. He looked amazing. I unbuttoned his shirt, slid off his pants, and admired him. Before doing anything else, I snapped a few photos with my camera. Some for each of us.

Then, everything came together as we joined as one. He liked it. I know he did, and God, it was the best thing that's ever happened to me. Before the morning came, I snuck a few Polaroids into his suitcase in a spot I knew his wife would see, or at least I hoped. I stayed there, waiting for him to wake up. He would be happy to see me in the morning, I knew it.

But when he woke up, he was pissed. We had our first fight. I don't even care enough about Roy to fight with him. I told him he said he loved me last night, which is what I think he mumbled. And Chris said he was sorry, couldn't remember anything that happened, and he loved his wife.

That's when I threatened to tell her.

A tear slid down his cheek, and he said he didn't understand how it happened. He said he must have had too much to drink and wasn't thinking straight. He got up and left my room without saying another word.

He'll come back to me.

Love,

Viv

P.S. Of course I didn't wear my diaphragm. God, I hope we make a beautiful baby.

"Oh my God," Maggie said. "I've been angry at him for cheating. He was as trapped as we were. He must have known she was dangerous."

Emily nodded her head. "But by the time you realize Marie or Vivian are dangerous, it's too late. Poor Dad."

Maggie shut the diary. "I don't think we should read

anymore. His last months must have been so conflicted and scary. We came for the answers we got. How Marie got how she was, or what happened to Vivian to do this to her? It's not our concern anymore. She mentioned it wasn't the first time she killed. I'll turn this over to the police. So, any idea what's next for you, Em?"

Emily said, "Well, I shut down my social media accounts and already there's a huge weight lifted. And, I've reached out to the school advisors and they said on account of what has happened, I should be able to catch up. They'll work with me. Maybe I'll call Josh again someday, but for now, I think I want to be on my own. Figuring out what's next."

Maggie gingerly put her arms around her daughter, careful with her slinged shoulder. Emily's head rested on her mother. Maggie let out a contented sigh.

"Mom, you have to let go."

"I'll never be the one to let go first." And she kissed the top of her daughter's head.

The End

who is vivian?

Vivian is dead. She was dead before Chapter One. But was she always a villain? What made her who she was? Was she created, or born that way? If you would like a free electronic copy of the diary Maggie found in Emily's dorm, **go here (if reading ebook)** or scan the QR code below.

Trigger warning–someone who winds up as damaged as Vivian had a lot of things happen in her life to bring her to that point. So, if The Watcher had enough information for you on who Vivian was, then I hope you'll join my reader group by visiting https://avapage.com/lets-connect/. There we can connect to other freebies, advanced sneak peeks into the Kat Eland Series ... and more.

free novella download

One Last Call

One Last Call - **FREE**

He'd followed her home before. Things happened in Mary's part of town, sometimes terrible things. Animals went missing, people got robbed, and unless they were teenagers who thought nothing could happen to them, no one walked alone

Scan to download
your copy today

at night. She wandered from the protection of her friends, and now it was time to pay for laughing at him. The lion stepped out from behind the bushes.

After forty-two years, it was time to retire. He'd had so many girls that they blended together. But Morgan with those moss green eyes with flecks of gold, she'd be his grand finale. Free to download <u>here</u> **(if reading ebook)** or by scanning the QR code above.

acknowledgments

Thank you to my Beta Readers Jon Corsini and Heath Anderson. You both made this book infinitely better. To my editor Edmund Pickett, thank you for your keen eye for detail and ways to tighten the overall pacing. Finally, Crystal Wren, thank you for your proofreading expertise.

a conversation with ava page

The Watcher *is a critical look at the relationship between mother and daughter. Why did you tackle this topic?*

I have a daughter who is college age. The relationship between Maggie and Emily is not ours (thank goodness). However, I've had many conversations with peers, families, read many books, and scoured the Internet and found a common thread of a lot of between mother and daughter as the relationship changes to more of a mentor or confidant. It can be hard for the mother (and possibly the father too, but that wasn't the subject of this book) to step aside and allow their child to grasp the reigns of their own life. Admittedly, this was difficult for me. Sometimes it is still difficult. I know I'm not alone in feeling this way.

Where did the idea of **The Watcher** *come from?*

After being accepted into college, my daughter was searching for a roommate. I found it fascinating how times evolved from randomly being placed with another human being to speed-dating/matching on different social media channels. This pre-matching made me think of how someone could hide in plain sight based on observing another's social media and becoming like that person.

There seemed to be a lot of conflict between Emily and Maggie. Why was that?

While Paul was in Emily's life, Maggie tried too hard to be everything for Emily (mother, father, sister, and friend). Emily needed to push against her mother to evolve and become the adult she was supposed to be. A nefarious plan interrupted Emily's process of growth, which was the basis of the plot.

Maggie has serious opinions on social media. Are they yours?

This is a good question. Not all of them, I do think social media has its uses, but social media is dangerous. Especially for young women. The phones and social media make it easy to see inside the worlds of teenagers and for them to compare the highlight reels of others to their everyday life. As a Generation X person I am eternally thankful that I was not raised to contend with social media.

What do you hope readers take away from The Watcher?

First, I desperately hope I kept you guessing, and you were entertained. From a broader perspective, I hope that readers of my book think hard about their involvement in their children's lives, and how much social media can creep in and just make things kind of... well creepy. The idea that she, and others, can see Emily and Maggie on Snapchat, Facebook, Instagram, texting, and a tracking application should seem weird to us. It doesn't anymore, but it should.

What's next?

I am currently writing a thriller series that I can't wait to share more about. Go to www.avapage.com to subscribe to my reader group to hear more.

about the author

Ava Page

Ava is a veteran civil servant who has worked for nearly 20 years in the government in various roles. When not reading or writing, she enjoys walking the beaches of San Diego, which she calls home.

Ava's latest novel, The Watcher, takes the reader through a gripping story told through the lens of the Generational differences between X and Z with the rise and impact of social media.

f facebook.com/TheAuthorAvaPage
© instagram.com/avapageauthor
g goodreads.com/avapage